SENSUAL STORM

Also available from Headline Liaison

Voluptuous Voyage by Lacey Carlyle
Dark Deception by Lacey Carlyle
Magnolia Moon by Lacey Carlyle
The Journal by James Allen
Love Letters by James Allen
Aphrodisia by Rebecca Ambrose
Out of Control by Rebecca Ambrose
A Private Affair by Carol Anderson
Autumn Dancing by Adam Chandler
Portrait in Blue by Lucinda Chester
Vermilion Gates by Lucinda Chester
The Paradise Garden by Aurelia Clifford
The Golden Cage by Aurelia Clifford
Green Silk by Cathryn Cooper
Sleepless Nights by Tom Crewe and Amber Wells
Hearts on Fire by Tom Crewe and Amber Wells
Seven Days by J J Duke
Dangerous Desires by J J Duke
A Scent of Danger by Sarah Hope-Walker
Private Lessons by Cheryl Mildenhall
Intimate Strangers by Cheryl Mildenhall
Dance of Desire by Cheryl Mildenhall

Sensual Storm

Lacey Carlyle

Copyright © 1996 Lacey Carlyle

The right of Lacey Carlyle to be identified as the Author of
the Work has been asserted by her in accordance with
the Copyright, Designs and Patents Act 1988.

First published in 1996 by
HEADLINE BOOK PUBLISHING LTD

A HEADLINE LIAISON paperback

10 9 8 7 6 5 4 3 2 1

All rights reserved. No part of this publication may be
reproduced, stored in a retrieval system, or transmitted,
in any form or by any means without the prior written
permission of the publisher, nor be otherwise circulated
in any form of binding or cover other than that in which
it is published and without a similar condition being
imposed on the subsequent purchaser.

All characters in this publication are fictitious and any
resemblance to real persons, living or dead, is purely coincidental

ISBN 0 7472 5274 2

Typeset by Avon Dataset Ltd, Bidford-on-Avon, Warks

Printed and bound in Great Britain by
Cox & Wyman Ltd, Reading, Berks

HEADLINE BOOK PUBLISHING LTD
A division of Hodder Headline PLC
338 Euston Road
London NW1 3BH

Sensual Storm

Chapter One

From her seat on the ancient, honey-coloured stone sill high up in the turret of the castle, Lisa could see out over the purple-stained moors and the blue-green pine forest to where the sea shimmered under the midsummer sun, a cold metallic sapphire.

It felt warm for once, the sun shining through the narrow slit of the window and falling directly onto her, making her waist-length hair flame an even more vivid shade of red. It was an exceptionally hot June day and Lisa revelled in the warmth as she sat on the sill, staring dreamily out of the open window.

It wasn't often she had such an uninterrupted vista. For most of the year the castle lay wreathed in mist, blotting out all but the immediate surroundings. But her mind wasn't on the familiar view of the Scottish Highlands, it was on another country half-way around the world – *Malaya*.

The name itself sounded so exotic, so mysterious and so imbued with sensual promise that just saying it made her shiver with delighted anticipation. It conjured up images of gracious colonial houses with thatched verandahs overlooking gardens reclaimed from the dense tropical undergrowth that surrounded them.

She envisaged wooden-bladed fans turning in the languid evening heat as the elegantly-dressed occupants sipped cocktails and prepared to greet dinner guests. How very different it would all be from her life so far.

At eighteen, Lisa had seen little of the giddy, hectic world of the early 1930s and most of what she knew of it came from conversations with her school friends.

Orphaned when young, she'd been left a ward of a distant cousin, Mr Varonne, who as far as she knew was her only living relative. She spent most of each year at a select boarding school and the holidays here in a remote castle rented by her guardian, in the care of Mrs Ross, a widowed relation of his.

She'd finished her last year at school a couple of weeks before and had returned to the castle as usual, eager to know what lay ahead of her. Would her guardian send her to finishing school in Switzerland perhaps? That was where several of her erstwhile school friends were heading.

The strange thing was, she'd never actually met him. He was a rubber planter who lived in Malaya and his instructions were carried out by an Edinburgh solicitor who paid her school fees, arranged staff for the castle and visited her once a term to take her out to tea.

She wrote dutifully to her guardian each month as she'd been bidden and in return received the occasional scrawled note and expensive presents for her birthday and at Christmas – until today.

The letter in her lap crackled and she picked it up and read it again. Although she'd only received it that morning, she already knew the contents by heart and it opened up a whole different future for her.

SENSUAL STORM

She was to go to Malaya to meet him at last.

He'd arranged a travelling companion for her who would arrive at the castle tomorrow to take her to London and then on to Southampton to join the *S.S. Orient* for the long journey by ocean liner.

Lisa wished the letter had gone into more detail. Who was her travelling companion to be? Where would they stay in London and what would she do once in Malaya?

Since being brought to Scotland ten years ago, the only city she'd visited had been Edinburgh. She had a dim and confused memory of London because she'd been there with her parents several times while they were still alive and she was looking forward to staying there again.

After her quiet and secluded life the idea of seeing something of the world was almost too thrilling to contemplate.

She'd always compensated for her quiet, often solitary, existence during the school holidays by sitting in the turret and weaving dreams. But recently the dreams had changed. Where once they'd been of romance, now they were charged with deep, dark yearnings which made her sex pulse and her Directoire knickers moist.

It was here in the window seat that she'd first learnt how to satisfy herself by stimulating the little bud of flesh which protruded between her sex-lips, until her slender body was convulsed by wave after wave of tingling pleasure.

And often, as she stroked herself, she thought of the man, unknown, dark and faceless, who appeared sometimes in her dreams at night and who used her body in a way which left her weak, shaking and drenched in perspiration.

Lisa blushed at the memory of a particularly disturbing dream last night, stirred restlessly on the hard, stone sill and decided to go for a walk. She swung her long legs to the ground and adjusted her white school dress with its sailor collar and navy blue silk bow at the neck, then strode along the gallery and down the steep, winding flight of stairs which led down from the turret.

'Take your hat, dear, if you're going out,' called Mrs Ross as Lisa passed the open door of the small sitting room they used. 'The sun's very strong at this time of year.'

Mrs Ross was to return to her cottage in a small village outside Edinburgh with a generous pension. Over breakfast, she'd confessed that she was relieved.

'Not that I haven't been glad to look after you during the school holidays,' she'd said in her soft Scottish burr. 'But the cold and damp in the castle are getting too much for me during the winter. I'll be glad to spend next Christmas in my warm, comfortable cottage. But I'll miss you, Lisa, and I hope you'll come and see me whenever you return to Scotland.'

Lisa had thanked her gratefully. She was fond of Mrs Ross who'd always treated her with kindness but she'd never been the most stimulating of companions, content to spend her days by the fire busy with her tapestry work.

Lisa took her hat from the hall table and hurried outside. The sun was beating down strongly so she pulled her hat on, aware that her delicate ivory skin burned easily and that the sun was prone to bring out a smattering of the freckles she disliked so much on the bridge of her small, straight nose.

Even in her shapeless school dress her appearance was very striking. Her red-gold hair was gloriously thick and glossy, dark lashes and brows framed her pewter-grey eyes and her full, wide mouth curved beguilingly upwards at the corners.

She took long strides as she walked through the castle's overgrown gardens. The elderly gardener did his best, but there was too much work for one man and he concentrated most of his attention on the kitchen garden.

When Lisa reached the moors she slowed her pace a little – it really was very hot that afternoon. It took her almost half an hour to get to the edge of the pine forest and as soon as she stepped into the resin-scented shade she removed her hat and pulled her hair free of the navy-blue ribbon which held it back.

She loved the forest and when she was far away in another country she knew she'd miss it and the solitude it offered. But she was eighteen and also hungry to experience whatever life had to offer.

She wondered what her guardian would be like. Mrs Ross was unable to enlighten her because she'd never actually met him, nor had the solicitor.

She hoped she'd like him and that he'd like her, or her life might be about to take a turn for the worse. But there was no point in worrying about it at this stage – she'd know soon enough.

When she'd walked about another mile she decided to stop for a while and sank down onto a bed of soft emerald-green moss under the thick, spreading branches of a pine tree.

She lay on her back luxuriating in the stillness and silence, watching a tiny puff of cloud meandering across the small patch of sky visible through the tree tops. Only a few thin lances of sunshine penetrated the shade, making splodges of gold on the moss and bracken.

As she lay there, the dream she'd had the night before came back to her.

She'd been sitting on an upright chair in a luxuriously furnished room where fashionable, well-dressed people were circulating with drinks in their hands.

She herself was also fashionably dressed in a crimson silk cocktail dress, her hair styled, her face discreetly made-up. A man appeared in front of her, dark and in evening dress, but although he was standing in front of her, somehow she couldn't see his face.

He produced a ruby bracelet and fastened it around her wrist, but he also fastened it around the arm of the chair so her wrist was secured and she couldn't move it. He produced a matching necklace and wound it twice around her other wrist and the chair arm, effectively pinioning her in position.

With a sudden rough gesture he wrenched at the front of her cocktail dress, ripping it down to the waist and exposing her firm, high breasts. The other people in the room gathered in a loose half-circle around her, still chatting and sipping their drinks, but watching avidly.

The man's hand grazed over one alabaster breast, skimming the coral nipple in an arousing circular movement. It hardened in an immediate shaming response and Lisa felt her pale cheeks colour with embarrassment.

The man bent his dark head and took the nipple in his mouth, flicking at it with his tongue then sucking slowly until it became hard and swollen. He stroked her other breast with his hand, tweaking and tugging at the crinkled nub of flesh until that too jutted proud from her aureole.

His caresses were making a sly, insidious heat build in her

sex. She pressed her thighs together and shifted uneasily on the hard seat of the chair.

His hand travelled down over her flat belly to the narrow waistband of her satin camiknickers, then his long fingers slipped under the edge and slid lower.

By this time the memory of her arousing dream had made Lisa's breathing ragged and she was unable to stop herself pulling up her skirt and slipping her own hand down the front of her Directoire knickers.

Her little bud of flesh was already slick and responded eagerly to her touch as she stroked it along the shaft. She could feel more warm moisture trickling out of her velvety interior until her fingers became wet and sticky.

A sudden cracking noise made Lisa's head jerk round and she saw Douglas, the ghillie's son, crouched in the bracken staring at her, a flush of excitement on his tanned cheeks.

'Lisa,' he said hoarsely, getting to his feet and stumbling over to her to kneel by her side. He laid one large hand on her breast over the cotton of her dress and looked at her imploringly.

She'd known Douglas since they'd played together as children and three months previously, during the Easter holidays, she'd succumbed to his urgent pleadings and they'd coupled among the fragrant but scratchy hay in the old barn.

Lisa had been eager to try this new and very adult experience, but although she'd had some pleasure, it was considerably less than that she could give herself.

They'd repeated the experiment a couple of times, and although she found it pleasant to be held and stroked and to feel a man's hard body against hers, his shaft buried deep inside her, the ultimate pleasure always seemed to slip away almost before it had begun to build.

But now Douglas had come across her unexpectedly and was obviously wildly excited to have seen her caressing herself. Perhaps this time, aroused as she already was, she would experience the heady release she could bring herself when she was alone. She opened her arms and he ripped open the buttons on his tweed plus-fours and fell clumsily on top of her.

He plunged inside her with no preliminaries and began a vigorous thrusting, sweat beading his forehead, the veins standing out on his temples. It was over almost as soon as it had begun, leaving Lisa feeling edgy and dissatisfied.

'Is it true you're going away?' he asked her as he rolled to one side and buttoned himself up.

'Yes, tomorrow,' replied Lisa, surprised that the news had already reached him.

'When will you be back?'

'I'm not certain – I don't know what my guardian has planned for me.'

'I'll miss you,' he said awkwardly.

'Why thank you, Douglas.' Lisa was touched. 'And I'll miss you too. It would have been lonely here in the holidays without you.'

The distant sound of a dog barking made him sit abruptly upright.

'I'll have to go – Pa will be wondering where I've got to.' He kissed her, scrambled to his feet and hurried off.

Lisa was watching from the window when the large black

Hispano-Suiza drew up outside the castle in the late morning.

'She's here,' she announced to Mrs Ross, who laid her tapestry aside and rose to her feet. Together the two women went to the door and waited while a petite, dark-haired woman stepped gracefully from the car, the door held open for her by a uniformed chauffeur.

Lisa decided immediately that she'd never seen a woman so elegantly dressed, not even Merle McImrie's mother who was always immaculately turned out in the latest couture clothing.

The visitor, who looked to be in her early thirties, was wearing a beautifully tailored black linen suit over an ochre silk top. She had a matching black cloche hat and her gloves, shoes and bag were of the finest, supple black suede.

She walked gracefully up the steps, her hips swaying and extended her hand. 'Good morning,' she greeted them, 'I am Madame Solange Valois.'

'Good morning,' Lisa murmured, taking the extended hand. 'I'm Lisa Cavendish and this is Mrs Ross.'

'Have you travelled far today?' asked Mrs Ross, shaking her hand in turn.

'From Edinburgh.'

'You must be ready for some tea then. Will you come in for a while?'

'Thank you. A cup of tea would be very welcome.'

Lisa hadn't expected her travelling companion to be French, or so exquisite, or so young. For some reason she'd expected her to be middle-aged and matronly. The prospect of travelling half way round the globe with the elegant Madame Valois was an alluring one.

An hour later when the time came to depart, Lisa was torn between sadness and excitement. She hugged Mrs Ross and promised to write to her and then followed the Frenchwoman into the huge black car into which her own modest amount of luggage had already been loaded.

Lisa was wearing another of her school dresses, virtually identical to the one she'd worn yesterday, with her hair tied neatly back and her hands encased in white cotton gloves. Next to the stylishly attired Solange she felt gauche and unsophisticated.

When eventually the castle was out of sight she stopped looking back and turned to Solange.

'When will we arrive in London, Madame Valois?'

'Call me Solange, *chérie*. We should arrive there tomorrow. Travelling non-stop is too fatiguing so we shall break the journey and spend tonight in a hotel in York.'

'And where will we be staying in London?'

'A house belonging to a friend of mine.'

'How long will we be there?'

She studied Solange as she spoke, admiring her beautifully waved, bobbed dark hair and perfectly applied make-up. The other woman had large brown eyes and a slightly upturned nose. Her luscious, pouting mouth was painted a deep red and now she'd removed her gloves Lisa saw that her nails were varnished the same colour.

'Just over a week and then we must join our ship. Will you be sad to leave Britain?'

'A little,' said Lisa truthfully, 'but it will be wonderful to travel and see foreign countries. Do you live in Malaya?'

'No, this will be my first visit.'

'Do you have friends or family there?' she asked.

'No. I'm going to inspect a rubber plantation I own and to oversee its sale.'

'Oh, you own a rubber plantation too,' exclaimed Lisa. 'So does my guardian. How long have you had it?'

'My husband left it to me when he died.'

Lisa stared at her in consternation. How awful to be a widow when she was so young. Afraid to ask any more questions she sat back in her comfortable seat and looked out of the window. She intended to enjoy every moment of their long drive to London.

Chapter Two

Lisa enjoyed their overnight stay in the hotel in York. Used to a rather spartan life both at school and in the castle, it seemed like the height of luxury. There was even time for a brief stroll around the narrow cobbled streets and then the Minster before an early dinner in the hotel's restaurant.

The following day was spent on the rest of the long journey and in the late afternoon they arrived at the house that was to be their home for the next few days.

Lisa couldn't believe how well appointed her bedroom was. A thickly woven, fringed carpet in shades of dusky-pink and cornflower-blue covered most of the floor, except for a two foot strip of highly polished wooden boards around the edge. A huge four poster bed dominated the room, hung with gauzy white muslin curtains which were moving slightly in the breeze wafting in through the open window.

A blue silk spread covered the bed and curtains of the same shade hung at the tall windows which overlooked a quiet London square. The furniture was old-fashioned but comfortable and, luxury of luxuries, there was an adjoining bathroom of her own.

Solange followed her in and sank onto the *chaise-longue* which was covered in blue-sprigged silk.

'I regret, *chérie*, that tonight you must dine alone as you are not yet correctly attired and groomed. Tomorrow I shall take you shopping, to the hairdresser and the beauty salon, then at night we will go to a restaurant. Will you be able to amuse yourself here this evening?'

'Yes, I'll be fine, thanks. Do you have friends in London?'

Solange smiled enigmatically.

'Indeed I do – and tomorrow you shall meet some of them.'

Lisa was tired after the journey and quite happy to take a long bath, eat a light meal and then retire to bed. It took her a while to go to sleep and soon after she did, she began to dream.

She was in a boat on a river, leaning back on comfortable cushions next to a dark, broad-shouldered man, who had an arm thrown nonchalantly around her shoulders. She was unable to turn her head to look at him, but she knew that she found him exceptionally attractive.

The boat was drifting slowly through some lush, beautiful meadows where modishly attired people were strolling in couples and small groups. She was wearing a printed silk georgette afternoon dress splashed with scarlet poppies, a matching sash wound once around her head and trailing down to her waist.

The man removed his hand from her shoulders and placed his hand on her knee. She could feel it through the thin silk of her dress and underslip as slowly, unhurriedly, he began to edge her skirt up. He pushed it so far up her thighs that the tops of her parchment-coloured stockings and then her ribbon suspenders came into view.

The sides of the boat were just high enough to prevent

people sauntering along the tow-path from seeing what he was doing, but even though she felt excited beyond measure, she wanted him to stop. But she seemed unable to tell him that or to demand he remove his hand. He kept raising her skirt until to her horror she saw he'd exposed her tawny fleece.

She didn't know why she wasn't wearing any underwear or why she was allowing him to do this, she only knew she was powerless to restrain him.

He laid his hand over her mound in a gesture of absolute possession, then slid his fingers into the damp groove of her flesh-valley.

A hot, tingling wave of excitement washed over her as they found the little bud of flesh which lay hidden among the soft folds of her sex. He stroked it until it began to swell and the blunt end protruded beyond her inner sex-lips.

He pushed her thighs apart and in a sudden unexpected movement slipped his forefinger deep inside her, making her gasp in shock and arousal.

To her horror she saw that the river was about to pass under a bridge where groups of people were gathered watching them approach.

She knew that within seconds everyone would be able to see her exposed mound and the fact that her companion had his hand between her legs and was touching her very publicly and very intimately. She closed her eyes and waited for the moment when her humiliation would be total and . . .

Lisa sat bolt upright in bed, dazed and disoriented, awakened by what she was sure had been a cry. Her cambric nightgown was clinging to her damp body and her hairline was beaded with perspiration.

She reached for the bedside lamp and switched it on, looking wildly around the room. But there was no-one there and she couldn't hear anything except her heart pounding in her chest.

She was thirsty and realised that more than anything she wanted a glass of milk. She swung her legs off the bed and padded silently on bare feet to the door. A dim light was burning in the corridor and another in the black and white tiled hallway at the foot of the wide sweep of the stairs.

As she descended them she wondered what time it was. It could have been only an hour after she'd gone to bed, just before dawn, or any time inbetween.

She was passing the dining room on her way to the green baize door she assumed led to the kitchen, when a soft moan from within made her stop dead. Her heart began to pound again as she heard another moan, and then a hastily suppressed cry.

The door was open just a crack and a narrow shaft of light spilled into the hallway. Nervously, Lisa padded to the door and peeped through the crack. Her hand darted to her throat and her eyes flew wide open at the scene which met her eyes.

Solange was kneeling up on a cushion on the dining-room table, naked except for a peach silk camisole, matching suspender belt and bone-coloured stockings. Her back was half turned to Lisa who could see the well-rounded curve of her creamy buttocks, the cleft between them deeply shadowed in the lamplight.

Two men were with her, one was holding her buttocks apart and as Lisa watched, he bent his fair head and flicked his tongue between them.

The other man was dark, his face was in shadow and he was

holding a riding crop. With the tip he slowly traced the full circles of Solange's silk-veiled breasts, then the smaller ones of her nipples. Lisa could see the jutting profile of Solange's left nipple and how it pushed at its silk and lace covering.

The dark man drew the leather crop down her cleavage until it caught in the flimsy fabric of her camisole, then lifted it free and continued inexorably down her belly.

When it reached her mound, Solange turned slightly towards the man and Lisa could see him stirring the sable fronds of her silken fleece, before slipping the crop even further down and then probing between her parted thighs.

The fair-haired man moved to the side and bit softly on one of Solange's shapely buttocks, sucking hard. He began to caress her breasts, squeezing and fondling them, rolling her nipples between his finger and thumb.

Solange's breath was coming in little gasps and as Lisa watched she saw the end of the riding crop appear from between her thighs at the back. The dark man moved it steadily backwards and forwards and even from the door Lisa could hear the slight noise it made as the leather slid over what was obviously wet, slippery flesh.

Solange's head fell back and she moaned again, her hips jerking as she bore down on the crop, her thighs wide apart.

Somehow the sound dragged Lisa back to reality and, afraid of being detected spying on this strange and disturbing scenario, she turned on her heel and fled back upstairs, all thoughts of milk forgotten.

In her bedroom she threw herself under the covers and lay there trembling, unable to go back to sleep for the insistent pulsing in her sex.

* * *

The following morning, she half thought that what she'd seen – or imagined she'd seen – was part of her own unsettling dream.

After the unprecedented luxury of breakfast in bed brought to her by a cheerful maid, it was with some trepidation that she dressed and went downstairs, afraid of what she might find.

But nothing could have been more normal than the sight of the sunlight slanting in through the windows or the quiet bustle of the servants going about their allotted tasks.

Certainly Solange gave no sign that anything untoward had taken place the previous night. She greeted Lisa pleasantly, asked her if she'd found everything she needed in her room and then bore her off to the hairdresser.

Monsieur Pierre ran his fingers through Lisa's luxuriant red-gold hair, considered its weight and thickness and then turned to Solange.

'I think for Mademoiselle, not the bob – it would be a criminal thing to cut off all this beautiful hair. Instead I will make it chic without being short.'

Solange nodded her agreement and then settled down to read a magazine while Monsieur Pierre got to work. He trimmed several inches off Lisa's hair so it fell to just below her shoulder blades instead of her waist, then snipped away at the front and the sides so it waved becomingly around her face.

He coiled it into a deceptively simple knot at the nape of her neck then beckoned to Solange.

'Perfect,' was her opinion. Lisa had to agree. She turned her head from side to side, pleased to see how the new style accentuated her cheekbones and the firm lines of her jaw. At least from the neck upwards she didn't look like a schoolgirl any more.

Their next stop was a beauty salon where her thick, dark eyebrows had a few stray hairs plucked from beneath them to give them a more fashionable shape and then vaseline was brushed through to keep them tidy and make them gleam.

She was given a facial and a manicure and shown how to apply a little discreet make-up. She left carrying a small pink striped carrier bag containing a selection of cosmetics chosen to suit her colouring and various face creams and scented lotions.

'I can't wait to buy some clothes,' she told Solange. 'Where shall we go first?'

'Lunch first,' said Solange firmly. 'We'll purchase just a few things this afternoon and then return to the house – I want to take a nap before tonight. We have over a week to buy you a new wardrobe, we don't need to get it all in one day.' She yawned slightly, a little cat-like yawn which showed the tip of her pink tongue.

Lisa had a fleeting image of her new companion kneeling on the dining table, her thighs wide apart, while two men touched her lewdly and lasciviously, and she had to suppress a shiver of excitement. She told herself again that she must have dreamt it, but somehow she wasn't quite convinced.

She found Solange intriguing, but since learning that the other woman was a widow she hadn't liked to ask her any more questions in case she touched a raw nerve. But it was frustrating because there was so much she wanted to know.

Who had her husband been? Where had they lived? When had he died and what of? She hoped that during the course of their voyage together she would learn more about her. To date, all their conversation had been either fairly general or about herself.

After lunch they visited several shops and Lisa, who'd never given much thought to her clothes, was enraptured by her new purchases. Most things had to have minute alterations to give them the perfect fit Solange demanded, but Lisa insisted on wearing an afternoon dress in yellow toile from the shop. She left her school dress behind saying airily she'd never wear it again.

Whenever she caught sight of her reflection in a window she felt a little thrill of pleasure. As well as the draped afternoon dress she was wearing a white linen jacket with a matching white bandeau around her hair. On her feet were a pair of supple kid leather shoes and she was carrying a slim clutch bag in exactly the same shade.

Her new set of silk underwear seemed to be slithering pleasurably over her skin with every movement she made and her long, slim legs were now encased in silk stockings.

'Where are we going tonight?' she asked as they climbed into the Hispano-Suiza which had been trailing them all day and into which all their purchases had been loaded. Solange too had bought several new outfits with the casual abandon of a woman used to spending vast sums of money on herself.

'Dinner and then on to a club if that would please you.'

'Oh, it would,' said Lisa fervently.

'Then I shall ask Roland – a friend of mine – to escort us. Tonight is the night you make your debut into the adult world

– I hope you find it lives up to your expectations.'

There was a tinge of sadness in Solange's prettily accented voice as she spoke which made Lisa shoot a swift sideways glance at her. Had Solange's life not lived up to expectations? Presumably not if the Frenchwoman had been widowed so young.

But if the strange scenario in the dining room had in reality taken place last night, Solange obviously didn't lack male company.

When they arrived at the house Solange yawned, and said she was going to take a nap. Half way up the stairs she turned and looked back.

'I would advise you to do the same, *chérie*. It's a good habit to get into, particularly as we're about to embark for a much hotter climate which can be very fatiguing.'

But Lisa was much too excited to sleep. Instead, she ran a deep bath and tossed a handful of rose-scented powder into the water before immersing herself up to her shoulders. She lay back and closed her eyes enjoying the sheer unaccustomed luxury of it.

By the time the water reached the ancient bathroom in the castle it was at best tepid and at worst stone cold. At school, baths couldn't be more than six inches deep and the time spent in them restricted to ten minutes – hardly conducive to the sort of sybaritic pleasure she was experiencing now.

She picked up the pink tablet of rose-scented soap and worked up a rich lather with her hands, pausing for a moment to admire her manicure and the coat of clear, pink-tinted polish that had been applied.

She began to soap her breasts, lingering on her coral nipples, circling and toying with them. She felt the small, crinkled nubs becoming hard and more sensitive and tingling little jolts of sensation began to shoot down to her sex.

She wondered what it would feel like to have a man draw the end of a riding crop across her breasts, touch her nipples and then run it down her belly to her mound.

Had the lewd stimulation of the leather being drawn backwards and forwards between her thighs brought Solange to a climax last night?

Later on, perhaps while her sex was still hot and moist from a shuddering release, had the dark-haired man bent her over the table and then taken her from behind while the other man watched?

Lisa was shocked by her own thoughts and even more shocked to discover that the idea made her catch her breath and a hard knot of excitement form in her chest.

With her eyes closed, she ran her knuckle down her body to where her silken fleece formed a soft triangle and toyed with the wet fronds, tugging at them gently and separating them.

She could feel an urgent pulsing in the kernel of her clitoris and brushed over it with her fingertips. An answering tingle of carnal sensation made her gasp.

What would it feel like to be touched there with a riding crop?

She opened her legs wide and rubbed her fingers backwards and forwards, imagining the sensation of warm leather, soon becoming damp with her juices, arousing her, exciting her.

Her little bud was becoming swollen and the engorged

folds of her sex felt slippery. She pushed two fingers deep inside herself and felt her internal muscles tighten around them.

The tingling in her bud was becoming unbearable and she rubbed at the shaft with increasing urgency. A wave of heat washed over her and then there was a soft little explosion of pleasure which made her spine arch and her head drop back.

A slight sound made her open her eyes to see Solange standing in the doorway, a white satin robe wrapped around her slender but voluptuous body. The older woman smiled at her, an enigmatic, knowing smile.

'I'm sorry, *ma petite*, I did knock. I wanted to tell you that my maid – Celeste – will come and help you to dress. Then please would you come to my room just before eight – I have something for you.'

She turned around and walked away, her hips swaying seductively beneath the sensuous satin. Lisa felt a hot flush of embarrassment flood her already warm body.

Had Solange realised what she was doing? What on earth must she have thought?

But if Solange *had* been involved in the wanton, three-way scenario Lisa thought she'd witnessed last night, watching her young charge pleasuring herself would seem no more shocking than seeing her apply lipstick.

After drying herself and pulling on a new pearl-grey silk robe edged with rolled slate-grey ribbon, Lisa was still too excited to sleep.

Instead she experimented with her new make-up. It was amazing what a difference just a few subtle touches made. No-one looking at her now would guess that yesterday she'd been an unsophisticated schoolgirl. She particularly liked the enamel powder compact inlaid with mother-of-pearl she'd bought, and the fact that a light application of powder hid the dusting of freckles across her nose.

After that she tried on all her new clothes, wondering what to wear that night. She could only assume they'd be going somewhere smart – she couldn't imagine Solange ever going anywhere that wasn't – and she wanted to be a credit to her. Eventually she curled up on her bed with the latest copy of *Vogue* until it was time to get dressed.

Just before eight Lisa tapped on the door of Solange's room.

'*Entrez*,' she heard Solange call. The Frenchwoman was sitting at her dressing table with her white satin robe open to show she was wearing a black charmeuse slip lavishly trimmed with lace.

She was touching perfume to her neck with the frosted glass stopper of a small cut-glass bottle in front of her. As Lisa watched she also touched her wrists, her cleavage and the inner crook of her elbows. Then she pulled her slip up and dabbed a few drops onto the soft skin at the top of her thighs above her sheer black stockings which were held up by lacy black garters.

She replaced the stopper in the bottle and turned to face Lisa. 'You look beautiful, *chérie*, absolutely beautiful.'

Lisa was quite pleased with her appearance. Celeste had helped arrange her hair and had given her some helpful tips on applying her make-up.

She was wearing a plain, sleeveless sheath in eau-de-nil silk with a vee neckline cut low enough to give a hint of cleavage. There was another vee at the back and the material was gathered slightly on her shoulders so it was about an inch wide. Cut on the bias so it hugged her slim hips and slender thighs, the dress was a triumph of elegant, understated design.

With it she'd bought an evening bag made of the same fabric sewn with crystal beading, as were the heels of a matching pair of silk evening slippers.

Beneath the dress she had on a cream silk camisole, camiknickers and a suspender belt which was holding up stockings of a pale, translucent buff-white. Her new clothes felt wonderful as she walked, slithering around her breasts, hips and bottom like the caress of a lover.

Solange rose to her feet and kissed Lisa's cheek. Her lips felt soft and her heady perfume which smelt of jasmine and orange flower enveloped Lisa in a seductive cloud. Lisa could see the voluptuous swelling of Solange's breasts under her slip and was seized by a sudden urge to caress them.

But Solange moved away and picked up a bottle-green Moroccan leather case from the bed.

'On the instructions of your guardian I had this sent round from the bank today. It was your mother's jewel case and it's now yours.'

She handed Lisa a small key and sank onto the edge of the bed. Taken aback, Lisa struggled to fit the key in the lock then fumbled with the catch.

She lifted the lid to see that the interior was divided into compartments. She opened the first one to reveal several rings slotted neatly into slits in the velvet lining. Other compartments held bracelets, necklaces, chokers and brooches.

'These are lovely,' said Lisa, holding up a long strand of

pearls, their lustre enhanced by the evening sunlight still pouring in through the window.

'You should wear those tonight – they'll set off the dress very well.' Solange drew them carefully over Lisa's head and knotted them. 'Knotted with this particular dress, I think, but you could also wind them around your neck two or three times, or wear them just as a single strand with some outfits. Now, let's see what else you could wear.'

Solange examined all the jewellery carefully. 'Some of the settings are rather old-fashioned, but there's no reason why you shouldn't take them to a good jeweller and have them altered. You could buy some new pieces as well. What about the gold and emerald bracelet and matching ring for tonight?'

Lisa agreed and was pleased by the finishing touch they gave to her appearance, adding to her apparent sophistication.

'Roland will be arriving shortly to take us out to dinner,' Solange told her, rubbing some scented lotion into her hands.

She slipped out of her robe and into a black velvet gown with a scooped neckline which just showed her collar bones at the front. It had tight, full-length sleeves and swooped down to below her waist at the back where there was a large, floppy black bow, the ends of which trailed seductively over her curvaceous *derrière*.

She added diamond eardrops and a diamond bracelet then pronounced herself ready. She slid her arm around Lisa's waist and drew her over to the pier glass.

'We look good together – *non*?'

Lisa had to admit it was true – they did make a striking couple. Her red-gold hair and ivory skin made a vivid contrast to Solange's dark, sophisticated beauty.

Solange turned her head and kissed Lisa on the lips.

'Let's go down. I think I heard Roland arriving a few minutes ago.'

Chapter Three

They found Roland in the drawing room, engaged in mixing cocktails in a silver shaker. Lisa knew him immediately – he was the fair-haired man who'd had his tongue buried between the creamy globes of Solange's bottom the night before.

'H... how do you do?' she stuttered after Solange had introduced them. There was a flush creeping over her cheeks at the memory of what she'd seen.

'Charming, absolutely charming,' he drawled, bending over her hand and kissing it. He was tall, slim and good-looking in a languid sort of way. His fair hair was worn rather long for the fashion of the times and he had a patrician nose and pale-blue eyes.

He was also easily the most attractive man Lisa had ever met.

'Solange should have brought you along last night,' he continued, agitating the shaker vigorously.

'I... was rather tired after the journey,' she told him, hoping Solange hadn't said anything about her not having the right clothes.

Roland poured a pale, almost colourless liquid into three chilled cocktail glasses and passed them both one. Was this a martini? She'd heard of the drink from friends at school, but it was the first time she'd ever seen one. She took a cautious sip and tried not to cough. Goodness – it was strong, the fumes alone were enough to make her feel woozy.

She wasn't sure if she liked it or not, but she certainly liked the feeling of enjoying pre-dinner cocktails before leaving for one of London's smartest restaurants.

She was shrewd enough to refuse a refill. Just half a glass had made a warm, golden glow flood her body and her head was already spinning slightly. She didn't want to make a fool of herself in any way.

Roland glanced at his watch.

'Shall we go?' he asked. 'I booked the table for nine.'

His car was waiting at the door, a chauffeur-driven Daimler. Roland sat in the middle, an arm stretched out along the back of the seat behind each of them. He smelt faintly of some sort of spicy cologne and she couldn't help but notice that his nails were immaculately manicured.

He was very different from Douglas whose grooming, to say the least, had always been cursory. She knew intuitively that Roland would know how to give a woman pleasure. She imagined his smooth, strong hand on her bare skin, perhaps caressing her breast or sliding up her thigh to her . . .

'Is this your first visit to London?' Roland asked her, interrupting her erotic reverie.

'Since I was a child, yes.'

'Do you find it much changed?'

'It seems noisier and there are more cars, but other than that – not really.'

He was easy to talk to and she found herself chatting away

quite happily on the short drive. The Daimler drew up outside a restaurant and a liveried doorman leapt forward to open the car door. Roland offered them both an arm and they walked into the restaurant together.

Lisa was instantly dazzled by the array of attractive people already dining. Sumptuously dressed women, their bare arms and throats glittering with jewels, sat with soberly clad men, their black and white evening clothes the perfect foil for their more colourfully dressed companions.

A dozen or more different perfumes scented the air, mingling with the appetising smell of perfectly cooked food. The *maître d'hôtel* led them to a secluded alcove table and the wine waiter immediately appeared to take their drinks order.

'Champagne,' said Roland immediately. He held a brief conversation about vintage with the man, who then hurried away to reappear very quickly with a bottle in an ice bucket.

Lisa hadn't been altogether sure whether she liked martinis, but she knew instantly that she loved champagne. She resisted the temptation to drink it as though it were lemonade and was careful to sip it slowly.

The food was superb too. Accustomed to very plain, unimaginative cooking she was unsure what to choose, but Solange helped her to make a decision without making it obvious she knew Lisa hadn't a clue what most of the dishes on the menu were.

Several people stopped at their table to chat. It was an experience just watching Solange flirt with the men, her large, dark eyes sparkling and her luscious, crimson mouth pouting provocatively. Lisa wondered if she'd ever become as adept at sparkling, vivacious conversation. She doubted it somehow.

She felt her head beginning to spin, as much from the heady excitement of being out in such sophisticated company as from the champagne.

She only hoped that no-one looking at her would guess that she'd woken that morning looking like the schoolgirl she'd so recently been and that an amazing transformation had been effected in the space of one short day.

After the meal Solange and Roland had a prolonged discussion about which nightclub to go on to and eventually decided on the Glass Slipper.

As they pulled up outside the club, faint strains of jazz floated up the stairs, making Lisa long to dance. They'd had a gramophone at school and often played jazz records, even though they were strictly forbidden. Lisa was thankful that she knew how to dance to the hot, sexy music.

They were shown to a tiny table crammed in among dozens of others around the dance floor and just a few yards from the small stage where a negro jazz band was performing.

Solange turned to Lisa and murmured, 'I hope you're wearing underwear, *chérie*.'

Lisa didn't know what she meant, until Solange nodded at the highly polished dance floor, which was made of glass laid over a silvered base.

Immediately Lisa realised that the underwear – or lack of it – any woman was wearing, would be reflected in the glass as soon as she stepped onto the dance floor.

Roland, meanwhile, had decided that the table was too cramped and noisy and instead indicated to the waiter that they'd take a larger, more secluded one in the far corner.

As she sank into the chair held out for her, Lisa was

practically bubbling with excitement. A nightclub with a jazz band. This really was living.

'There's Alex,' Roland said and raised a languid hand to a tall, broad-shouldered man making his way through the crowded room to them. Lisa's heart skipped a beat.

She realised she'd been half expecting this.

It was the other man from last night – the one who'd wielded the riding crop with such erotic expertise. She felt a carnal fluttering somewhere high up in her sex, and almost let out a moan as Roland said, 'Alex Campion – Lisa Cavendish.'

He took her hand and kissed it. Every downy hair on the back of her neck stood on end in unabashed response to his sexuality and a surge of sheer lust jabbed through her slender body. She found Roland very attractive, but Alex made her feel practically molten inside.

Roland asked Solange to dance and they vanished into the crowd. Alex sank into the seat next to Lisa and turned towards her so she was able to get a good look at him for the first time.

He was probably about ten years older than her and his face wasn't classically handsome, but it was strong with winged dark brows which almost met in the middle over long, narrow eyes. His dark hair was slightly untidy, as if he'd been out in a strong wind, and even in the dim light she could see the dark-shadowed jaw-line that indicated a virile beard growth.

'Have you recovered from your long journey?' he asked her, pouring her a glass of champagne from the bottle which had appeared on their table only moments after they'd sat down.

'Y . . . yes thank you,' she stuttered, barely able to speak for the strength of the sexual attraction she felt for him. She blushed and cursed herself. She couldn't imagine Solange ever behaving so gauchely. She tried to think of something light and amusing to say, but nothing came to mind that didn't sound inane.

'Which part of Scotland did you live in?'

She told him and then began to describe the area, desperate to appear self-possessed in front of him. Her natural enthusiasm for the beauty of the Highlands came to her rescue and she found to her relief that she was able to talk with a reasonable degree of fluency.

She was just congratulating herself on handling the situation with adult aplomb when she saw his eyes flickering appraisingly over her shoulders and breasts. She immediately lost the thread of what she was saying and her voice tailed off.

He smiled suddenly, showing extremely white teeth. His canines were very pointed and longer than the teeth on either side of them, giving him a predatory air which she found half-frightening, half-fascinating.

'How lovely you are,' he said, taking her hand and kissing it again. 'Or should I say bonny? Tell me, lovely Lisa, did you have many admirers up in the wilds of Scotland?'

'N . . . not really,' she murmured. 'I was at school until a couple of weeks ago.'

'But you must have met people during the holidays?'

'No, it was just Mrs Ross – the lady who looked after me when I wasn't at school – and me.'

'What about your neighbours?'

'We didn't really have any, other than the people who worked on the estate. I was friendly with Douglas, the ghillie's son. We used to play together when I was younger.'

'And did you . . . play together when you were older?'

Intuitively Lisa realised that this was a loaded question.

'We remained friends,' she replied evasively. She saw him weighing her reply and then he leant across, put his hand on her neck under her glossy knot of hair and pulled her towards him. His face was so close that even in the dim light she could see his thick, dark lashes half-veiling his narrow eyes which gleamed between them.

She caught a faint whiff of his eau-de-Cologne and found herself staring at him, mesmerised by his closeness and the raw sexuality which emanated from him.

'Are *we* going to be friends?' he murmured.

Without waiting for a reply he brushed her lips with his, making her glad she was sitting down because if she'd been standing she was certain her legs would have trembled so much, they would have refused to support her.

The kiss became more intense, sending hectic messages of arousal feathering down her spine. She became aware of a pleasurable ache in her sex which soon turned into a demanding throbbing that made her press her thighs together.

His lips against hers were igniting a spark which threatened to consume her, particularly when he bit softly on her lower lip. He drew away, but looking directly into her eyes he placed his hand on her silk-clad knee beneath the cover of the tablecloth.

She inhaled sharply and then held her breath as it glided inexorably upwards and under the skirt of her eau-de-Nil dress. She knew she should tell him to remove it at once, but she could no more have told him to than she could have levitated from her seat and then flown around the room.

His fingers found the smooth skin above her stocking tops and caressed it softly. She felt herself becoming moist and squirmed slightly on her seat, half-hoping he would continue the indecorous caress and half-dreading her reaction if he did.

But he withdrew his hand and sat back in his seat, leaving her wide-eyed and breathing erratically through parted lips.

'Would you like to dance?' he enquired blandly. Confused and not certain her legs would support her if she stood up, she merely stared at him and then managed to nod. 'Go to the powder room first and discard any underwear you have on,' he directed her.

For a few seconds Lisa thought she must have misheard him and that her fevered, over-stimulated brain had made something lewd out of a perfectly innocuous remark. But then she saw the expression on his face and realised that she'd heard him correctly and he *had* just made an unforgivably indecent suggestion.

She should have told him sharply to remove his hand when he'd first laid it on her knee. Her passivity had obviously convinced him that she welcomed his attentions.

She sat frozen to her chair, aware that she should slap his face, but somehow powerless to do so. Even worse, she felt a stealthy trickling sensation which indicated she found the idea so unbearably exciting that her honeyed juices were already soaking into her camiknickers.

Maybe it was the champagne, maybe it was the memory of him stroking Solange with the riding crop, or maybe it was her own over-stimulated state, but Lisa found herself rising numbly to her feet and heading in the direction of the powder room.

Even when she'd locked herself in one of the cubicles and was stepping out of her flimsy lingerie, she couldn't quite believe she was doing it. She stuffed the camiknickers in her bag, automatically tidied her hair, powdered her nose and then returned to the table.

Alex rose to his feet before she reached it and led her on to the dance floor. Her face was hot and she didn't dare meet his eyes. Instead she stared at his lapels as she began to move to the insistent, undulating, percussive rhythms, well aware where he was looking and hoping no-one else was looking too.

'Your sex is as beautiful as the rest of you,' he told her in a low voice. 'I look forward to stroking your red fleece and then parting those exquisite petals to observe the parts still hidden. I can see they're already swollen and shining with your female dew, waiting for my caresses.'

Lisa's face burned with a combination of arousal and shame as she listened to his words. The awful thing was she *wanted* him to touch her. Her sex flesh seemed to be throbbing with a demanding heat she'd never experienced before – not even in her dreams.

The music stopped and he took her hand and led her back to the table where they were joined by Solange and Roland a few minutes later.

'Shall we go on to the Horseshoe?' asked Roland, his arm around Solange's shoulder, his fingers stroking the smooth skin over her collarbones.

'Lisa is tired,' replied Alex smoothly, 'if you like I'll take her home while you go on somewhere.'

'Are you ready to go home, *chérie*?' asked Solange.

'Y . . . yes, I think so,' she stuttered.

They left the club together, the blaring of the tenor saxophone following them up the stairs. Solange patted Lisa's cheek and said 'Goodnight,' then she and Roland slid into Roland's Daimler and sped off into the night.

A long black Rolls pulled up beside Alex and Lisa and a chauffeur leapt out and opened the door. Lisa stepped in and sank into the deep, comfortable seat, very aware that to all intents and purposes she was alone with this man.

He didn't waste any time.

He drew her into his arms and kissed her until she was aware of nothing but how much she wanted him.

'Lie down and pull your skirt up around your waist,' he directed her, releasing her and sitting back.

Mesmerised by his sexuality, she lay down on the seat half propped up against the side of the car, and lifted the front of her dress to reveal her ivory suspender belt and damp, tawny fleece.

'All of it.' She wasn't sure what he meant at first, then unsteadily, she raised her backside for just long enough to flip the back of her dress up too, then sank down again. The soft suede of the seat felt wonderful against her bare bottom and seemed to transmit the purring of the engine directly to her quivering bud.

He put his hand on her thigh and she trembled.

'Open your legs.' His voice sounded deep and slightly hoarse and she felt her thighs parting before she'd made any conscious decision to obey him.

He lifted her by the hips so she was lying across his lap, her legs along the seat on the far side of him. She could feel the hardness of his manhood between her buttocks as his hand slipped up her thigh then settled on her mound before beginning a soft, insidious stroking of her damp fleece. She felt as though her silken triangle were a nervous little animal he was soothing into quiescence.

Except his touch was also making her red-hot with sheer carnal desire. She had a sudden vivid memory of her dream last night; this was so similar it was unnerving. Was Alex the dark, faceless man who'd plagued her sleeping hours in recent months?

His long fingers moved further down and dabbled carelessly among the unfurling folds of her labia. She felt her bud throbbing, but he didn't touch it. Instead two fingers probed the slippery entrance to her sex and then slid very slowly inside.

He moved them around as if assessing her tightness, making her gasp. She could feel more of her female dew trickling out and briefly hoped she wouldn't leave a damp stain on his trousers, then her full attention was reclaimed as he began to slide them in and out of her. Could he tell she wasn't a virgin?

As well as moving his fingers in and out, his thumb found her aching bud and stroked it skilfully. A wave of tingling heat washed over her and she bit her lip hard to stop herself moaning as she shuddered into a lengthy climax that left her weak and trembling.

She lay for a while, her eyes closed, expecting him to roll on top of her and thrust inside, but he merely stroked her thighs gently. She wondered confusedly why he wasn't continuing with their amorous encounter and found she was putting off the moment when she had to open her eyes and face him.

He pre-empted her by saying, 'We're here.'

She turned to look out of the window and saw that the car had pulled up outside her temporary home. With an effort she swung her legs to the ground, pulled her skirt down then groped around for her bag while Alex got out of the car and held the door open for her, just beating the chauffeur to it.

Was he planning to come in and make heady, breathless love to her in the house? Lisa wasn't quite sure what the form was on an occasion like this. What did you say to a man who'd just brought you to an earth-shattering climax in the back of his chauffeur-driven car?

She was sure that Solange would know, but she herself was at a loss. Was he waiting for an invitation and if he was, should she offer it?

The decision was taken out of her hands because he bent to kiss her full on the lips then got back into the Rolls-Royce. He waited with the door open until she'd stumbled up the steps and let herself in, then as she watched she saw the long, black car gliding silently off.

Chapter Four

Lisa half expected her sleep to be disturbed by more erotic dreams or the sounds of further licentious activity from downstairs, but it was nine o'clock the following morning before she woke up.

She stretched languorously, suffused by a feeling of well-being which vanished abruptly as the events of the previous night came flooding back to her in a series of terrifyingly vivid images.

Dancing on the mirrored nightclub floor, displaying her most private parts to anyone who chose to look.

Lying along the suede back seat of the Rolls-Royce, her skirts bunched up around her waist, her thighs wide apart.

Shuddering into a glorious orgasm which had been by far the strongest she'd ever had.

She let out a little moan of shame and buried her face in the pillow. Whatever could have possessed her?

Was it the unaccustomed alcohol that had made her lose all sense of propriety? She would have liked to have blamed it on the champagne, but a strong streak of realism made her uncomfortably aware that something in her nature, something she barely recognised, craved whatever it was Alex had offered her.

She wondered how many other men beside Alex had caught glimpses of her russet fleece and furled sex-folds. The thought made her want to curl up in a tight ball of embarrassment and stay like that, but at the same time it made her sex moisten and throb.

There was one shred of comfort to be had from the situation – that within a few days she'd be embarking on a journey of several thousand miles and need never see Alex again. She could feign illness and refuse to leave the house until then and spare herself a great deal of embarrassment.

But was that what she really wanted?

She had to admit that it wasn't. Last night had merely whetted her appetite for more of the erotic stimulation she'd enjoyed and now she wanted more.

Her couplings with Douglas in the old barn which at the time had seemed so daring and adult, now appeared positively wholesome in contrast.

She wanted to see Alex again and she wanted to experience everything he could teach her in her remaining time in England. After that she could set sail for the Orient and her new life.

Partially reconciled to the situation, Lisa swung her long, slender legs from the bed, discarded her new shell-pink silk nightgown and went to run a bath. Bathed and with her hair hanging carelessly around her shoulders, she slipped back into bed and rang for her breakfast.

'Madame Valois would like you to join her for breakfast in her room,' the maid announced when she arrived. Hoping that Solange had no inkling of what had taken place between her and Alex last night, Lisa pulled on her grey silk robe and went along to her bedroom.

The Frenchwoman was propped up against a pile of downy pillows, a bed jacket of aqua satin with a ruffled neckline open over her nightgown. There was a contented, sated air about her that made Lisa wonder exactly how she'd spent the night.

'Did you sleep well?' Solange enquired in her husky voice.

'Yes, thank you. Did you?'

'Certainly I did. There's nothing like a few hours in the arms of a lover to ensure a good night's sleep.' Lisa must have looked taken aback at Solange's frankness because she laughed and patted her hand.

'Have I shocked you, *chérie*? Did you not amuse yourself *bien* with Alex?'

'Well yes, but . . .' Her voice trailed off as there was a tap at the door and the maid entered the room carrying a heavily laden breakfast tray. Somewhat to her surprise, Lisa found she had a hearty appetite and helped herself to eggs, bacon and tomatoes, while Solange merely nibbled on a croissant and drank several cups of strong coffee.

'What did you think of Roland and Alex?' she asked when they'd finished eating.

'I . . . I think they're both very nice,' replied Lisa lamely.

'Nice?' echoed Solange. 'You are mistaken Lisa, they are neither of them *nice*. But they are attractive, *amusant* and both exceptionally gifted at pleasuring a woman. Did Alex not pleasure you?'

'Well . . . yes,' admitted Lisa, blushing.

'Good. Now, we have much to do today so I'll meet you downstairs in an hour.'

Lisa was young and in excellent health, but even so she found shopping all day tiring enough to be relieved when Solange announced that it was time for afternoon tea, after which they would return home for a rest before the evening.

They went to a tea room on the edge of the park and ate tiny sandwiches and cakes served by elderly waitresses in severe black dresses, starched white aprons and ribbon-threaded white caps.

The tea room was in a conservatory adjoining an orchid house and the tables were separated by banks of potted palms, aspidistras and weeping figs. A three-piece orchestra played in the background over the muted hum of decorous conversation and the chink of bone china.

Exciting though Lisa found the prospect of sailing for Malaya, she wished their stay in London was to be longer. She was enjoying her entry into adult life and the new pleasures she was experiencing on a daily basis.

She was also flattered by the way in which men now looked at her, but put most of it down to her new wardrobe and hairstyle. Today she was wearing a severely cut heather-pink linen dress with a matching jacket and a tiny frivolous cloche hat.

'What shall we do tonight?' asked Solange. 'We've been invited to a recital and three parties.'

Lisa didn't like to ask if Alex and Roland were included in the invitations, so she said, 'Whatever you want to do. It's all new and exciting for me.'

'*Bien*. I think the recital will be dull and we will amuse ourselves better at a party. Oh look – there's Alex. Unfortunately he's with Emily Galton, who is the most ghastly woman.'

Lisa blushed a vivid pink at the mention of Alex's name and wondered how on earth she was going to face him after her wanton behaviour the previous night.

She glanced up and saw that he'd just entered the tea room with a beautiful blonde-haired woman on his arm. She looked to be in her mid-thirties and from her carefully styled hair to her elegant high-heeled shoes, she exuded a sophisticated, brittle glamour. She was clinging to his arm with an air of possessiveness, laughing at something he'd just said.

Solange waved and Alex began to make his way through the tables to them. His companion looked sulky when Solange invited them to sit down. Lisa could tell that the glamorous blonde would rather have kept Alex to herself.

Solange performed the introductions, but although Emily smiled coldly at the Frenchwoman and asked her how she was, she barely acknowledged Lisa's presence. Instead, she inserted a cigarette into a tortoise-shell holder and held it poised at her carmine lips for Alex to light.

He proffered the light with a gallant, graceful flourish then asked her what she'd like him to order for her.

'I want a cocktail,' she drawled. 'A Tom Collins.'

'They don't serve them here,' replied Alex, pocketing his lighter.

'Then we'll have to go somewhere else,' announced Emily triumphantly. 'Come along, darling.'

'Have some tea now and we'll go somewhere for cocktails later,' suggested Alex.

Lisa could tell that Emily was tempted to demand that they move on immediately, but wasn't certain that Alex would accompany her if she insisted on leaving. She hesitated, then apparently decided to make the best of a bad job and sat back in her seat.

'I didn't see you at the Fortuneys' party last week,' she said to Solange.

'*Non*, I was out of town on business.'

'Business! What an odd creature you are, Solange. Don't you have people to handle that sort of thing for you?'

'Certainly I do. But we French are a practical race and know that taking a personal interest in our affairs generally gets the best results.'

'Really? I'm afraid I'd consider it vulgar to interest myself in anything like that.'

'Then that is probably why you're so impoverished that you're forced to spend all your time and energy looking for a rich husband,' retorted Solange sweetly. 'I, on the other hand, can enjoy dalliance where I please with no such constraints. Poor Emily, it must be so fatiguing for you.'

Emily flushed an ugly red.

'I think you've been misinformed,' she snapped. 'I've no intention of ever marrying again.'

Solange smiled at her, her dark eyes gleaming, and said, 'Remind me – what happened to your first husband?'

As the two women continued to exchange barbed words, Alex leant towards Lisa and asked, 'Have you seen the orchids?'

'N . . . no,' she stuttered, unable to meet his eyes as she remembered lying across his lap, her skirt around her waist, while he toyed skilfully with her private parts.

'May I show them to you?' He rose to his feet and moved behind her, ready to help her from her chair. Lisa glanced appealingly at Solange who broke off what she was saying to Emily to smile encouragingly at her young charge.

'Yes, do go with Alex, *chérie*, the orchids are most beautiful. Emily and I will be quite happy exchanging gossip.' She shot a triumphant look at Emily, obviously delighted that Lisa appeared to be stealing him from under the other woman's nose.

Lisa didn't dare look at the blonde. Instead she rose to her feet, took Alex's arm and accompanied him silently from the room.

The orchid house was warm and humid and a narrow winding path led them past dozens of different varieties of the flowers which were in full and exotic bloom. A fountain played in the centre, the musical notes of the droplets of water providing a pleasant background for the strolling visitors.

'Did you dream of me last night?' enquired Alex. 'Did you dream of the things we did together . . . the things we might do together in the future?'

Lisa blushed again, wondering how he could be so ungentlemanly as to refer to their erotic interlude, but she was stirred nevertheless.

'If I had any dreams, I don't remember them,' she said shortly, trying not to let him see that his words had affected her. She felt an itch high up in her sex and a tantalising tingling in her bud.

'I dreamt about you,' he told her. 'I dreamt that you appeared in my room, wearing only a simple white nightgown of the finest muslin. There was a lamp on behind you and I could see the soft contours of your body through the filmy material.'

He paused by a waist-high mossy bank where a dozen creamy orchids with trembling, pollen-heavy stamens grew among delicate ferns. Lisa nearly jumped a foot in the air when she felt his caressing hand brush lightly over her bottom.

She looked agonizedly round to see if anyone had noticed, but they were both hidden from the waist down by the mossy bank in front of them and there was a wall directly behind them.

Alex's hand continued its unhurried exploration of her *derrière* as he went on, 'I could see the hard points of your nipples pushing at the thin material and the dark triangle of your silken fleece, a tantalising shadow between your thighs.'

His hand slipped down to the hem of her short heather-pink skirt and then glided up her thighs underneath it. Lisa gasped as his fingers made contact with the bare skin above her stocking tops and stroked it slowly.

'I reached out, took hold of the neckline of your nightgown and ripped it from your body with one swift pull, so you stood naked before me. Your breasts were such perfect creamy orbs that I wanted to worship them. I covered them with my hands and felt the pebble-hard points of your nipples pushing against me.'

The sensations his caressing hand were evoking were so delicious that Lisa almost moaned aloud.

'I drew you down on to the bed and made slow, gentle love to you until you were soft and yielding in my arms. And that is exactly what I intend to do in reality as soon as the opportunity presents itself.'

Lisa could feel her sex-flesh swelling and moistening at the idea. She swayed against him, her knees trembling and then bit her lip as she felt his hand pushing her thighs apart.

'Bend forward and smell the flowers,' he directed her. Barely able to breathe, she did so and felt his fingers moving under the loose leg of her camiknickers to make electrifying contact with the slick folds of her vulva.

Afterwards, Lisa couldn't have said whether the exotic blooms had any scent, the only thing she was aware of was Alex's fingers rimming her outer sex-lips then briefly gliding over her throbbing bud before slipping inside her to explore her sex.

She was aware of hot liquid seeping into the crotch of her camiknickers as he subjected her to a thorough internal exploration. His thumb began to rub her swollen bud until hot shivers of fast-mounting excitement coursed through her. It was only when he suddenly withdrew his hand and then bent forward to smell the flowers too, that she came back down to earth with unwelcome abruptness.

'Emily's coming this way,' he told her, as she looked at him in bewilderment, wondering why he'd stopped the caresses which were giving her so much pleasure. Startled, she glanced up and saw the older woman, her forehead wrinkled in a frown, making her way towards them. Lisa hastily smoothed her skirt down and tried to pull herself together before Emily reached them.

'Alex! Whatever's taking you so long?' demanded the blonde.

'I didn't realise I was supposed to be hurrying.'

She tapped her foot impatiently. 'I'm ready to leave now. Come along.' If Alex resented her high-handed attitude, he gave no sign of it. He merely escorted Lisa back to Solange, kissed their hands then allowed Emily to shepherd him from the tea room.

The party was in full swing when Lisa, Solange and Roland arrived. There was a crush of people in the hall and they had to push their way through to reach the relatively less crowded drawing room. Roland grabbed three glasses of champagne from a circulating waiter and they stood by the window chatting.

Roland had dined with them at the house, but Lisa had been disappointed that Alex wasn't able to come. Solange had mentioned that he'd had a prior engagement, but would see them at the party.

Lisa was wearing a dress of printed chiffon in black and white from Paquin. It was an elegant creation with a draped waist, low vee-neck and handkerchief points at the hem. It seemed to mould itself subtly to her slim figure, emphasising her delicate curves and long legs.

Solange was in a pair of black crêpe-de-Chine pyjamas with appliquéd velvet flowers in scarlet and emerald green on the back. The pyjamas were belted around the waist and she wore them with a pair of black velvet evening shoes with very high heels. Every time she moved it was possible to catch an intoxicating glimpse of her alabaster cleavage and Roland was obviously having difficulty in not staring at it.

Lisa was trying to concentrate on what the man who had just joined them and was talking to her was saying. But it was difficult, not only because he was talking about farming in which she had no interest whatsoever, but because she couldn't help but look round to see if Alex had arrived.

When at last she spotted him she saw to her dismay that Emily was still with him, hanging onto his arm, pressing herself close to him, obviously determined not to be separated.

Lisa immediately turned away and tried to look as though she was finding her companion's conversation absolutely fascinating.

When at length he came to the end of his rambling discourse on intensive farming he said, 'I say – would you like to dance?'

She nodded and allowed him to lead her into the room which had been set aside for dancing. They passed close to where Alex and Emily were standing but Lisa pretended not to have seen them.

Determined that whenever he caught a glimpse of her, it would look as though she was having a wonderful time, she laughed, flirted and drank several glasses of champagne.

It was getting late when at last he approached her. Her dancing partner had gone to get her another drink and she was standing alone when Alex came up.

'Shall we?' he said, indicating the dancing couples.

'I'm already dancing with someone, thank you,' she returned coolly. 'He's gone to get me a drink.'

Alex took no notice but drew her into the crowd, put his arm around her waist and pulled her close. She started to protest but it was a slow number and the feeling of his lean body against her own was too seductive to resist.

She wondered what had happened to Emily but wasn't about to give him the satisfaction of letting him know she'd noticed them together. He'd managed to get rid of her and that was the most important thing.

At the end of the dance, her former partner rushed forward and handed her a drink. Alex took the other from his hand, said 'Thanks,' and then steered her from the room.

'Wh . . . where are we going?' she asked as he led her upstairs.

'Somewhere we can be alone.'

He opened a couple of doors leading off the first floor gallery and then backed out, indicating that they were already occupied. The room he took her into was dominated by a four-poster bed and lit only by the moonlight shining in through the window.

Lisa was dismayed. Although she'd eagerly anticipated this moment, she'd assumed it would be in the privacy of the house she and Solange were staying in. It seemed . . . squalid somehow to make love at a party.

As well as that, she knew that they were taking a risk of discovery by someone stumbling in, but the glasses of champagne she'd consumed had made her reckless.

Alex took her into his arms and quelled any fleeting uneasiness by kissing her until she felt weak and giddy.

'Much as I'd like to rip this off you,' he muttered, his hands busy at the fastenings of her dress, 'it wouldn't do to have you leaving a party wearing only the tatters of a frock. I think I'll buy you a gown for the sole pleasure of tearing it from your beautiful body.'

Something intense and primitive in his words made her shiver, just as the printed chiffon fluttered to the floor around her ankles, leaving her clad in only her ivory camisole, camiknickers, suspender belt, stockings and shoes.

He lifted her into his arms and kissed her again, a hard

demanding kiss that set her senses aflame. When he laid her on the bed she let out a little cry as she felt something furry beneath her, thinking for a moment that it was a cat. But it was a fur coat thrown carelessly on the bed and adding another ingredient of pleasure as she felt its sensual softness against the bare skin of her arms and shoulders.

Alex began to kiss his way over her body, beginning with her lips, then working his way downwards, brushing aside the silk of her lingerie to press burning kisses on her skin until she was in an erotic daze.

He drew the thin straps of her camisole down her arms, exposing her breasts for the first time. He gazed at them in the moonlight and then breathed, 'Your breasts are even more beautiful than they were in my dream.'

He kissed her nipples, flicking at them with the tip of his tongue, then drew one into his mouth to commence a soft sucking which had her writhing voluptuously on the bed. He massaged her belly, sending lances of sheer lust down to her vulva and making her ache for his touch there.

When both her nipples were hard, throbbing peaks of aroused female flesh, he drew her camiknickers slowly down her hips and tossed them to one side.

He covered her mound with the palm of his hand and gently massaged her silken russet fleece, making her moan. Warm moisture trickled stealthily from her, soaking into the already damp fronds curling around her vulva. Unable to stop herself she opened her legs invitingly, then froze in shock as he bent his head and kissed the throbbing bud of her clitoris.

'Don't,' she protested weakly, horrified by this unknown and unexpected development, but unable to stop a shiver of desire passing over her as his warm lips and tongue explored her most intimate parts. What on earth was he doing? She'd never heard of such a thing, let alone imagined it happening to her.

'Shhh,' he murmured, raising his head for a moment, then pushing his tongue between her inner sex-lips to find the furled entrance to her concealed chamber.

It felt, if possible, even better than when he'd explored her with his hands. Initially tense, the delicious sensations he was evoking soon made her forget her reservations as he skilfully worked her towards a climax with his persuasive mouth.

When at last she lay poised on the brink, he strummed the head of her clitoris with firm strokes of his tongue and she clutched desperately at the fur beneath her as her back arched and she convulsed into a hot, urgent climax.

She was barely aware of him stripping off his clothes, and was just spiralling slowly back to earth when he positioned himself over her. She felt the hard, smooth head of his manhood pushing gently against her sex-flesh and then he slid it slowly, tantalisingly into her an inch at a time.

Lisa was gripped by such an urgent need to have him completely inside her that she lost all inhibitions and wound her legs around his thighs, thrusting her pelvis upwards and opening herself to him.

His member was big, very big. She could feel it stretching her to her fullest extent, giving her time to accommodate it by a slow, measured entry.

When it was deeply embedded, he withdrew slightly and then began an unhurried, steady thrusting. She thought briefly that it was a good job she was so aroused, so running with honeyed juices, or it might have been uncomfortable. As it was, she relaxed and began the heady, inexorable climb to another climax.

The fur under her felt wonderful as she writhed ecstatically beneath him, loving the sensation of him moving in and out of her. Her hips rose and fell to meet each thrust until he accelerated the pace and the bed shook beneath them.

It was a hot and heady coupling and Lisa found herself digging her nails into his back and biting her own lip in an attempt not to cry out.

At last, in an explosion of pleasure that left her weak and trembling, she convulsed into another orgasm only moments before he made three last, very fast thrusts and erupted into her.

She clung to him, her internal muscles clutching at his shaft as he finally slowed to a halt and rolled her over so she was lying on top of him. They lay silently in the moonlit room, only dimly aware of the noise from the party drifting up to them until Lisa regretfully eased herself away, suddenly self-conscious.

He pulled her back and tried to kiss her, but she was uncomfortably aware that she would be able to taste herself on his lips. The idea unnerved her so she averted her face.

They dressed in silence after that and then she said awkwardly, 'Why don't you go downstairs? I need to find a bathroom.'

'There's one next door,' he told her, fastening his shirt and then stepping into his trousers.

Luckily there was no-one in sight when she nervously pushed open the bedroom door and peered round it. She washed as best she could in the opulently appointed bathroom and then studied her reflection in the mirror.

She looked very different from the schoolgirl of only a few days before. Her high cheekbones were stained with a hectic flush and her grey eyes looked almost black and glittered like anthracite. Her full, wide mouth was slightly swollen from Alex's kisses and although there was no trace of lipstick left, it was very red.

She suspected that Solange would know immediately what she'd been doing and as she left the bathroom and made her way downstairs, she hoped it wouldn't be as obvious to everybody.

Chapter Five

After another full day of fittings and shopping, Lisa's head was spinning. She lost track of the number of clothes she'd purchased and began to wonder when she was going to wear them. At Solange's suggestion she bought what seemed to her to be a vast amount of lingerie, nightgowns and robes as well as yet more clothes, accessories and toiletries.

'It may be years before you're able to buy couture clothing again and many things will undoubtedly not be available in Malaya,' said Solange wisely. 'Stock up now while you have the chance. It's a great pity we don't have time to go to Paris for your clothes, but we must do the best we can.'

Lisa also purchased an enormous steamer trunk and half a dozen new cases of varying sizes to hold them all.

'Surely I have enough now?' she said to Solange, as she sank exhaustedly into the back seat of the car in the late afternoon.

'The voyage lasts for five weeks and on board ship everyone changes their clothes several times a day, particularly in the tropics,' explained Solange. 'But I agree we have done enough for one day. What would you like to do tonight, *ma petite*?'

'I . . . I'm not sure,' said Lisa blushing.

'Alex has invited us to dinner at his club. Shall we accept?'

'Yes – if that's what you'd like,' mumbled Lisa, pretending to search in her bag for something. Solange smiled enigmatically and rested her head against the back of the seat.

When Lisa had made her way back downstairs the night before, it was to find that Alex had already left the party.

'The ghastly Emily was drunk and began to make a scene,' Solange had explained. '*Pauvre* Alex felt he had to take her home as he'd brought her, but you could see he was not happy.'

Lisa had been half relieved. Making love was one thing, but knowing how to act afterwards was another. Perhaps if she studied Solange she'd learn to behave with the same total poise. She'd never seen her companion even mildly flustered.

When Lisa descended the stairs that evening her heart was pounding. She'd tapped on Solange's door, but the Frenchwoman had said she wasn't quite ready and asked Lisa to go and entertain Alex and Roland who'd arrived a few minutes earlier.

Lisa was wearing a dress of panelled ash-blue satin which swirled around her legs as she walked. A silver bag, belt and shoes completed the ensemble. From her mother's jewellery box she'd chosen an intricately worked silver bracelet set with a large sapphire and she was wearing the string of pearls hanging as a single strand to just below her breasts.

'Enchanting,' was Roland's reaction when she entered the room. He walked around her and examined her from all angles, while Alex leant back against the sideboard, his legs crossed, a drink in his hand. Lisa couldn't bring herself to look at him and kept her eyes averted.

'Molyneux?' asked Roland and she nodded surprised – she'd thought men didn't know anything about clothes. 'Very chic.' To her surprise she felt his hand glide appraisingly over the satin-clad contours of her bottom. Before she could react he stepped away, brushing back a lock of fair hair. 'Drink?' he enquired.

'Yes please.' The liquid which bubbled out of the cocktail shaker was darker than a martini. She took a sip and had to stop herself pulling a face because it tasted foul. 'What is it?' she asked.

'A Bosom Caresser,' said Alex, leaving his position against the sideboard and coming over to her.

'Th . . . that's a funny name for a cocktail,' she stuttered, a moist heat already forming in her sex.

She felt like a rabbit in the presence of a fox as he smiled at her showing his pointed canine teeth, a smile which seemed in equal measure to carry both threat and promise. He put his drink down and with his eyes holding hers he began to undo the small, satin-covered buttons of her bodice.

It wasn't that she didn't want him to push open her dress and reveal her breasts, then touch and caress them. She just didn't want him to do it in front of Roland, with Solange about to join them at any moment.

In a reflex reaction she raised her hands to push his away, only to have them seized from behind by Roland. Alex continued to unfasten her bodice until it hung open, leaving her coral-tipped breasts exposed to his gaze.

There was complete silence in the room broken only by the

sound of her own ragged breathing. Strangely, it didn't occur to her to struggle or call out for Solange.

Alex took the strand of pearls and drew them over her breasts, then let them dangle down her cleavage. He made a loop of the end and captured one crinkled nipple with it, lifting it slightly. It was a curiously voluptuous sensation to have her bared orbs caressed by the cool, smooth pearls as he rolled them over her ivory skin.

Alex left the necklace looped over one nipple then bent his dark head and took the other in his mouth. Lisa thought she was about to pass out from sheer pleasure as he tugged at it with his lips, then sucked hard. He flicked at the rapidly hardening nub with the tip of his tongue, making her long to be alone with him so he could make love to her again.

When he removed his mouth the whole of her aureole was glistening with his saliva and the nipple was much harder and more swollen than its twin.

He cupped her other breast in his hand, flattened it slightly then glided his palm over it in an arousing circular movement. He pinched her nipple with his long fingers, coaxing it into tumescence.

A slight sound from the doorway made Lisa's eyes dart in that direction as Solange entered the room in a whisper of elegant, slate-grey moiré which showed a lot of her creamy cleavage.

'You've helped yourself to drinks I see – *bien*,' she greeted them, strolling over to the cocktail shaker and pouring herself one. 'Does anyone want another?'

Lisa couldn't work out what was going on. Hadn't Solange noticed that her charge had her wrists held behind her by one man while another was openly fondling her breasts?

Solange wandered over to them and watched the proceedings with mild interest for a few moments and then said, 'As I thought, that shade of blue is most becoming on you, *chérie*.' She glanced at her watch. 'We should be leaving soon,' she added.

With a last tweak of Lisa's nipple, Alex moved away from her and Roland released her wrists. She turned her back and with fumbling fingers fastened her bodice, feeling confused and disoriented.

Confused, disoriented and *very* aroused.

Alex's club was opulently furnished in heavy Victorian style with a lot of deep red velvet and mahogany furniture. The period feel was enhanced by gloomy oil paintings of former members, many of them sporting the mutton chop whiskers and luxuriant moustaches of an earlier era.

Solange saw Lisa's expression as an elderly waiter led them upstairs to the bar.

'The food here is quite passable – at least for London,' she murmured, 'but it's not the most cheerful of establishments, is it?'

They had drinks in a wood-panelled bar and then were shown to the dining room and a table in a high-backed booth. The waiter departed to fetch the champagne Alex ordered and Lisa immediately opened her menu so she didn't have to look at anyone.

To her relief the menu was in English. After some deliberation she opted for asparagus and then cutlets, eschewing the soup and fish courses.

Solange and Roland were both in high spirits, exchanging

gossip and witty banter in a way that made Lisa laugh several times, even though she didn't know any of the people involved. Alex contributed the occasional remark, but most of the time he was silent, though Lisa was aware of his eyes beneath their thick, dark lashes resting on her more than once.

Lisa thought the food was delicious. Her asparagus came dripping with a lemon butter dressing, perfectly cooked to just the right degree of tenderness. Her cutlets in port and redcurrant sauce tasted like the best thing she'd ever eaten and she couldn't help but exclaim at the tiny sautéed potatoes that accompanied them along with florets of broccoli.

When they'd finished their main courses Alex told the waiter they'd wait for a while before deciding whether to order puddings. It was a warm evening and stuffy in the dining room. Solange took a small ivory and rice paper fan out of her bag and began to fan herself.

'You'd be cooler if you undid your dress,' remarked Roland. 'Then I could fan your breasts for you.'

'Are you not hot too?' she enquired sweetly.

'Very.'

Without a word Solange reached across and deftly unbuttoned Roland's fly, pushed aside his undergarment and drew out a large, de-tumescent shaft, which at the touch of her fingers at once began to swell.

From across the table Lisa watched wide-eyed as Solange fondled it with one hand and fanned it with the other.

'Cooler?' enquired Solange huskily.

'No – much, much hotter,' he said, putting his hand on her silk-clad knee and stroking it. 'So hot that I think I might have to have you right now – here on the table.'

SENSUAL STORM

Lisa's eyes, which had been fixed on Roland's rearing member, now flickered nervously around the room, but as their booth was high-backed, someone would have to come right up to their table to see what was going on. A couple of people had already stopped to exchange a few brief words, so it seemed to Lisa her companions were taking quite a risk.

Alex was lounging back, his hand around his champagne glass, watching the proceedings with mild amusement. Lisa found her eyes drawn back to the swollen rod Solange was caressing so expertly, mesmerised by it.

It wasn't that she'd never seen one before – she had. Last night it had been too dark to see Alex's penis, but she'd caught a couple of glimpses of Douglas's during their interludes in the old barn. She'd been too shy to examine it in detail at the time, but all she knew was that if the sensations evoked were anything to go by, Alex's was bigger. Roland's looked strong, thick and was marbled with blue veins.

Lisa found herself wondering what it would feel like to have it sliding inside her, stretching her, filling her up. She shifted on her seat, uneasily aware that her sex-lips felt engorged and heavy.

Roland suddenly removed Solange's hand, buttoned up his fly and rose from the table. Without a word she rose too and took his arm. They left the room leaving Lisa confused at their sudden disappearance and nervous at being alone with Alex.

'Wh . . . where have they gone?' she asked, taking a gulp from her glass of chablis, a bottle of which had followed the champagne.

'To find somewhere they can be alone – or almost alone.' Lisa felt she needed a few minutes alone too to get herself in hand and not reveal her embarrassing naivety.

Murmuring that she needed to powder her nose, she left him at the table and went into the corridor outside where she'd seen a powder room. But when she opened the door of the room she thought it was, it turned out to be a broom closet.

She hurriedly closed it and then opened the door next to it – if it wasn't that one it was certainly the next because there were only three doors in the corridor other than that leading to the dining room.

But she found herself in a some sort of office with a large leather-topped table piled high with musty looking books. About to back out and try the last door, she noticed that although three of the walls were wood-panelled, instead of a fourth there was a plush red velvet curtain.

Surely the powder room couldn't be through there? But if she glanced quickly around the curtain she'd know for sure and wouldn't have to try the third door.

Just as her hand reached out to push the curtain aside Lisa heard a faint noise, somewhere between a mew and a moan. Her heart beating fast, she bent forward to put her eye to the half-inch gap between the curtain and the wall.

It seemed she was destined to spend most of her waking hours in a state of shock, because there on the other side of the curtain were Roland and Solange.

Her companion was seated on the broad back of a leather armchair, the skirts of her slate-grey dress bunched up around her waist. Her pearl-grey camiknickers lay in a tiny crumpled pool of satin on the floor and her shapely legs in their sheer grey stockings were locked around Roland's neck.

He had his head between her thighs and what he was doing

with his mouth and tongue was obviously giving her great pleasure because her eyes were closed and Lisa could hear her erratic breathing from across the room.

Solange was holding onto the top of the chair and her bare bottom was making voluptuous circles on the highly polished leather. It seemed that Roland was indeed skilled at giving a woman pleasure because she suddenly stiffened, her head fell back and she let out a moan as she enjoyed what was obviously a strong, long-drawn-out climax.

She unlocked her legs from around his neck and wound them around his waist as he straightened up, his face wet with her female juices. He ripped open his trousers with impatient fingers, his other hand covering the silken sable triangle of Solange's mound.

His shaft looked even bigger than before as he positioned it at the entrance to her sex and thrust it swiftly in. Solange wound her arms around his neck and they commenced a feverish, urgent coupling.

Lisa knew she shouldn't be watching, knew she should immediately withdraw, but somehow she remained rooted to the spot, unable to tear herself away. She was disconcerted to realise that a hot little flame of lust was licking at her vulva in libidinous response to the abandoned scenario she was spying on.

Solange's hips moved in an undulating rhythm, her arms now about Roland's neck, their mouths together in a deep kiss. Lisa was mesmerised as the coupling seemed to go on for a very long time. How long had she and Alex been making love last night? It had felt like an eternity, but she had no way of gauging it accurately.

With Douglas it had usually lasted only seconds and then it was over. Watching Roland and Solange was almost like watching an erotic dance, their movements were so perfectly synchronised.

At last, with a cry that echoed around the room, Solange came again and then Roland made three last accelerating thrusts and was still.

Lisa found that her mouth was dry and that there was moisture beaded on her upper lip. Fearful of discovery she backed away from the curtain and hurried to the door. Luckily the elderly waiter was passing and directed her to the powder room which was not next to the dining room as she'd thought, but next to the bar.

She splashed cold water on her face and wrists and then dusted some powder on her face. She was just applying some fresh lipstick when the door opened and Solange came in. Lisa blushed a deep pink, but Solange didn't appear to notice because she smiled at her and said, 'Did you enjoy your meal?' then went into the cubicle.

Lisa wondered how the other woman could look so poised and well-groomed when she'd just been in the throes of a passion so heady she'd taken a terrible risk of discovery by making love in a deserted office in a gentlemen's club. Anyone could have walked in and Solange was obviously unaware that someone had.

'Yes, it was delicious,' Lisa managed to call over the top of the door separating them.

'I believe the food on the *S.S. Orient* is among the best in the world outside France,' Solange told her, emerging from the cubicle and washing her hands. 'I have friends who have travelled on the ship and they spoke of it very highly.'

The two women returned to the dining room to find the men studying the list of puddings available that evening.

'Let me warn you, *chérie*,' said Solange, 'the puddings here are absolutely disgusting and no woman with any delicacy would ever eat one.'

'That's not the case at all,' protested Roland. 'They're wonderful grub.'

'Nursery food for little boys,' said Solange dismissively. Lisa glanced curiously at the list and saw immediately what Solange meant. Steamed jam roly-poly, spotted dick and treacle tart were not what she'd have chosen to eat after the previous courses. Puddings like that had been served at school and she'd never cared for them and had vowed when leaving that she'd never eat such food again.

'Anyone?' asked Roland.

'Not for me,' said Alex, replenishing glasses with the last of the wine.

'Ladies?' They both shook their heads. 'One jam roly-poly,' he said to the waiter.

They went on to a club and then later were on their way to another when Alex suggested a walk in the park. It was a balmy night and everyone found the idea appealing after the heat and smoky atmosphere of the nightclub. The car trailed them at a discreet distance as they walked in silence, passing several other people out for a late night stroll.

After a few hundred yards Solange declared she'd walked far enough and she and Roland returned to the car. Lisa glanced sideways at Alex. He'd seemed pre-occupied most of the evening and she wondered what he was thinking about.

He took her arm and led her onto the grass leading down to the lake. The air was heavy with the perfume of roses and newly mown grass and the more subtle night scents of earth and the breeze playing over the water.

'I regret to say that this is the last evening in London I'll be able to enjoy your company,' he said, as they passed under the spreading branches of an oak tree. 'I have to return home to see my family tomorrow and it's unlikely I'll be back until the day the *S.S. Orient* sails.'

Lisa's heart plummeted. She'd been hoping to learn so much from him. Even though his behaviour earlier that evening had disturbed her, she'd still found it deeply arousing and both that and what she'd later witnessed between Solange and Roland had left a lingering warmth and moistness between her thighs that wouldn't go away.

'I'm sorry to hear that,' she said awkwardly, wondering why he couldn't come back a day earlier to spend a final evening with her.

He stopped and turned to face her in the shadows below the tree. Lisa's heart beat faster as she wondered if he were about to kiss her.

She was taken aback when he took her hand and laid it on his crotch. She could feel a hard bulge and tried to snatch her hand away, but he held it firmly in place.

'It's been like that since last night,' he told her. 'Hard and ready for you – take it out.'

Lisa wanted to refuse such a peremptory command, but curiosity and desire got the better of her. With trembling fingers she undid his trousers then jerked away as she made contact with a warm, throbbing column of flesh.

He caught her hand and placed it back on his shaft and this time she began a tentative, tactile exploration. It felt like silk-covered steel; very big and with a heavily knobbed end that reminded her of a firm plum.

While she explored it Alex drew her into his arms and kissed her, the sort of deep, protracted kiss that made her giddy with desire. His hand glided down over the ash-blue satin of her skirt, found the hem and slid under it and up the back of her thighs, pausing to stroke the bare skin just above her stocking tops.

Lisa wasn't sure which she found the most exciting, the throbbing of his member in her hand, his mouth on hers or when his hand moved upwards to clasp her bottom over her silk underwear.

He slipped his hand under the waistband of her camiknickers and caressed her backside in a way that made her feel as if her sex-valley was practically bubbling with excited moisture. As if of their own volition her legs parted and she felt his fingers glide between them.

His mouth left hers and he murmured in her ear, 'You saw them, didn't you?'

Startled, she stiffened and her hand froze on his rod.

'What do you mean?' she asked.

'You saw Roland and Solange making love and you found it exciting – didn't you?' His cool fingers traced the rim of her outer labia, lingering among the slippery tissues, then probed her inner sex-lips until they made contact with her clitoris.

Unable to help herself she gasped and parted her legs further.

'Didn't you?' he repeated, skilfully stroking the little nub of flesh.

'Y . . . yes,' she moaned.

'Did you wish you were Solange? Did you want Roland's arms around you, his shaft deep inside you?' He stroked her bud more urgently, increasing the pressure, making Lisa feel she was about to explode.

'Yes,' she moaned again. Her hand began to squeeze his manhood in an answering rhythm, enjoying the feeling of power it gave her as he groaned in response. Heat built in her groin, a tingling, disturbing heat. It suddenly broke in a dizzying wave as she shuddered into a climax that seemed to go on and on.

In a swift movement, almost rude in its abruptness, he dragged her skirt up around her waist and her camiknickers down around her thighs.

His hand covered her own which was still clutching his penis and guided it to her sex. When she felt the glans pushing against the soft, fleece-covered entrance to her inner-chamber she gasped and then gasped again as he thrust it slowly and smoothly into her.

Time lost all meaning as, with her back against the tree, Lisa lost herself in an ecstatic coupling.

She found her hips moving to meet each thrust with one of her own, wanting more. The heat began to build again making her think she couldn't stand so much pleasure. Her knees buckled and she clung to him, coming again just before he did.

They leant against each other, breathing hard. Lisa eventually became aware that there was a cool breeze playing over her bare bottom and that goosepimples had formed on her upper arms.

Alex drew away from her, their separation making a faintly obscene plopping sound in the silence. She drew her camiknickers back up her legs and straightened her dress as best she could in the darkness. They walked back towards the car without speaking, his arm around her shoulders.

With a sinking heart Lisa realised that this was to be their last carnal interlude if he was leaving town tomorrow and she was embarking for the Orient in only a few short days. But at least it had given her a pleasurable memory to carry overseas with her.

There was still Roland of course, but she wasn't sure whether he was exclusively Solange's lover.

When they returned to the car Roland and Solange were enjoying cognac from the Rolls-Royce's tiny bar.

'Where to now?' asked Roland.

'*Chérie*! Your dress!' exclaimed Solange. Lisa glanced over her shoulder to see the back of her ash-blue satin covered in moss and bark stains.

'You'd better take me home,' she said ruefully.

'I'll buy you another dress,' said Alex carelessly. 'Choose whatever you like and have the bill sent to me.'

When the car drew up at the door of the house Lisa felt almost bereft but managed to assume a creditable air of nonchalance as she said her good-nights. Solange suggested she change her dress and come with them to another club, but she felt drained by all the excitement and declined politely.

The car drew away as she went into the house, cursing fate for having thrown such a sexually mesmerising man her way for such a short space of time.

Chapter Six

Solange announced that she had business to attend to on the following day, so Lisa decided to wander around and explore London. Much as she was enjoying shopping, she was quite pleased to have a break from it.

She walked briskly through the park enjoying the warm sunshine on her face even though there was a cool breeze blowing. When she came to the spot where she'd behaved with such abandoned licentiousness the night before, she paused for a moment to savour the memory.

Celeste had whisked her ash-blue satin dress away after pursing her lips in disapproval, but Lisa doubted if she'd be able to restore it to its former pristine state.

As she continued with her walk she pondered the relationship between Solange, Alex and Roland. It was pretty much unfathomable as far as Lisa was concerned. The three of them had obviously enjoyed erotic games together, although Roland appeared to be the one who was Solange's regular lover.

Lisa had found it most unnerving to have Alex caress her so intimately in front of Roland last night. It had been even worse when Solange had appeared, but the older woman hadn't seemed to find it anything out of the ordinary.

It was all a bit much to take in. But what did it matter? She'd never see Alex again and in a few days she and Solange would be joining the *S.S. Orient* and leaving Britain far behind. Let life bring her what it may. – it was all new and exciting.

She was striding down a pretty street full of quaint little houses and shops selling antiques, paintings and fine china when she saw a sign outside a small gallery announcing an exhibition of sculpture by someone whose name rang a bell.

Trying to place the name she went inside, accepted a catalogue from a woman just inside the door and stood on the edge of the room. A couple of dozen people were circulating, studying the exhibits and chatting.

They were an artier and more bohemian crowd than Solange's friends. Generally less fashionably dressed, they lacked the stylish edge of the people she'd socialised with in the last few giddy days.

But she nevertheless found them fascinating. Some of the men were wearing corduroy jackets instead of tweed and several of the women seemed to be festooned with unusual, ethnic looking jewellery.

She turned her attention to the first sculpture then blushed to the roots of her hair when she saw that it was of a naked man with a huge, erect phallus.

She moved hurriedly on and then was taken aback to discover that the second one was of a man and woman entwined and enjoying intercourse in what seemed to Lisa to be an imaginative – if not impossible – position.

She was just about to walk past, her eyes averted, when a

voice from behind her said, 'Lisa! Is it really you?' She turned round to see Fiona MacLaine, one of her old school friends.

Of course. No wonder the name of the sculptor had rung a bell. It was Andrew MacLaine's exhibition.

Fiona had always been proud of her older cousin who had apparently made a name for himself in artistic circles and often mentioned him. She and Lisa had always been friendly but not close.

'Fiona – what are you doing in London?' asked Lisa. The last time the two women had seen each other they'd both been in school uniform, but now Fiona was wearing a shapeless dress made of hessian, with a raffia belt around her waist and a necklace of what appeared to be painted acorns around her neck. She had flat, thonged sandals on her bare feet and her dark blonde hair was worn untidily long and loose.

'I came down for Andrew's exhibition, but I was having such a wonderful time I thought I'd stay,' Fiona told her. 'What about you? I thought you were going back to your castle for the hols then off to a finishing school. You . . . you look very smart,' she added, glancing doubtfully at Lisa's clothes.

Lisa was in a garnet-coloured suit made from lightweight wool with a belted jacket and military style revers. Her skirt was tight and tapered to a kick pleat and her shoes, bag and gloves were of mole-grey suede.

'That's my companion, Solange's, doing rather than mine. She's been sent by my guardian to travel with me to Malaya to stay with him. We're just here for a few days so I could buy some clothes and then we sail for the Orient.'

Fiona clasped her hands together, her eyes shining.

'The Orient – how exciting! I thought I was being daring

staying in London. Come and meet Andrew.' A few days previously Lisa would have been dubious about meeting the creator of such explicit sculptures, but even her brief exposure to Solange's friends had made her more worldly.

Fiona took Lisa's hand and led her over to where a group in the corner were talking and laughing.

'Lisa, this is my cousin Andrew. Andrew, I want you to meet an old friend of mine, Lisa Cavendish.'

He was stocky and of medium height with sandy hair and a lot of freckles. His look as he shook hands was frankly appraising, but she didn't allow it to fluster her, merely murmured, 'How do you do?'

'Hello, Lisa Cavendish – do you believe that women enjoy sex as much as men?' he boomed at her. A muffled titter rippled around the room and Fiona flushed a deep, embarrassed red.

A couple of weeks previously Lisa would have wanted the ground to open and swallow her up, but somehow she managed to reply with perfect composure, 'If you approach making love to a woman with the same lack of subtlety as making conversation, then with you – no.'

Someone laughed out loud and then the room seemed to erupt into mirth. Andrew had the grace to join in then handed Lisa a glass of red wine and said, 'You must stay to lunch. I want to get to know you better.'

Lisa didn't particularly want to get to know *him* better, but Fiona tucked her hand through her arm and said, 'Let's look at the rest of the exhibition.'

Lisa was proud of herself because although the sculptures became even more overtly erotic as she worked her way through the catalogue, she managed to scrutinise them all and even make a few light comments without blushing again.

Lunch was served in a room upstairs and was accompanied by more of the red wine which was so robust it burnt a fiery trail down her throat. She sipped it cautiously wishing there were some champagne. As soon as the thought passed through her mind she castigated herself. A couple of weeks ago she hadn't even tasted champagne and now here she was thinking it ought to be served with every meal. She was in serious danger of becoming spoilt.

Andrew sat down next to her and proceeded to monopolise her and ignore Fiona who was sitting on his other side and hanging onto his every word. He was obviously a man used to dominating the conversation, because despite his avowed assertion that he wanted to get to know Lisa better, this seemed to take the form of talking about himself.

Only half listening, Lisa studied him idly as he held forth. She supposed that some women might find him attractive – Fiona obviously did – but he undoubtedly wasn't her type. There was a hole in his sweater, his nails were dirty and she found his habit of talking and eating at the same time off-putting.

'I'm throwing a party on Saturday – you must come,' he urged her enthusiastically. 'I'm giving a talk on "Form and Energy – Are They Valid Influences?" then the floor will be thrown open for discussion.'

'I'm sorry, by Saturday I'll have left the country,' she said politely.

'That's too bad.' He seized her hand and leant close to her. 'Come back to my house after lunch – I want to make love to you. All women should be introduced to the erotic arts by a man who knows what he's doing and I'm a very skilful lover. Afterwards you can sit for me – I'll create a sculpture for you.'

Lisa wondered why he assumed she needed an introduction to the erotic arts. She noticed that he had food between his teeth and that the wine had left an unpleasant looking crust around his mouth.

'Thank you but I really can't,' she told him firmly. 'In fact I must be going. Thank you so much for lunch. It was lovely to see you again, Fiona.'

Fiona looked deeply relieved that Lisa was leaving. She walked with her to the door, promising to write if Lisa would send her address in Malaya once she'd arrived.

As she made her way back to the house Lisa pondered the nature of sexual attraction and wondered why she found Alex – and Roland – so physically compelling, but Andrew quite the opposite. Hopefully there would be men on board the *S.S. Orient* she would find attractive. It was to be hoped so, or it would be a very dull voyage.

She returned home just in time for tea, an English custom Solange had embraced wholeheartedly. In their absence the tickets for the voyage had arrived and Lisa pored over the accompanying literature excitedly.

'Who else will be on board, do you think?' she asked.

'People rarely travel for pleasure to the Far East. Our fellow passengers will be mostly people going out there to work. Army officers to take up postings, colonial civil servants, company men, rubber planters, tea planters. There will probably be very few female passengers, just the wives and families of some of the men and perhaps a few nurses – which should give us much scope for dalliance.'

Solange paused just before biting into a tiny scone to give her a look of such wicked sensual anticipation that Lisa couldn't help but smile. It hadn't taken her long to discover that the pleasures of the flesh – at least on the surface – were everything to the Frenchwoman.

'It is a great pity Alex couldn't be with us tonight,' continued Solange. 'Shall I ask Roland to bring a friend or shall he squire us both?'

'He'd probably like you to himself for once,' Lisa suggested.

'Believe me, he will be delighted to escort two women instead of one.'

'If you don't mind, Solange, I'll have an early night tonight. Perhaps tomorrow.'

'As you wish, *ma petite*.'

In fact, what Lisa really wanted was to be alone so she could remember everything that had passed between herself and Alex in every lascivious detail. She wanted to dwell on it and to milk the last drop of pleasure from her memories before they faded.

As she headed for the door Solange added, 'The clothes you left for alterations earlier this week and the lingerie you ordered have been delivered – they're in your room.'

Lisa ran eagerly up the stairs to find Celeste unpacking the clothes from their swathes of tissue paper. Even with the help of the maid it seemed to take for ever to stow all her new purchases away. When at last she was alone, she took a bath and then tried on some of her new underwear.

She'd never seen anything as beautiful as the fragile silk, satin and cotton-voile lingerie she now owned. Embroidered, be-ribboned or trimmed with lace, she found the delicate garments almost as lovely as her dozens of new dresses.

She slipped into a camisole of the palest jade-green, edged with white Brussels lace and posed in front of the pier-glass wearing only that and a pair of high-heeled white satin slippers.

The pale shade of jade set off her red-gold hair, alabaster skin and tawny fleece. Her hair looked tousled so she picked up her silver-backed hairbrush and smoothed it back into place. As she looked at her reflection she noticed that the crimson tip of her clitoris was visible, standing proud from her sex-lips like the stamen of an exotic flower.

She touched it dreamily with the silver handle of the brush and thought how pleasing was the contrast between her warm sliver of flesh and the cool metal. She stroked the shaft gently, watching how it soon became swollen and even more prominent.

It began to tingle and pulse and she felt a tiny jolt of sexuality jab upwards and outwards through her belly. She sank slowly onto the bed and leant back against the pile of downy pillows, moving the silver handle sensually up and down the responsive bud.

Her sex-flesh began to feel warm and engorged and she could tell by the easy way the metal slipped over it that a fine dew of moisture was already forming. She ran the end of the handle along her sex-valley, tracing the furrows of her labia and then paused at the entrance to her hidden channel.

She couldn't resist the temptation. Slowly she slipped it

inside her a couple of inches, enjoying the feeling of the cool, smooth metal, then another couple of inches, squeezing gently with her internal muscles to maximise the stimulation.

As she slid it rhythmically in and out, she thought of Alex and how hopelessly erotic she found the things they'd done together. She could feel a fine beading of perspiration forming on her cleavage and more of her female dew gathering in her private parts at the memory.

As her excitement mounted she recalled how he'd entered her; his strong, throbbing shaft filling her up, satisfying her. Her hand moved faster and faster, working the handle in and out, causing a delicious friction against the hood of her clitoris with every stroke.

Just as she knew she was on the verge of an explosive release and the first ripples were already passing through her body, her eyes fluttered open. To her absolute horror she saw Solange and Roland framed in the open doorway.

It was too late to stop her climax, she'd reached the point of no return. She could only close her eyes, lie back and give herself up to it as spasm after spasm of pleasure washed over her.

The bed beside her dipped and she smelt Solange's jasmine and orange flower perfume. The other woman's lips were warm on her cheek as she breathed, 'That was beautiful, *chérie*.'

'Beautiful,' she heard Roland's deep voice echo in agreement.

Still weak and breathless after her climax, Lisa didn't have the strength to ask them to leave, although she wanted to.

She was shocked when Solange laid a shapely hand on her silk-covered breast and stroked it. She made a move to push the other woman's hand away, but her nipple hardened in an immediate response which made a shiver of sheer carnality ripple down to her sex.

Solange intensified the caress by slipping Lisa's strap from her shoulder and gliding the palm of her hand over the bared orb. Her touch was delicate and arousing as she toyed with the swollen nipple and then cupped the whole breast.

To her shame, Lisa realised that the pleasure she was experiencing was greater than her reluctance to be part of such a decadent scenario, so she didn't protest when Roland knelt by the side of her parted thighs and bent his fair head to kiss her damp floss.

Like Solange's, his touch was delicate and arousing and Lisa shifted her bottom slightly on the bed's silk spread. She felt the warmth of his tongue make contact with her swollen kernel and it made her gasp and splay her legs further apart, wanting more of the same.

While Solange continued to caress her breasts, Roland commenced a thorough exploration of her vulva with his lips and tongue.

It felt marvellous to have a man stimulate her in that way again. The fact that her breasts were also being fondled doubled the pleasure. He probed her hidden entrance with his tongue, pushing it in as far as it would go and swirling in circles that made her hips shift in avid response.

He took her throbbing bud between his lips and sucked hard, then stabbed at it with the tip of his tongue. A loud moan she didn't even recognise as her own was wrenched from her as for the second time in the space of a few minutes she convulsed into an urgent, rippling climax.

SENSUAL STORM

There was a protracted silence, which to Lisa soon became awkward as she came back down to earth and realised exactly what had just happened. She gave a little moan of mortification and covered her face with her hands.

'What is it, *ma petite*?' asked Solange, her voice soft with concern. But Lisa was too embarrassed at not only having been observed pleasuring herself with a hairbrush handle, but in having been so far gone in the throes of passion that she'd allowed them to do as they wished with her.

Goodness knows how long they'd both been standing there until she opened her eyes.

She felt she could never look either of them in the face again. The bed shifted slightly as Solange stood up and Lisa heard her murmur something to Roland, who thankfully then left the room.

'Open your eyes – I want you to look at something,' Solange bade her.

Reluctantly Lisa allowed her eyes to flicker open. She saw that Solange had moved the pier-glass so it was at the foot of the bed and tipped at the correct angle for Lisa to see her own reflection.

'What you see, is what a woman *should* look like,' Solange told her firmly.

Lisa found what she saw in the mirror infinitely disturbing. She was reclining against the pillows, legs apart, one breast bared, the other still covered in jade-green silk, the nipple prominent under its thin covering. Her hair was dishevelled, her eyes glittered and there was a hectic flush staining her cheeks and breasts.

She looked abandoned, wanton and sated.

Solange allowed her to study herself for a few moments then said, 'There is nothing wrong with enjoying yourself or taking pleasure where you can find it. Life often has many sorrows lying in wait, so you should indulge yourself whenever you can.'

Lisa was silent, uncertain what to say as Solange continued, 'There is much in you that reminds me of myself a few short years ago. We've both known unhappiness – you lost your parents when you were so young and I've lost my husband – so life owes us something. Seize anything that comes your way with both hands, *chérie* – you never know if it may be your last opportunity.'

Lisa sat up and pulled her camisole over her exposed breast, then slipped off the bed and donned a robe.

'In a few days we shall be setting sail for the exotic East and spending several weeks on a ship where every conceivable luxury will be ours,' Solange told her. 'I intend that it shall be a time of total and absolute pleasure because I think we may find Malaya primitive in the extreme. I suggest that you decide to do the same.'

Lisa felt oddly comforted by the older woman's words, recognising the inherent wisdom of them. It suddenly seemed like a good time to ask her the question that had been bothering her.

'Solange . . .' she began.

'Mmm?'

'Do you think Alex will be back before we sail?' It had occurred to her that he might – just might – come and see them off.

'He is returning from the country on the day of embarkation – why do you ask?'

'Will . . . will he come and say goodbye, do you think?' she asked diffidently.

Solange looked startled. 'Say goodbye? Didn't I tell you? Both Alex and Roland will be sailing with us.'

'Wh . . . what?' gasped Lisa joyfully.

'Alex has business in Malaya and Roland is to take up a prestigious posting in the colonial service in Singapore for a few years. That is partially why I introduced you to them as soon as we arrived in London. Now we already know two delightful men who will be on board the *S.S. Orient* and I'm certain we shall soon meet many more,' she ended with a wicked smile.

She leant across and kissed Lisa's cheek. 'Don't worry, *ma petite* we'll have a wonderful time,' she said, then glided gracefully from the room.

Chapter Seven

The next few days passed in a whirl of activity. At last the day of embarkation came and the two women departed for Southampton in the Hispano-Suiza with two further cars carrying the rest of their luggage.

It was a cool and blustery day and Solange had chosen to wear a tweed suit which was unlike one Lisa had ever seen before. Most of her school friends' mothers wore tough, shapeless Scottish tweeds designed to be warm, hard-wearing and not show dog hairs.

Solange's Chanel suit was in a subtle pinkish-grey and heather mix with soft, fluid lines that accentuated her narrow waist and well-rounded bottom. The material felt soft to the touch instead of rough and scratchy.

She wore it with a tiny grey hat which sported a flirtatious pink feather. She looked so stylish that Lisa was deeply envious, aware that however hard she tried she could never carry off clothes with the same *chic* as the Frenchwoman.

She herself was wearing a cobalt-blue and white printed crêpe day dress which buttoned down the back with large black buttons. Over it she wore a matching plain cobalt-blue jacket, fastened by one single large black button at the front.

When shopping, overwhelmed by the choice and uncertain what suited her, she'd always taken Solange's advice. She hadn't regretted it. With consummate ease the other woman had steered her away from colours and styles that weren't flattering and encouraged her to try some shades Lisa thought would be death with her hair and colouring, but which had turned out to be very becoming.

Even on the busy dock which was teeming with hordes of people, the two women attracted a lot of attention. As she got out of the car, Lisa stared upwards at where the massive side of the ship towered high above them. A gangplank protected from the elements by a canopy led to what seemed like a very small hole in the black, riveted steel of the ship's side.

She was grateful for Solange's total poise as, taking no notice of anyone, she walked to the bottom of the gangplank and spoke briefly to the uniformed officer standing there. Within seconds their luggage was being unloaded while Solange returned to the car and thanked the chauffeur, pressed some money discreetly into his hand and then turned to Lisa.

'Are you ready to board?'

Lisa nodded and was suddenly overwhelmed by apprehension at the thought of leaving the country where she'd lived all her life, to set sail for the unknown.

Solange must have sensed her feelings for she tucked her arm through hers and drew her forward. As she stepped onto the gangplank, Lisa tried not to think that this might be the last time she set foot on British soil. Together the two women stepped through the narrow entrance and into another world.

Attended by a ship's officer, two stewards who carried their hand luggage and Celeste who clutched their jewellery cases as if afraid they would be wrested from her, they were led along a maze of gleaming corridors, up in an elevator and along more corridors until they reached their suite.

Lisa was too dazed to notice anything except how clean and sparkling everything looked and that there was a faint smell of paint, disinfectant and the unmistakable tang of sea air.

She was immediately dazzled by the opulence of their suite which consisted of a sitting room and two bedrooms, each with its own bathroom. She could hardly believe that such luxury was going to be theirs and theirs alone for the next few weeks.

She sank into a chair while Solange allowed the officer to show her round, thanked him and the stewards prettily and ushered them to the door.

'So, what do you think?' she asked. The sitting room seemed to be filled with flowers, three huge arrangements scented the air with their heady perfumes and the table held champagne, chocolates, biscuits and other small gifts.

'From Alex and Roland,' announced Solange after glancing at two of the cards, 'and this one is from your guardian wishing us a safe journey.'

The sitting room had a floor of highly polished, honey-coloured parquet strewn with richly woven rugs. Three of the walls were covered in cream watered-silk and on the third was a fanciful mural depicting a forest glade with a sun-dappled pool where voluptuously naked women bathed while unicorns pranced on the mossy banks around them.

Two squashy, modern, low-backed sofas were covered in glazed printed chintz and the rest of the furniture was an eclectic mix of rattan and more traditional pieces inlaid with marquetry.

Even to Lisa's untutored eye the beautifully chosen paintings, lamps and vases were the perfect complement to the clean lines of the furnishings.

Double doors behind willow-green silk curtains could be thrown open and led out onto a semi-circle of teak which was their private verandah and where two lounging chairs and a glass-topped rattan table awaited them.

There was a knock at the door and Celeste hurried to answer it. The rest of their luggage lay in the corridor and the steward immediately began to carry it in.

'I think this would be a good time to go for a drink while Celeste unpacks,' Solange decided. 'Celeste – please ring for a stewardess to help you and then start with those three cases.'

Although Lisa was eager to examine the suite in detail – she'd only glanced at her bedroom and bathroom for a few seconds – she had to agree that they'd be better out of the way for a while.

Lisa thought that the voyage would be almost over before she found her way around the ship – it seemed enormous and immensely confusing. As they strolled along in search of a bar they passed a long line of people queuing outside the first class dining salon.

'What do you think they're waiting for?' asked Lisa with mild interest.

'To choose their table at dinner – the best ones get snapped up very quickly.'

'Shouldn't we join them, then?' she said in alarm, having a

sudden mental picture of them sitting at a table next to the kitchens.

'No need – Roland was travelling down early this morning and he will have ensured we're well seated.'

'Do you think Alex will be aboard too?' enquired Lisa eagerly.

'I'm not sure – he didn't say what time he was planning to get here.'

They entered the crowded cocktail bar where passengers about to set sail, often to be away for years, were enjoying last drinks with friends and relatives. Some of the people present looked tearful, but generally there was a party atmosphere.

The cocktail bar had been recently refurbished in the style made popular by the exhibition of the Arts Décoratifs a few years previously. The bar itself undulated along one wall in three sweeping serpentine curves, the shelves behind it laden with bottles of every type of drink available.

The front of the bar was made from alternating panels of brushed and mirrored aluminium and high black stools with waist high back-rests which were placed along it at intervals.

A steward hurried over to ask what they wanted to drink.

'A split of champagne,' ordered Solange immediately. Lisa felt a hand on her shoulder then Roland planted an exuberant kiss full on her mouth before leaning over to greet Solange in the same way.

Lisa felt herself blushing, it was the first time she'd seen him since he'd used his lips and tongue to bring her to a climax that day in her bedroom.

'I say – this is something like,' he commented, having asked the steward for a whisky sour, 'five weeks of hedonism on the open seas before buckling down to work. Seen Alex?'

'Not yet,' said Solange, removing her gloves in a way that was far sexier than most women removing every item of clothing.

Their drinks arrived and Lisa sipped her champagne appreciatively, enjoying the effervescent tingle of the chilled wine against her tongue and the roof of her mouth. The room was suddenly silent as three mournful hoots sounded, signalling that it was time for all non-passengers to leave the ship.

'Can we go up on deck?' asked Lisa.

'You go, *chérie*,' said Solange, 'I wish to discuss something with Roland.'

Not unwilling to spend a little time alone as she saw the last of her country – at least for a while – Lisa picked up her bag and gloves and followed the hordes of people along the corridors towards the stairs, although she supposed they were called something different on a ship.

She was just about to turn a corner when she heard her name called. Her heart seemed to skip a beat and when she turned around she saw Alex, looking broad-shouldered and athletic in a tweed jacket, white shirt and flannels.

He caught her to him and kissed her, both of them oblivious to the crowds still hurrying by. Lisa was the first to break the kiss by pulling away, rather embarrassed at having behaved so boldly in public and determined not to wear her heart on her sleeve and let him know how glad she was to see him. But she couldn't ignore the electrifying effect his touch had on her.

'Where are you heading?' he asked.

'Up on deck to wave goodbye.'

'Come to my cabin – we can watch from my verandah without being jostled.' He took her hand and led her along the corridor, then stopped and unlocked a door. Although well appointed and spacious, his cabin wasn't quite as lavishly furnished as their suite.

He opened the door leading outside and they stood together leaning against the verandah's white-painted rail overlooking both the deck and the dock where crowds had gathered to wave goodbye.

There was a band playing and people throwing paper streamers, the ends of which were caught by the ship's passengers as their only link with those they were about to leave behind.

Lisa stood looking down, feeling both sad and elated at the same time. Alex stepped behind her and then he was pressing her against the rail with his strong thighs, his arms around her waist. Within a few seconds she could feel the hard bulge of his manhood swelling against her bottom.

With one hand he began to caress her hip, skimming over the soft crêpe of her dress, sending urgent signals of arousal shooting through her belly. She couldn't stop herself pressing back against him and swivelling her hips slightly, feeling a slight ripple of contractions in her sex.

He eased away from her and his hand slid down to cup her bottom and then stroke it.

'Alex,' she said warningly. She wanted him to caress her but not in front of all the crowds below them. He seemed to have a penchant for touching her intimately in public.

'No-one can see,' he murmured, lifting her hair and kissing the back of her neck, 'I just look as if I'm standing behind you.'

It was true. As long as he confined his attentions to her back, his caresses were a private matter between them. Even so, she stiffened when she felt his hand sliding down her skirt until it reached the hem and then stroked the back of her stocking-clad leg.

A hot, tingling excitement shot up her thigh and her sex-valley began to feel moist. She felt him unbutton the lowest button on the back of her dress, then the next two, until it was undone almost up to the waist. She wanted to protest but the desire to have him continue was stronger.

His hand slipped inside her skirt, drifted over the backs of her thighs then fondled the soft, bare skin just above her stocking tops. It felt tremendously exciting to know that he was doing it in front of so many people but that none of them could see.

His long fingers slipped up the loose-fitting leg of her camiknickers and brushed the lower slopes of her buttocks. His touch made her feel that her blood was zinging effervescently around her veins and despite the fresh and blustery sea breeze in her face she felt dizzy.

The ship began to edge away from the dock and the crowd went wild, waving and shouting to the passengers milling on deck.

Lisa felt Alex cupping the cheeks of her bottom, kneading them gently, then he slipped his fingers between her legs and massaged her vulva through the thin strip of satin covering it. The satin was swiftly soaked with her female honey and she had to clutch the rail hard with her gloved hands to stay upright.

When he brushed the satin to one side and stroked her

swollen clitoris, she gasped. She gasped again when he pushed two fingers deep inside her and rotated them, making her long to bear down on his hand and move lewdly and lasciviously against him. He worked his fingers in and out of her, brushing her throbbing bud with each stroke.

She didn't realise he'd freed his shaft or what his next intention was, until she felt the heavily-knobbed end wedging itself into the cleft between her buttocks.

The ship was now several yards from the dock and the multi-coloured streamers stretched between ship and dock began, one by one, to snap.

But Lisa had lost interest in everything but the virile, throbbing organ lodged between her buttocks. As he slid it down then probed the moist entrance to her female channel, she realised that he actually intended to take her here in front of all these people. She was moved to protest, despite her urgent need to have him inside her.

'Alex – not here,' she entreated huskily.

His only answer was to tighten his grasp on her waist and inch his manhood inside her so the plum-like glans was nestled tantalisingly just within her.

Her internal muscles clutched at it spasmodically and she moaned, her reservations melting away as she wondered why he was keeping her waiting when she was more than ready for the first ecstatic thrust into her very depths.

She butted her bottom demandingly back at him, but he remained motionless and said softly, 'We'll wait until that party of officers has moved down the deck.'

Glancing down, she saw what he'd seen but she hadn't – three ship's officers strolling slowly along just below them.

Even as she looked down Lisa saw one of them glance up, his eyes meeting hers briefly. But he couldn't have noticed anything untoward because he raised his hand in a polite salute and continued on his way with his companions.

No-one else on deck had looked up, they were all too engrossed in waving to friends and family on the other side of a rapidly widening gulf of choppy water.

A few seconds later when the officers had passed out of sight, Alex suddenly entered her with a seductive rocking movement that had her molten with lust. She leant further over the rail and began to move her hips rhythmically against him to meet each carefully measured thrust.

'Keep absolutely still,' he advised her, 'or someone might notice.'

Lisa discovered that keeping still was no easy matter. She clung onto the rail trying to look relaxed and nonchalant while behind her Alex plunged in and out of her, setting her sex alight and making her breasts feel tender and swollen although he hadn't actually touched them.

She wanted him to touch them, she wanted him to touch every part of her and she wanted to do the same to every part of him. But even so she found the sheer audacity of coupling in public had lit a fire in her loins that burned hotter than anything she'd ever experienced before.

The ship moved faster and the gap widened so much that the individual faces had become indistinguishable. A sudden sizzling wave of heat passed over Lisa and then she came, a glorious sweeping climax that made her feel that until this moment she'd only been half alive.

She felt Alex accelerate his movements and then he paused

for a moment before reaching his own satisfaction in half a dozen last, compulsive thrusts.

Lisa felt so weightless that she was certain if Alex hadn't had her by the waist she could have soared upwards to join the seagulls flapping and squawking noisily overhead.

She came back down to earth when Alex withdrew and she heard the sound of him zipping himself up.

'Back away from the rail,' he suggested, 'then you can adjust your clothing inside the cabin.'

She did as he suggested and then, self-consciously aware that their combined juices were trickling down her thighs, asked if she could use his bathroom.

It was tiled throughout in gleaming black and white with a huge pile of snowy white towels on a rack at the end of the bath. Someone had unpacked Alex's toilet kit and she spent a few moments examining his silver-topped bottles before turning her attention to her own appearance.

She used the pristine white toilet with the black wooden seat then washed herself. Several strands of red-gold hair had escaped from the smooth coil at the nape of her neck and she pinned them deftly back into place. She powdered her nose and adjusted her clothing and then went back into the cabin.

Alex was out on the verandah, smoking. He extinguished his cigarette when she came out.

'I'll go back to our suite now,' she said awkwardly. 'If I can find it.'

'I'll take you and then I'll try and locate Roland.'

Lisa found it difficult to walk along the corridors without lurching now they were actually in motion. It made her feel clumsy and as though she had no control over her own body.

'Wait until we're away from these sheltered waters,' he said, steadying her as she stumbled. 'This is nothing in comparison.' Lisa devoutly hoped that she wouldn't waste any of their time afloat by being seasick.

They turned a corner and she saw to her amazement that two dark-skinned men in turbans, brightly woven tunics and embroidered slippers were standing on either side of a door. They both seemed to be standing stiffly to attention and as she and Alex approached, she noticed with shock that they had large sheathed knives hanging from their belts.

Neither man gave any indication that they'd noticed the passing couple. As soon as they were out of earshot, Lisa murmured, 'Who do you think they were?'

She'd never seen men so exotically garbed – they looked like something out of the Arabian Nights.

'I believe we have a Maharajah travelling with us,' Alex informed her. 'That must be his suite and they must be part of his entourage.'

'A Maharajah,' breathed Lisa, 'how amazing.'

She couldn't wait to tell Solange, but when she and Alex eventually found the suite she was to share with the Frenchwoman, Solange wasn't there.

She saw her briefly during the lifeboat drill, but they didn't get chance to exchange more than a couple of words. Never mind, she would tell her later over cocktails.

Stretched drowsily out on her stomach on the bed in Roland's cabin, Solange jumped when she felt him place something cold on her voluptuously curved bottom.

'What's that?' she asked, trying to look over her shoulder.

'A martini.'

'I can't reach it there,' she pointed out.

'No. but I can.' Roland resumed his position beside her. 'Don't move or you'll spill it and it's very cold,' he warned her. He spoke the truth. His movements made the bed bounce slightly and an icy splash of the drink sloshed over the rim of the glass and into the cleft between Solange's creamy buttocks.

'*Merde*! It's freezing!' she exclaimed as it trickled down and ran over her swollen vulva. Roland lifted the glass from its unorthodox resting place and passed it to her.

'You take what's left in the glass and I'll make do with what splashed out.' Solange drained it in one swallow and set it down on the bedside table, before lying back down on her stomach.

He knelt between her parted thighs and dipped his tongue into her drenched delta. He licked up all the droplets of martini from her smooth-skinned globes and then delved deeper. Solange squirmed deliciously as she felt his tongue lapping at her outer sex-lips and parted her thighs wider.

'It lacks something,' he told her, sitting up and reaching to one side of the bed.

'What?'

'An olive.' As he spoke he deftly inserted an olive into her hidden core and pushed it gently inside her with his forefinger. He picked up the silver martini shaker and poured some more over her buttocks, making her yelp and swear again.

But as his warm tongue traced the icy trickles which cascaded over her heated private parts she made a little mewing sound of satisfaction and wriggled delightedly.

When he'd finished he made her turn onto her back and went in search of the olive. It proved more difficult to get out than it had to put in and Roland was forced to perform contortions with his tongue which sent Solange into ecstasy. At last he managed to retrieve it and washed it down with another swallow of the cocktail freshly poured from the shaker.

'I think it tastes better from you than a glass,' he decided.

'Don't you dare—' her warning went unheeded and she shrieked as Roland tipped the last of the drink straight onto her vulva.

He bent his head and busied himself between her thighs for a while, then sat up. 'It's not cold enough,' he complained. He picked up an ice cube and ran it teasingly over her sex-lips and then lapped at them. 'That's better,' he decided. For the next few minutes Solange enjoyed the exquisite contrast between the heat of Roland's mouth and the chill of the cube of ice until eventually it melted.

'Don't stop now,' purred Solange. 'Finish what you've started.'

Obligingly, Roland took her blunt little arrow of sensitive, highly responsive flesh between his lips and sucked and nibbled it until she moaned and her head rolled from side to side on the pillow.

He stabbed at it rhythmically with his tongue and then made teasing swirling movements around it. At last he strummed the head until Solange let out a cry and her body went rigid as she convulsed into a lengthy, liquid climax.

When she opened her eyes she glanced at the clock on the bedside table.

'Nearly time to dress for dinner,' she commented.

'No-one dresses for dinner on the first night,' he teased her.

'*Vraiment*? You mean everyone will be naked?' she enquired, her large brown eyes wide. 'That I must see, but it may be too much for Lisa, who is not as worldly-wise as I am.'

'You know very well what I mean.' Roland tugged gently on one distended, brown nipple. 'Bathe here with me – the bath's certainly big enough,' he invited her.

'Very well – on condition that you bathe me.'

'It will be my pleasure,' he told her, his eyes gleaming with anticipation at the prospect of soaping every inch of Solange's lovely body. 'I'll go and run it.' He stubbed his toe on the raised sill between the bedroom and bathroom and swore. 'I'll never get used to this thing,' he complained. 'What's it for anyway?'

'Presumably to stop water sloshing out of the bath in rough weather and soaking the bedroom carpet,' suggested Solange, sitting up, stretching like a cat and then walking gracefully over to the mirror to pin up her hair.

When the bath was full she sat between Roland's thighs with her back to him while he worked up a creamy lather from a bar of ivory soap. He rubbed it into her back and shoulders then reached in front of her to massage her breasts, lingering on the full orbs, teasing the already swollen nipples into even greater tumescence.

He turned his attention to her belly, making her laugh as he inadvertently found a ticklish spot. He soaped her mound, then spread her thighs and washed carefully between her legs to rinse away any lingering traces of martini.

Solange turned to face him and relieved him of the soap,

before bathing him in turn. His member was already hard when she took it in her hand and rubbed her thumb tantalisingly over the glans.

'Ready again so soon?' she marvelled. 'I thought I'd exhausted you until this evening. Is it the sea air?'

'No, it's your bewitching body. By the time we reach the Orient I probably won't have the strength to rise from my bed.'

Solange fondled the twitching shaft in her slender hand, tracing the veins and then manipulating it skilfully in an up and down movement. She adjusted her position so she was poised over it, then slowly, an inch at a time lowered herself until it was embedded deep inside her.

Roland let out a heartfelt sigh of satisfaction and his hands found her breasts. Steadying herself by holding onto his shoulders, Solange began to rise and fall to an erotic rhythm.

She started slowly, but Roland's strong, thick member felt so good that she was soon moving faster and faster. He seized her by the waist, steadying her and then when at last he came, he jammed her down hard while he pumped his juices into her.

The water was cooling around them as Solange rose, the water streaming alluringly from her curvaceous body. She reached for a towel and wrapped herself in it, throwing another to him.

'I must hurry myself,' she said, 'it's later than I thought.'

She dried herself thoroughly and then dressed, while Roland, wrapped in a towel, watched appreciatively.

She went over to him, patted his manhood over the towel and said, 'We will meet for cocktails – no?'

He grabbed her wrist and pressed her hand firmly against

his member. Amazingly she felt a responsive stiffening, but regretfully pulled away.

'Later,' she promised, before blowing him a kiss and slipping from the room.

Chapter Eight

Lisa adjusted the ribbon-suspenders holding her pale silk stockings in place and straightened up. She shivered with pleasure as she slipped an ivory silk camisole over her head and felt it flutter over her breasts, catching caressingly on her swollen coral nipples.

She drew a matching pair of camiknickers up her slender legs and fastened the two tiny pearl buttons on one hip.

Sinking onto a stool in front of the dressing table of inlaid rosewood, its angled mirrors edged with an etched geometric design, she couldn't help but look around her airy stateroom with satisfaction.

From the wide, comfortable bed with its quilted amber satin eiderdown, to the thick Broadloom carpet woven in shades of dusky-green and buttermilk beneath her bare feet, she was surrounded by luxury.

She picked up her silver-backed hairbrush and drew it through her hair wondering how long it would take before she became accustomed to the vibration of the engines, inescapable even up here in one of the ship's most opulently appointed suites.

The throbbing of the engines was echoed by another

throbbing of a much more intimate kind. The whole of her sex seemed to be pulsing with a hot lingering pleasure, reminding her of the intensely carnal interlude that had taken place earlier that afternoon. The memory caused a surge of heat to wash over her, making her hot and breathless.

Feeling the need for some fresh air, she pulled on an ivy-green satin robe, opened the door which led out onto the suite's private verandah and stepped outside.

A cool, blustery breeze was blowing which whipped at her hair and robe, but the clean sea air smelt good and she breathed in deeply. Accustomed to living in a cold climate, she wondered whether she'd enjoy the heat and humidity of the tropics.

The sea was rough and choppy, furrowed with deep-green troughs over which cream-crested waves broke in a relentless, undulating rhythm.

She leant over the verandah rail and was immediately lost in an erotic reverie which had her sex aching demandingly as she was reminded of the events of the last few days.

She was jerked back to reality when the ship's siren hooted and she shivered, half at her memories and half from cold, then glanced at the face of her gold filigree cocktail watch.

Only another few minutes and it would be time to join the others for drinks and she still had to dress and have Celeste arrange her hair.

It already felt like a long time since she'd left the Scottish castle that had been her home for the last ten years. Was it really less than two weeks ago?

And now she was on her way to Malaya to begin a new life she could only begin to imagine. Thank goodness she had Solange as a companion. Perhaps Mr Varonne would invite the older woman to stay with them for a while before she attended to the business of selling her rubber plantation. Lisa certainly hoped so. It would make it much easier for her to settle into her new life.

She went back into her stateroom and pulled the door to behind her, then wondered what to wear. She opened the wardrobe door and doubtfully surveyed the dozens of frocks hanging there. Solange would know.

She opened the door into their shared sitting room, just as Solange let herself in from the corridor, still in the tweed suit she'd had on earlier, her hair curling in damp fronds around her piquant face.

'Hello, *chérie*,' Solange greeted her. 'Have you settled in? Do you have everything you need?'

'My stateroom's lovely,' Lisa assured her. 'It's very comfortable. Have . . . have you been for a swim?'

Solange laughed, a low musical sound.

'*Non* – I bathed in Roland's bathroom, so all I need do is dress and attend to my face and hair.'

'Solange – what do you think I should wear tonight?'

'Dress is informal on the first night so a cocktail dress would be most appropriate.' She followed Lisa into her room and after a few moments consideration lifted down two dresses. 'Perhaps this one – or this one.'

Lisa studied them both before deciding on the lapis lazuli tulle. The skirt billowed out from a tight-fitting bodice to form overlapping petals of the gauzy fabric. The bodice was sleeveless and edged with tiny seed pearls around the scooped neckline. Solange nodded her approval. 'I'll send Celeste to do your hair while I apply my make-up.'

Celeste arranged Lisa's hair with her customary skill and then suggested the addition of a silver circlet laid on top of her hair and resting against her forehead under her fringe. She pinned it deftly into position so it was firmly secured and fluffed the fringe around it more becomingly.

Lisa wound her pearls twice around her neck, added her aquamarine bracelet, then went to see how Solange was doing.

Solange was just stepping into a cowl-necked dress of pansy-purple crêpe. 'You look as beautiful as you always do,' she complimented her charge, putting her hands on her hips while the maid fastened her dress.

'Celeste, will you take our jewellery cases to the Purser's office please,' said Solange as soon as the maid had made a minute adjustment to the way the dress fell and then handed her a sequinned black bag.

'*Oui, Madame.*'

'So, are you ready to go and look over our fellow passengers in the cocktail bar?' asked Solange, studying herself critically in the mirror.

'I think so,' replied Lisa, suddenly nervous. 'How will we find our way?'

'I should think there will be plenty of crew members to give us directions,' said Solange airily.

She was right of course. A respectful steward they encountered only a few yards from their suite, led them deferentially along acres of carpeted passageways until they found themselves in the bar where they'd drunk champagne that afternoon.

A silence fell for a few seconds as the two women walked

in and then a ship's officer stepped forward to greet them. The first thing that Lisa noticed was that there were very few other women present, the second that everyone seemed to be looking at the two of them.

She moved a little closer to Solange and glancing at her saw that her companion's large, dark eyes were sparkling at the attention they were receiving.

She barely heard the officer welcoming them aboard, she was so busy looking around.

'What would you ladies like to drink?' he asked them.

'A martini please,' said Solange, then when Lisa didn't say anything, 'And for you, *chérie*?'

'The same please.'

'Is this your first voyage?' the officer asked Solange, as the hovering steward went to fetch their drinks.

'*Mais oui*, except for the cross-channel ferry,' Solange told him.

'And where are you heading?'

'Malaya.'

'We have many passengers disembarking there. I'm sure some of them will be able to tell you a great deal about the country.'

He chatted to them until Lisa spotted Roland making his way through the crowd and waved at him. The ship's officer, seeing they now had an escort, excused himself and went to greet some of the other passengers.

'Roland!' Solange greeted him with a kiss. 'I forgot to ask you – did you secure us a good table in the dining room?'

'One of the best,' he assured her. 'I told the chief steward that my companions would undoubtedly be the two most beautiful women on board and he was happy to accommodate me.' He turned to Lisa and raised her hand to his lips to kiss it. 'Shall we sit down?'

They retired to a table by the window, but the spray was so strong that most of the view was obscured and instead Lisa turned her attention to the other people in the room.

More women had appeared now but the men still out numbered them by about five to one. Many of the men were in uniform but she wasn't altogether sure which of them belonged to the ship and which were in the armed forces. Still, five weeks would be plenty of time to find out.

Disappointingly there was no sign of the Maharajah, but she told Solange and Roland about seeing the two exotically garbed men guarding the entrance to his suite.

'A Maharajah, eh?' was Roland's response. 'It's to be hoped that he doesn't set eyes on you two gorgeous ladies or he'll be wanting you for his harem.'

'Do Maharajahs have harems?' asked Solange.

'Damned if I know,' he replied. 'But he'll have a fight on his hands if that's what he wants. Here comes Alex, at last.'

Alex sauntered into the bar and Lisa's heart lurched at the sight of him. She thought he was easily the most attractive man in the room with his lean athletic frame, dark hair and strong jawline and had to press her thighs together in an attempt to suppress a wayward tingling in her sex at his appearance.

He joined them at their table. 'I'm starving,' he announced, having ordered a Sidecar. 'Shall we dine unfashionably early tonight?'

'Certainly not,' Solange remonstrated with him. 'We shall

enjoy our cocktails like the civilised people we are and then make a late entrance.'

'In that case, would you like to do a little exploring, Lisa? If Solange won't allow me to eat, I need distraction. Bring your drink with you,' he added.

'We'll meet you in the dining salon in about an hour,' Solange proposed.

Lisa and Alex left the cocktail bar and went in to the lounge next to it. Lisa had to hurriedly close her mouth which threatened to hang open at the sight of the opulently appointed room.

Decorated in orchid-white and gold it was two decks high, the ceiling supported by pillars finished in gold leaf. Gilt panels lined the walls and the windows were hung with oriental brocade draperies. A richly patterned Chinese carpet covered the floor and chandeliers of polished brass and crystal blazed overhead.

Brocade-covered easy chairs and sofas were arranged in inviting groups and several parties of people were seated and exchanging small talk. The overall effect was one of sumptuous luxury which dazzled Lisa.

They wandered through the room and then out into the corridor again. As they explored, Lisa felt that she must have stumbled into another world, it was so far removed from the simple life she'd enjoyed at school and in the spartan Scottish castle.

The gorgeously furnished public rooms became practically deserted as people drifted towards the dining salon. At last they found themselves alone in what appeared to be the writing room.

Alex led the way past the leather-topped tables laid with every conceivable writing accoutrement, to a sofa in front of the fireplace where he sat down. Lisa joined him and was startled when he took her hand and laid it over his groin. A shiver of desire fluttered up her arm as she felt the hardness of his manhood which had been the instrument of so much enjoyment earlier that day.

'I want you to give me pleasure,' he told her, his long, narrow eyes glittering with excitement.

'Wh . . . what, here?' she said. 'Anyone could come in.'

'Perhaps. But that's what adds spice to the proceedings. Besides, if anyone does come in they won't be able to see anything unless they walk over to the fireplace because the back of the sofa will obscure their view. Take out my shaft and caress it.'

He sat back on the sofa and stretched out his long legs in front of him. Lisa hesitated, aware of a moistening in her vulva at the idea of exposing Alex's manhood in a public room and caressing it into hungry tumescence. Although judging by the hard bulge she could feel under the fabric of his trousers, it wasn't far from being fully erect now.

While she was still mentally weighing the possibilities, her hand moved as if of its own volition and she found herself drawing down his zip. It was the work of a moment to free his penis and without actually having made a conscious decision to do so, she discovered she was holding it in her hand.

Blushing at her own daring she squeezed it gently and felt it twitch. She ran the tips of her fingers down the full length of it and then circled the glans with her forefinger.

She wished Alex would stop watching her so intensely. She

could feel his eyes on her face and it was making her uncomfortable.

Hoping to distract him she closed her hand around his shaft and moved it up and down. He swallowed and his eyelids drooped closed as she intensified the pressure. A strange feeling of power welled up in her as she fondled him experimentally, trying different things to see what sort of reaction she got.

As she touched him she remembered how he'd used his lips and tongue to stimulate her most private parts and the thought leapt into her mind that she might try the same thing on him. Without daring to consider the idea too carefully in case she lost her nerve, she slipped to her knees and placed the very tip of his rod between her lips.

The result was electrifying. He groaned audibly and buried a hand in her hair, pressing her face closer. Cautiously, she drew more of his shaft into her mouth and sucked it. It was warm and very smooth and she could feel it throbbing excitedly. Fully erect now, it was too big to take more of, so she licked her way to the base, kissed her way back up to the glans then took it between her lips to suck again.

She was aware that touching him in this way was arousing her and that her sex was growing moister by the moment. She became so absorbed in her task that she forgot they were in the writing room of an ocean liner and could be disturbed at any moment.

It was only the sound of voices that suddenly jolted her back to reality, reminding her that they were in fact committing an act of indecency in a public place. She sat hastily back on her heels and then scrambled to her feet.

'Someone's coming!' she hissed. Alex's eyes flew open and he zipped himself up in a flash. He was just in time because the next moment a middle-aged man and woman came in, smiled at them and then took seats at the other end of the room.

Alex and Lisa sat in silence for a few moments and then he said, 'Are you ready to eat? We should go and find our table in the dining salon.'

'Yes – if you're ready,' she managed to say.

They left the room and walked slowly down the thickly carpeted corridor. There was a bank of elevators at the end and Alex studied the plan of the ship next to them to see which deck they needed. Lisa had only been in an elevator once before earlier that day and she felt nervous about it, but didn't want to let Alex know that.

They stepped into one and the doors glided silently closed. Lisa was just about to comment on the mahogany panelling in the hope of sounding blasé, when Alex grabbed her by the hips, turned her so she was facing one of the panelled walls and dragged her skirt up around her waist.

'Alex! What...' Her voice trailed off as his intention became plain. 'We can't – not here,' she said desperately.

'I've got to have you right now.' His voice was hoarse with arousal as he pulled her camiknickers around her thighs and felt swiftly between her legs, his fingers slipping easily over the slick tissues of her labia.

Satisfied that she was wet, he ripped his zip down and a moment later she felt the end of his penis poised against her whorled entrance. In one smooth movement he was inside her.

Lisa gasped as she was pressed forwards against the panelling and flattened her hands against it in an attempt to steady herself. Alex was like a man possessed, one hand finding her breasts and caressing them over the tight tulle of her bodice and the other around her waist, the flimsy layers of her skirt crushed between them.

He pistoned in and out of her, gathering momentum like a well-maintained engine swiftly reaching its maximum throttle. It was a fast and furious coupling and completely lacking in any sort of subtlety, but nevertheless Lisa was soon in the grip of as wild an excitement as he was.

The well-lubricated friction of his organ driving in and out of her was working her up to boiling point and she began to feel as though she would explode at any moment. He came in a series of last feverish thrusts and sagged against her, his head on her shoulder.

To her dismay, Lisa felt her own climax slipping away and her internal muscles clutched desperately at his member. She felt the arm around her waist slip lower and then his hand was between her legs, finding her urgently pulsing sliver of flesh. She moaned loudly when he rubbed it deftly, swiftly sending her climbing back up towards the satisfaction she thought had eluded her.

She felt her sticky juices trickling onto his hand and opened her legs wider. There was a heady fizzing sensation which suffused her entire groin and then she exploded into a release which swept over her entire body in great waves of hectic pleasure.

The only sound in the lift was her ragged breathing and then a slight squelching noise as Alex withdrew. Slowly, she tried to pull her camiknickers up, but the multi-petalled layers of her skirt got in the way.

'That was reckless,' she accused him. 'The doors could have opened at any time and although you presumably don't care about your reputation, I care about mine.'

He reached out and caressed her breasts through her tight bodice.

'You should have thought about that before you tantalised me with your mouth in that way,' he said softly. 'If those people hadn't come in I would undoubtedly have taken you on the sofa, regardless of the consequences.'

He smiled at her and she noticed again what a predatory appearance it gave him to show his white teeth with those long canines. Despite the warmth of the elevator she shivered. There was something primitive about Alex despite his excellent manners. His absolute determination to satisfy his appetites as they occurred half-frightened her, even as she responded to it.

'Let me help you,' he said, holding her skirts up so she could fasten her camiknickers back in position. She felt dishevelled and insisted he find her a powder room so she could tidy herself in there before they made their way to dine.

The powder room had a lavishly executed mural of an underwater scene where mermaids frolicked in the blue-green depths of the ocean, tails flicking in joyous abandon, bare breasts tipped with small, rosy nipples.

A large shell held a dozen miniature bars of soap and others a pile of individual linen towels and a selection of hairpins. A pink-hued cockle shell was heaped with talcum powder on which rested a large fluffy puff.

SENSUAL STORM

Lisa was glad there was no-one else in there as she washed, rearranged the flounces of her skirt and then tidied her hair. She barely recognised herself. Her eyes were glittering and her normally pale cheeks were flushed. She took her compact from her bag and dusted her cheeks and then splashed cold water on her wrists.

Alex was lounging against the wall when she came out and after a couple of wrong turns they found a steward who conducted them to the dining salon.

Three decks high, the salon rose to a massive glass dome in the centre around the bottom of which were stained glass panels depicting unicorns with flowing manes against a background of verdant green forests.

Graceful white Grecian pillars supported the ceiling and revolving brass fans sent a gentle current of air moving through the warm room. One wall was of Algerian marble into which had been set two massive mahogany doors and the others were hung with modern paintings interspaced by mounted fan-shaped lights.

Tonight the table linen was of the palest hyacinth-blue, against which the silver and crystal sparkled as it reflected back the light.

The chief steward stepped forward to greet them and Alex gave their names. The steward checked his book and took them up a carpeted staircase against one wall which led to a wide circular balcony directly beneath the dome and overlooking the rest of the salon.

It was here that the most desirable tables on board the ship were situated and Roland had done well indeed, theirs was against the parapet so they were able to look down on the other diners.

Solange and Roland were already seated and Roland rose to his feet as Lisa and Alex approached the table.

'The menu is excellent,' Solange told them with some satisfaction. 'I only hope the food is as good as it sounds.'

Lisa opened the leather-bound menu in front of her and realised immediately that if she were to read it thoroughly, it would take her about half an hour to work her way through. Her eye was caught by an exotic sounding dish and she saw that in addition to the usual cuisine there were curries and eastern delicacies on offer.

'I've never had curry,' she told the others. 'What's it like?' Solange pulled a face, wrinkling her small upturned nose.

'An acquired taste I have not yet learnt to acquire,' was her wry comment. 'I believe it is widely served in Malaya so I shall be forced to accustom myself to it there.'

'Curry's wonderful stuff,' observed Roland. 'There's nothing like it washed down by a few icy beers, particularly in a hot climate.'

'But it smells so terrible,' pointed out Solange. 'How can something with such a ghastly *odeur* taste good? Be warned, Lisa, it taints the breath most foully.'

Lisa decided that she'd wait until another evening before trying it; tonight she would choose something more familiar.

After long deliberation she ordered Ogen melon filled with mixed berries, followed by fillets of sole in champagne sauce. There were five courses available, but she was much too excited on this, the first night of the voyage, to eat much.

The food proved to be absolutely sublime. When she'd

finished her entrée, Solange dabbed delicately at her lips with her napkin and sighed contentedly.

'Almost as good as the food in my favourite restaurant in Paris,' was her opinion. 'The cuisine in London is most indifferent and it's a relief not to be forced to eat it any longer.'

Lisa was amazed – she'd thought it excellent, but then after several years at boarding school hers was hardly a sophisticated palate.

They were just debating who wished to order a pudding when a tall, narrow-hipped man passing their table paused to say, 'Madame Valois?'

Was it Lisa's imagination or did Solange stiffen and suddenly go pale? But a moment later she was looking up at the man and smiling charmingly as he continued, 'Mark Channing – I was acquainted with your late husband.'

He looked to be in his late thirties or early forties and had a deeply tanned, hard-boned face. His hair was a sun-streaked tawny-brown and he had the build of a man who'd known hard, physical work.

'But of course.' She offered him her hand. 'How delightful to see you again.'

'Please accept my heartfelt condolences – I'm afraid I've been out of the country and have only recently heard about his death.'

Solange inclined her head as he went on, 'Where are you headed?'

There was an infinitesimal pause before she replied, 'Malaya.'

He appeared to be waiting for her to say more, or to introduce him to her companions, but when she didn't he remarked, 'I'm sure our paths will cross again,' bowed slightly and continued on his way.

There was silence at the table for a few moments. Lisa was sure that Solange must be upset to have been reminded of her husband and said hurriedly, 'Are you having a pudding, Solange? The chocolate mousse sounds very tempting.'

'No, thank you.' She rose to her feet. 'Excuse me, please.'

She walked away from the table and left the dining salon by the upper entrance. Lisa was tempted to ask Alex and Roland if they knew anything about Solange's husband, but it seemed an invasion of her privacy to do so.

She decided she'd eaten enough and ordered only coffee, but then consumed several of the chocolate mints served with it. Solange returned to the table looking her normal self and allowed Roland to coax her into trying a spoonful of his gateaux.

Alex and Roland were in high spirits and the four of them repaired to the lounge for cognac and more coffee. 'What about going back to your suite for a game of cards?' suggested Roland.

'I think not – you play too well and I've no wish to lose vast sums of money to you,' was Solange's abstracted reply.

'Who said anything about playing for money?' he protested. The Frenchwoman's attention was caught by an elegantly dressed woman who'd just entered the lounge.

'Excuse me a moment, I see someone I know,' she murmured. She and the woman exchanged kisses and stood chatting on the other side of the room while Roland began to flirt with Lisa, suggesting the various stakes they could use in a card game instead of money.

When Lisa next glanced that way both Solange and the woman had vanished. Lisa wondered if her companion had gone to use the powder room and then decided to go in search of the nearest one herself.

She was just passing the doorway of the Winter Garden when she caught the faintest whiff of Solange's jasmine and orange flower perfume, indicating that she'd passed that way only seconds earlier. Lisa glanced inside to see Mark Channing holding her companion's arm and talking to her in a low, urgent voice.

Solange had her back to the door but there was a rigidity about her stance that suggested she wasn't enjoying the conversation. Lisa paused, uncertain whether to join them. At that moment one of the ship's officers, possibly alerted by some sense that all was not well, moved over to them. Mark immediately released Solange's arm and walked off.

Deciding that it would be more discreet to slip away, rather than ask questions Solange might not want to answer, Lisa located the nearest powder room and then went back to the lounge.

It was a while before Solange returned and then when she did, she seemed preoccupied. Roland persisted in trying to persuade her to play cards, but she suddenly rose to her feet.

'I'm most fatigued. I shall say goodnight now.'

His eyes gleaming, Roland rose too and slipped his arm around her. 'I'll walk you back to your suite and we'll have a night cap,' he murmured.

'*Non!*' she said sharply. Roland looked taken aback.

'But I—' he began.

'Leave me alone!' she hissed, turned on her heel and walked swiftly from the room.

Chapter Nine

To Alex's evident annoyance, Lisa refused to accompany him back to his cabin.

'I want to make sure Solange is alright,' she explained.

'You'll probably get your head bitten off,' commented Roland gloomily. 'I'm off to the smoking room.' He waved a languid hand at them and sauntered away.

'He's right,' said Alex. 'She obviously wants to be on her own.' He leant towards her. 'Come back to my cabin – I want to undress you slowly, stand you on a chair and then admire every inch of your beautiful body.'

Lisa felt seared by the sheer carnal heat of his gaze. The way he was looking at her made her feel he could see right through her clothing and that to him, she was already naked.

Her mouth went dry with anticipation and she swallowed, tempted beyond measure by his words. But Solange was obviously upset and Lisa thought that after the kindness the older woman had shown her, the least she could do was go and see if she was alright, or if there was anything she wanted to talk about.

'I really can't – not tonight,' she told him with regret.

She was taken aback when his face darkened and he said

coldly, 'As you wish. There are other women an the ship, after all.' He stalked off leaving her sitting alone, biting her lip. She stared after him with dismay, half-tempted to run after him, but then she told herself not to be ridiculous – he didn't own her.

Resolutely she made her way back to their suite. Celeste was in the sitting room, plumping the cushions on the sofa.

'Is Madame Valois in her room?' asked Lisa.

'*Oui, Mademoiselle*, but she is not to be disturbed.'

'I must just speak to her for a moment,' Lisa told her, walking towards the door. To her surprise Celeste blocked her path.

'No, *Mademoiselle* – you must not – it is most unwise.' She spoke with such vehemence that Lisa was taken aback.

'Very well – if you think so,' she said, half convinced that if she persisted the maid would stand in front of the door to Solange's bedroom and refuse to let her past.

She suddenly felt very tired. It had been a long, eventful day and the prospect of curling up in her comfortable bed beneath the amber satin quilt was very inviting.

She'd talk to Solange tomorrow. For now, a good night's sleep was what she most needed.

She was following a narrow track through what appeared to be a jungle. The sunlight was all but blotted out by the interwoven branches of the trees high above and she was surrounded by dense, leafy foliage. The air was rent by strange cries and squawks and from time to time brilliantly-feathered birds flew across her path.

It was very hot, the sort of intense steamy heat which made her red-gold hair curl in damp tendrils around her face. She was wearing a strange garment – a type of sarong in gold-coloured silk which left one shoulder and one thigh bare.

She was obviously in a hurry because she was walking as fast as the rough terrain would allow, pushing aside trailing tendrils of greenery which tried to wind themselves around her and slow her down.

She reached a clearing in the jungle and paused to catch her breath. To her surprise there was a house there, a small wooden structure with a thatched roof and wide verandah.

Alex was lounging in a rattan chair, his feet propped up on a matching table, a chilled drink in his hand. She started to walk towards him, but he seemed not to have seen her, it was only when she stepped onto the verandah that he looked up.

'We've been waiting for you,' he said.

She glanced around, but there was no-one else in sight. His eyes travelled from her flushed, damp face, over her bare creamy shoulder and lingered on the swell of her breasts where they pushed against the fine silk of her sarong. It was only then she became aware that the silk was damp and had moulded itself to her form in a way which left little to the imagination.

'Take it off,' he directed her.

Her hands crossed protectively in front of her.

'No,' she defied him.

'Take it off, or I'll rip it off,' he said gently, placing his glass on the table in front of him.

She didn't move. His hand snaked out and with one swift movement he tore it from her, leaving her naked except for a small triangle of gold-coloured silk which covered her russet fleece.

'Beautiful,' he commented, sitting back in his chair and

surveying her appraisingly, the rags of her sarong still in his hand. 'Now that.' He indicated her remaining covering, the silk triangle held in place by ties on her hips.

She backed away from him, moving out of reach, but he rose lithely from his chair and followed her with the single-minded determination of a hunter stalking his prey.

When she felt the rough wooden rail around the verandah against the small of her back she had no choice but to stop. He stood in front of her and slowly drew the knuckle of his forefinger down between her breasts to her belly. The remains of her sarong were still dangling from his hand and the silk fluttered arousingly over her bare skin.

She half expected him to continue downwards and wrench the triangle from her pubic floss, but instead he circled her stomach and then ran his knuckle over her breasts. Despite the heat she shivered and her coral nipples hardened perceptibly.

With a sudden violent movement he tore the sarong in two, twisted it into impromptu bonds and deftly tied one of her wrists to the verandah rail. He secured her other wrist with the rest of the silk and then divested himself of his clothing in a leisurely fashion.

His penis was hugely engorged, the veins blue and swollen. It could not have been more obvious that he wanted her. His desire wreathed itself around her like sexual ether, making her legs feel weak and her sex hot and moist.

He caressed her breasts, covering the small orbs with his hands, savouring their firmness and toying lengthily with her coral nipples. His hands slid over her hips and stroked her thighs, then reached behind her to cup her peach-pert buttocks and massage them in an arousing circular movement.

As he fondled the smooth-skinned globes, his manhood pressed against her mound. Even through the silk triangle she could feel the heat and strength of it. His hands on her buttocks grew more demanding, lifting and easing them apart, then probing the cleft between them.

Lisa felt the heat in her groin growing more intense as he coaxed a response from her. Her sex-lips felt hot and heavy and there was a tingling in her tight little bud which was becoming more urgent by the minute.

She could feel the thin strip of fabric between her legs becoming wet as her female honey trickled into it. His fingers slid into the slick folds of her vulva from behind and eased themselves into her sex-furrow, exciting her beyond belief.

She opened her legs to him and inhaled sharply as he made contact with the tight knot of her clitoris, then slipped two fingers inside her. They moved steadily in and out of her slippery channel, while he rubbed his member arousingly against her mound.

She found that her hips were undulating in time to his movements and that there was a wanton throbbing in her female core which demanded more than he was giving her. Her clitoris was only being indirectly stimulated and she ached for him to make more immediate contact.

He stepped away from her, hooked his thumbs into the silken triangle and jerked it free, exposing the damp tawny fronds of her pubic fleece and the moist folds of her outer sex-lips.

It was only at that moment she noticed Roland. He was sitting in a chair watching them, his eyelids half-lowered and his blue eyes gleaming. He was naked and his erection towered up between his thighs, paying mute testament to the strength of his arousal.

Then Mark Channing stepped out of the house onto the verandah and took up a position leaning against the wooden wall, his arms folded, an expression of anticipation on his face. He too had divested himself of his clothes and the virile column of his member showed that he was in a state of urgent excitement.

But somehow their presence only served to stimulate Lisa further. Instead of being horrified that there were now spectators of the licentious game being played out in the jungle clearing, she found herself opening her thighs even wider so they could see the gleaming vermilion folds of her vulva and the swollen kernel of her clitoris standing proud of her inner labia.

Alex reached out a hand and touched the throbbing bud, stroking it skilfully so that jolts of erotic sensation lanced through her body. She could feel the beads of perspiration covering her satiny skin turning into trickles as the heat inside her became at least equal to that in the steamy tropical jungle.

She was very aware of the eyes of all three men on her, devouring her, wanting her. Alex's touch on her sensitive sliver of flesh was sending her wild with excitement. Her hips thrust rhythmically against his hand as he manipulated it skilfully, his other hand on her breasts.

She began to strain at her bonds, but the fragile appearance of the twisted silk ties belied their strength and they didn't give, however hard she pulled.

She felt her excitement mounting to boiling point until

suddenly, in a great explosion of pleasure which seemed to reach every cell in her body, she came.

It was a wild and wonderful climax. Just as it began to ebb away, Alex seized her by the hips and then positioned his engorged rod at the pulsing entrance to her sex. One smooth thrust and he was inside her, filling her completely and prolonging the pleasure of her climax.

His hands closed on the silken spheres of her rump and he began to plunge relentlessly in and out of her; controlled, powerful, plunges which soon had her climbing the slopes of arousal again.

His hands on her buttocks lifted her to meet each thrust and she found herself gripping the verandah rail with her bound hands to steady herself. He paused briefly to lift her high enough to wind her legs around his waist, then resumed the movements which were giving her so much pleasure.

Holding onto the rail, Lisa was able to rock her pelvis to an erotic tempo and angle herself so that the stimulation of her sex was more complete. She lost track of time as they continued with their carnal dance until at last Alex let out a long, low groan and erupted into her, jamming her down hard with each spasmodic movement.

Lisa cried out as she toppled over the edge and convulsed into her own satisfaction, her legs gripping him tightly around the waist as the spasms of release took her over.

It was only as she came back down to earth that she realised how much her arms were aching from the strain they'd had to take.

'Untie me,' she murmured as he lowered her to the ground. He swiftly undid the knots and she sank to her knees on the rough wooden floor, rubbing her wrists.

Alex sat in a rattan chair, breathing hard, while Roland moved forward to kneel behind Lisa. He pulled her back against his hard chest and clasped her breasts, rubbing his thumbs over the cherry-hard points of her nipples.

She moaned, immediately on fire again, and arched her back voluptuously. He stroked her belly and hips, finding the soft skin of her inner thighs and caressing it until she burnt for him to touch her more intimately. He worked her gradually up the spiral of arousal, moulding her buttocks with his hands and then stroking her hips and letting the tips of his fingers trail teasingly over the damps fronds of her fleece.

She spread her thighs for him but still he didn't touch the swollen folds of her sex-flesh. She reached behind him and her slender hand closed over the throbbing rod of his manhood. She manoeuvred herself until she was astride it and then began to slide backwards and forwards, using it as an instrument for her pleasure.

She was so wet that it was soon drenched with her juices and the friction produced by her lascivious actions made an obscene squelching sound. Overhead a dozen birds with brilliantly-coloured plumage flew out of the trees, circled the clearing then vanished uttering loud, unearthly cries. But Lisa barely heard them she was so intent on her own amorous activities.

Roland groaned as she moved faster and faster on his organ, squeezing it gently as she did so. His desire became too urgent to withstand and he brought her to a halt by holding her tightly around the waist against his chest while he found the whorled entrance to her dripping sex.

She held her breath while he positioned himself and then penetrated her, embedding his shaft up to the hilt. It felt so good to be filled to capacity and she squeezed gently with her internal muscles, making him groan again.

They rocked against each other, establishing a mutually satisfying rhythm while he stroked her breasts and belly. Each time he withdrew he did it slowly, then pushed inside her again at a much faster pace.

Mark Channing suddenly left his position against the wall and fell to his knees in front of Lisa. He reached out, found the engorged nub of her clitoris and stroked it, making her squirm with excitement.

Sandwiched between them, Roland thrusting in and out of her and Mark manipulating her clit, Lisa's arousal became white-hot. The intensity of their combined attentions was making her sizzle internally.

She came in a glorious blaze of sensation which was heightened by Roland's determined plunges. Mark squeezed her clitoris again, but as she was still in the last throes of orgasm his touch felt painful on her over-sensitised nub.

She grasped his wrist to stop him, but Roland seized her arms and held them by her sides. Mark rubbed her bud between his finger and thumb, making her cry out, then she convulsed into another heady, liquid climax.

She felt she couldn't endure another – the sensations evoked were too strong, but she had no choice. Roland kept her arms pinioned while Mark stimulated her the few seconds it took to bring her to another orgasm which seemed to go on for an eternity.

Unable to hold back any longer, Roland discharged himself

into her with the force of a long dormant geyser bursting into renewed life.

He withdrew and Mark leant towards her, organ in hand, his intention to take Roland's place very plain.

Then suddenly Lisa was no longer on the verandah of a house in a jungle clearing. She was . . . where was she? She sat bolt upright in bed in a state of confusion. Was she in her narrow bed at school? Or in the ancient four-poster with the moth-eaten tapestry curtains in the castle?

Then she became aware of the incessant vibration of the engines and remembered that she was in neither of those places – she was on board the *S.S. Orient* on her way to Malaya.

She sank back against the downy pillows, aware of an urgent, frustrated throbbing in her sex. What a deliciously erotic dream that had been. It made her yearn to feel Alex's hard body against hers in her bed. Or Roland's for that matter. In fact right at that minute any healthy, attractive male with an erection would have done.

A noise from outside made her stiffen and hold her breath. What was that? It sounded like someone on their private deck. She slipped silently from bed and padded across to the window on bare feet. Stealthily, she drew the curtain a couple of inches to one side and peered through the gap.

Solange was standing by the rail, looking out to sea, her dark hair blowing in the breeze. She had her back to Lisa, but there was a despairing slump to her shoulders Lisa had never seen before. She hesitated, should she go outside and join her?

But then Solange shivered, drew her robe more closely around her and glided away to the door leading back into her bedroom. Lisa caught a glimpse of her white, set face and her heart ached for Solange's distress, but she sensed intuitively that the Frenchwoman would not welcome her company.

She got back into bed and turned onto her side, wishing the demanding heat in her sex would die down. She pulled her nightgown up to her hips and slipped her hand between her thighs, then slowly, delicately, began to stroke her tingling clitoris.

Dawn was breaking when she next woke, but more sleep didn't seem to have assuaged the ache in her loins. She'd stimulated herself to a climax before dozing off again, but she still felt edgy with frustration. Even worse she was wide awake.

She suddenly felt that she'd like to take a swim. There was a loch near the Scottish castle and in summer she used to plunge into the icy waters and swim all the way across it. Occasionally Douglas would join her and they'd race each other, but more often than not she'd been alone.

There was something about cleaving through the deep, dark waters that had always cleared her head and satisfied the restlessness she'd sometimes felt.

On an impulse Lisa jumped out of bed and discarded her nightgown. She rummaged through the drawers of the dresser until she found one of the fashionable new swimming costumes she'd bought. It was very daring, much more so than her old navy-blue wool costume with elbow-length sleeves and legs that went all the way to her knees.

This one had scarlet and white stripes and was skimpy in the extreme. It left her arms, shoulders and thighs bare and dipped down at the front to give just a hint of cleavage. She pulled it on then fastened her grey robe over it. Slipping her feet into a pair of dainty leather mules, she darted into the bathroom for a towel.

The sitting room was lit only by shafts of dim light coming in through the closed curtains. There was no sound from Solange's room, so Lisa let herself out into the corridor. She had no idea where the swimming pool was, but she'd noticed a plan of the ship at the far end of the corridor near the companion-way.

She studied the plan carefully then ran down the stairs leading to the deck below. There were very few people around, but when she took a wrong turning she found a steward cleaning one of the brass rails which ran along all the passageways so passengers could hold onto them in inclement weather. He re-directed her and a few minutes later she found the door to the pool room.

She pushed it open and then blinked at the splendour which met her eyes. It looked like a film set.

Lit from beneath, the water glowed an unearthly, luminous green. On the bottom was a mosaic pattern portraying dolphins, sea-horses and turtles which seemed to move as the water shimmered, stirred by a fountain gushing from the mouth of a fat bronze fish at the far end.

The ceiling was supported by Pompeian pillars carved from greenish onyx and steps of the same substance led into the water at both ends.

Lisa shed her robe and leather mules, ran down the steps and plunged in. She swam several lengths in a graceful crawl, then turned and floated on her back, staring up at the ceiling where carved cream frescos depicted scenes from ancient Rome.

She swam over to the fountain and let the water cascade over her head and shoulders. The urgent pulse in her sex was still tormenting her and on an impulse she positioned herself so that the water played onto her mound.

It felt so good that she was tempted to remove her costume and let it fall directly on her sex, but there was always the danger someone would come in and see her.

She closed her eyes and lay back, keeping herself in position by paddling with her hands if she began to float away. A sound from behind her made her eyes flutter open to see Roland standing on the edge of the pool watching her.

She flushed a deep rose-pink which spread down to her breasts as his lips curved into a lascivious smile at the sight of her. He pushed a lock of floppy blond hair back from his forehead, dived into the water and surfaced a couple of yards from her.

The memory of her dream came back to her and she could feel hot moisture gathering between her legs. He didn't speak, just pulled her into his arms and kissed her. She could feel the strength of his erection against her and lewd images of him imprinted themselves on her over-heated brain.

Making love to Solange as she sat on the back of an armchair, her legs wound around his waist.

Kneeling between her own legs and bringing her to a climax with his lips and tongue after he and Solange had found her pleasuring herself with the silver-backed hairbrush.

Taking her from behind in her dream.

It appeared that he was in the grip of the same kind of

feverish desire – possibly because Solange had refused to let him share her bed last night – because the passion in his kisses left her weak with hunger for him.

He led her to the steps and in the waist-deep water laid his hand on her breast. The heat from his palm seemed to burn through the wet stuff of her bathing costume, so much so that she half expected to see steam rising from it.

Her nipples pushed against the striped fabric like small thimbles and she was so lost to everything except an all-consuming carnal pull that she didn't object when he pulled her costume down to the waist.

He kissed her again, stroking her breasts and shoulders, then the taut curves of her bottom. He tried to ease her costume down her hips but it was difficult under water. Lisa walked up a couple of the steps and, remembering her dream, knelt down. Roland knelt behind her and managed to peel her costume down around her thighs.

She tried to turn over so he could remove it completely, but the sight of her bare *derrière* was obviously too much for him, because he freed his member and thrust immediately inside her.

Pushed off balance and hobbled by the wet material clinging to her thighs, Lisa had to steady herself by placing her hands on the step above so she was on all fours. Roland was like a man possessed as he shafted her, fondling her breasts and then her vulva as he drove tirelessly in and out of her.

She jammed her bottom back to meet each urgent thrust, moaning as he worked them both towards satisfaction. She'd never been taken in this position before and found that not only did it feel deliciously wanton, but the angle of penetration was particularly arousing.

Her bare buttocks began to make wet slapping noises as they smacked against his thighs and she could feel the weight and heat of his testicles. It was too frenzied a coupling to last long and Lisa cried out as she spasmed into a womb-wrenching climax.

Roland came in a series of powerful spurts which felt molten in contrast to the cool water lapping against them. Bent over her, he went limp for a few moments and then withdrew. Lisa turned around and sat down, enjoying the sensation of the cool water immersing her private parts.

'Time for us to clean ourselves up,' he announced, taking her hand and towing her towards the fountain. He held her beneath it so that the water gushed over her naked vulva, cooling her and washing her sex clean of their juices.

He let the water play over his detumescent shaft for a few moments and then buttoned his costume back into position. Lisa tried to drag her striped bathing suit up her thighs, but he stopped her.

'I need to check and make sure you're quite clean,' he teased her, burrowing at her crotch with his hand and then slipping his fingers inside her. She closed her thighs over his wrist and splashed around in the water, enjoying the feeling of being so pleasurably skewered. The water made her so buoyant that he was able to propel her gently through it by the hand between her thighs.

It felt so gloriously lewd that she pushed hard against it and wriggled voluptuously. She felt his thumb on her bud and he rubbed it as they made their way down the pool. Lisa suddenly tensed in shock as a small, unexpected climax rippled through her.

He withdrew his hand and they embraced in the water, then both of them went under as it proved to be deeper than they'd anticipated. They came up spluttering and swam to the steps where Lisa dragged her costume back into position.

She was just in the nick of time. The door opened to admit a stewardess, her arms full of snowy towels.

Brought back to reality as she realised what a narrow escape they'd just had, Lisa climbed from the pool and pulled on her robe.

She really would have to be more careful in future if she didn't want to get a bad reputation. Roland however seemed indifferent to how close they'd come to being caught.

'I don't know about you, but that's certainly given me an appetite,' he drawled as they made their way to the door.

Chapter Ten

There was no sign of Solange when Lisa returned to their suite. But it was still only early and her companion usually slept late if she possibly could, so Lisa decided to dress and go in search of breakfast. Celeste arrived just as she was about to leave.

'The stewardess will bring *le petit déjeuner* here for you,' the maid informed her but Lisa didn't feel like breakfasting alone. She wanted to mingle with the other passengers and then stretch her legs on deck.

It was a cool, blustery day and she was wearing a cashmere twin-set in emerald-green, teamed with a skirt in a muted greenish-brown tweed. She wondered how soon the weather would become warm enough for her to wear something lighter. She had several ravishing sun dresses she was eager to show off.

Although he greeted her with the utmost courtesy, the chief steward seemed surprised to see her when she presented herself at the upper entrance to the dining salon. She soon realised why. From her vantage point at the table on the balcony she could see that she was the only woman present. All the other female passengers must be having breakfast in their cabins.

Roland arrived a minute after her and they both ordered grapefruit, followed by bacon, eggs, grilled tomatoes and mushrooms. Lisa couldn't manage toast and marmalade but Roland did, accompanied by several cups of coffee.

Lisa was half-sorry, half-relieved when Alex didn't appear. She wasn't sure whether he would mind if he discovered that she and Roland had enjoyed a carnal encounter that morning. She presumed Solange wouldn't, but if her companion did mind, she herself would just have to leave Roland strictly alone in future. She was already too fond of the Frenchwoman to want to upset her in any way.

After breakfast Roland went off to read the ship's newspaper in the smoking room while Lisa decided to do several perambulations of the deck.

As soon as she stepped outside she was assailed by a gust of fresh, salty air which almost knocked her off her feet. But used to spending a lot of time in the open air, she was undaunted and set off at a brisk pace.

The sense of space on the boat deck was breathtaking. The acres of polished wood flooring seemed to go on forever and it was only as she strode along that she realised just how massive the liner actually was.

The stacks towered high above her leaving a trail of charcoal-grey smoke which soon paled to silver-grey and then was lost as the wind whipped it away. She passed several other passengers also taking the morning air and returned their polite nods with a smile.

When she reached the bow she paused to lean over the rail and watch the boiling white wake trailing into infinity as it cut a swathe across the blue-green surface of the ocean.

How many miles had they come? How many did they still have to travel? She really must find out.

When she'd completed several circuits of the deck she returned to their suite, anxious to see Solange. But Celeste told her that Solange was still asleep and knowing how late the other woman had been up the night before, Lisa decided not to disturb her.

She wandered off to the ship's library and found herself a novel, then curled up in one of the large, burgundy leather armchairs with it.

At around eleven she went up on deck for a cup of bouillon and was joined by Roland, who tasted the salty brew, pulled a face and promptly threw the rest over the side.

'Prefer whiskey,' he explained. 'Have you seen Solange today?' he asked, once a steward had been despatched to bring him his drink.

'No, she was still asleep when I left the suite,' replied Lisa.

'Hope she wakes up in a better mood,' he commented.

Unsure whether to ask if Roland knew anything about Solange's past, Lisa tried an indirect approach.

'Have you known her long?' she asked.

'A couple of months or so.'

'Where did you meet?'

'A friend of mine introduced me to her at a party. Discovered we were both travelling east and I've seen a lot of her since then. She's a very alluring woman. Fancy some clay pigeon shooting?'

The day passed pleasantly enough. She ate lunch with Roland, but neither Solange nor Alex joined them. In the afternoon

Lisa played shuffle board and then went to take a long bath and spend some time trying to decide what to wear that night at the first formal dinner on board the ship.

She was concerned that Solange still hadn't emerged from her bedroom, but Celeste assured her that the Frenchwoman would be joining her for cocktails.

After spending some time agonising over her choice of gown, Lisa opted for a draped, cloth-of-silver sheath. Cut on the bias it clung to her like a second skin and fell in a shimmering circle around her ankles. Other than for two narrow shoulder straps, it left her shoulders and arms bare and dipped to the waist at the back.

It had a matching bolero-jacket with puffed sleeves and she added some silver bracelets that had been among the jewellery her mother had left her.

A tap on the door distracted her from trying on various pairs of shoes. Celeste handed her a white envelope.

'This was just delivered, *Mademoiselle*.' Excitedly, Lisa tore it open to find an invitation to the captain's cocktail party.

'I take it Solange has received one too,' she said to the maid.

'Certainly I have,' came Solange's prettily accented voice from the sitting room, then she swept into Lisa's bedroom. 'Good evening, *chérie*, I hope you have passed the day most pleasantly.'

Lisa had expected her to be pale and subdued and was unprepared for the radiant vision before her. Solange looked absolutely stunning in a gown of richly embroidered silk in vivid hues of crimson, blue and gold.

The dress swooped between Solange's full breasts to

expose a generous amount of creamy cleavage and then fell to the floor in fluid folds which accentuated her small waist and well-rounded *derrière*.

Her slender feet were encased in crimson satin shoes with a very high heel and there were diamonds at her throat and one wrist. Her dark hair had been caught up at one side with a diamond clip and several crimson feathers nodded flirtatiously from it. Her luscious mouth was painted a deep red and her large dark eyes were sparkling with gaiety under her winged dark brows.

She surveyed Lisa's appearance critically, then shook her head at the shoes she'd chosen.

'The black and silver shoes with the silver mesh bag would be better with that gown,' she observed.

Obediently Lisa changed them while asking, 'Are you alright, Solange? I was worried about you.'

'Nothing but a touch of *mal de mer*, but now I am absolutely fine. We have been invited to the captain's cocktail party. Let us hope there will be many interesting people there.'

'You look ravishing,' Lisa told her truthfully.

'And so do you, *ma petite*.' She kissed Lisa's cheek and then twirled in front of the mirror so that her skirt swung out around her, exposing her shapely ankles. 'Are you ready to meet the gallant captain who steers this ship so bravely across many oceans? Let us go.'

The party was being held in the main lounge and when they presented themselves at the door, a ship's officer took their invitations from them with a bow.

'Madame Solange Valois and Miss Lisa Cavendish,' he

announced in a booming voice. The captain stepped forward to greet them. Deeply tanned and with thick, greying hair and craggy features he shook their hands, saying, 'I'm Captain Saville and I'm delighted to have two such charming ladies on board my ship. Are my crew taking good care of you?'

Solange fluttered her silky eyelashes at him and Lisa saw immediately that he was captivated.

'Indeed they are,' murmured Solange huskily. He offered an arm to each of them and then led them forward to introduce them to various other guests. Lisa tried hard to remember all their names, but suspected she'd forget most of them within minutes. The captain drew Solange to one side and they were soon deep in conversation.

'And where are you bound?' enquired a burly, middle-aged man with a high colour. What was his name? Stephen Temple or Templeton, she thought Captain Saville had said.

'Malaya,' she said, accepting a glass of champagne from a tray proffered by a steward.

'Which part?'

'Penang, initially.'

'I have a plantation up-country from there myself. Do your family live in Malaya?'

'My guardian does. He's called Charles Varonne. Do you know him?' she asked eagerly, hoping she might learn something about him before they met. Stephen shook his head.

'I've heard of him of course, but our paths have never crossed. He's a member of the same club in Penang but our plantations are a long way apart. Phyllis, have you ever met Charles Varonne?'

His wife was a handsome, well-bred woman in her late

thirties with smooth, dark-blonde hair and large white teeth.

'Can't say I have,' she retorted. 'He your father?'

'No, my guardian.'

'Ever been out east before?'

'No.'

'Takes a bit of getting used to, I can tell you, particularly the humidity. Anything you want to know, just ask.'

'What's the countryside like?'

'Gloriously beautiful. Miles and miles of jungle, forest and marsh. But it's a harsh country – particularly for a woman. Take my advice and keep busy or you'll spend the day sitting on the verandah swilling gin and wishing yourself back in England.'

There was a sudden commotion by the door and all heads turned in that direction. Two ferocious-looking, dark-skinned men had just entered the room and were surveying the gathered throng suspiciously. They stood to one side and a dozen more marched in and then stood to attention in two rows.

They were all clad in similar garments to the ones Lisa had seen the day before and all had hands on the hilts of the large sheathed knives which dangled from their belts.

Silence fell and a rustle of expectation ran around the room. An overweight, turbanned man appeared in the doorway and then walked casually between the guards. It was hard to tell how old he was but Lisa guessed him to be in his sixties.

'It's the Maharajah,' Lisa heard someone whisper. He was clad in a gold brocade jacket and baggy white silk trousers which were gathered around the ankle. His white turban was embedded with a dazzling array of jewels and he wore a necklace of rubies, the largest of which was the size of a golf ball.

He held out a bejewelled hand to the captain.

'Good evening. I am the Maharajah of Panjore.' His appearance may have been exotic in the extreme, but nothing could have been more English than his accent.

'Captain Saville. How do you do? Glad to have you on board.' They shook hands and then the Maharajah turned to Solange.

'I need not ask your name because it is surely "beauteous one".' He possessed himself of her hand, held it between his and kissed it lingeringly. The captain's bushy brows drew together at the sight and it was obvious that he made the introduction reluctantly.

'May I introduce Madame Solange Valois.'

The Maharajah kissed her hand again. 'Enchanted,' he murmured. 'Let us go and admire the sunset together.' He bore her off towards the windows overlooking the bow, leaving Captain Saville looking very displeased. Lisa stifled a giggle. It looked as though Roland had not one, but two rivals for Solange's affections.

Her attention was claimed by another of the men she'd been introduced to and she chatted animatedly, shooting the occasional glance in Solange's direction to make sure she was alright.

But her companion seemed to be enjoying herself and was at her flirtatious best, pouting and fluttering her eyelashes in a way which would have enslaved any man with red blood in his veins. There was no sign of Alex or Roland and it suddenly dawned on Lisa that perhaps they hadn't been invited. She had a shrewd suspicion that she and Solange were there simply because they were probably the only two unattached women on the ship.

The party began to break up and Lisa saw Solange laughing and shaking her head at the Maharajah who seemed to be trying to persuade her to do something.

Captain Saville appeared at Lisa's elbow, cleared his throat and said, 'I'd be honoured if you and Madame Valois would dine at my table for the rest of the voyage.'

'Thank you, but I'm not sure...' Lisa cast a look of entreaty in Solange's direction, not sure whether her companion would wish to accept or not.

Hips undulating seductively, Solange made her way over to them leaving the Maharajah looking downcast. He snapped his fingers at the guards and they hurried to form ranks behind him as he approached the captain.

'Thank you for a delightful party, Captain Saville. I hope to return your hospitality very soon.' He bowed to Solange and Lisa then left the room with his entourage.

The captain repeated his invitation to Solange.

'How kind of you,' purred Solange. 'We'd be delighted to accept... for tonight.' It obviously wasn't the answer he'd hoped for but he beckoned to one of the ship's officers who offered his arm to Lisa and together the four of them made their way to the dining salon.

It was a lively meal, though Lisa found she kept glancing upwards hoping to catch a glimpse of Alex, but their table on the balcony wasn't in view from where she was sitting. It was only as they left the dining salon that she saw him. He was staring down with a grim expression on his face. Their eyes met and she smiled, but the smile wasn't returned.

Solange caught the exchange and murmured, 'He's jealous, *chérie*. But he and Roland can hardly expect us to limit ourselves to them, when there are so many charming men on board.'

Solange's lighthearted words reminded Lisa of how her companion had reacted to encountering Mark Channing yesterday. She felt a shiver of unease feather down her spine as they made their way to the main lounge where a formal dance was being held.

All evening she'd been dreading bumping into the man in case his presence had the same effect on her companion as it had last night. He hadn't been at the captain's cocktail party and she hadn't glimpsed him in the dining salon, but the odds were that he'd be at the dance.

An orchestra was playing on the raised dais at one end of the room and many couples had already taken to the floor. Lisa was immediately swept away to dance by the officer who'd taken her into dinner and as soon as that ended one of the men she'd been introduced to at the party presented himself as her next partner.

She caught sight of Alex standing by the bar, a drink in his hand, glowering at her. She wondered if he'd ask her to dance, but he remained morosely where he was.

Roland asked for the next dance and proved to be an accomplished and graceful dancer, a far cry from her last partner who'd stepped on her toes several times.

'Sorry you weren't able to join us for dinner,' he said. 'I should have guessed you'd be invited to dine at the captain's table as soon as he set eyes on you both.'

'How's Alex?' she ventured. 'I haven't spoken to him yet today.'

'Moody bastard, Alex,' returned Roland cheerfully. 'Seems to be in a rage about something. Not a bit like me, I'm always in good spirits.'

Lisa's hope that Alex would ask her to dance seemed to be doomed to disappointment. She tried waving at him and smiling again, but the scowl she received in return daunted her. Well, if Alex didn't want to dance with her, there were plenty of men who did.

Solange seemed to be having a wonderful time. She whirled around the room in her vividly-hued dress like some kind of gorgeous, exotic bird and Lisa noticed more than one man staring at her hungrily.

It was while Lisa was dancing with Stephen Templeton that she saw Mark Channing approach Solange. She tried to keep them in sight while Stephen steered her enthusiastically around the floor, but when she next passed the spot where they'd been, they'd vanished.

She bit her lip anxiously. If Mark Channing had a shred of sensitivity he'd keep his distance and leave Solange alone. Unable to concentrate on the dance she suggested to Stephen they pause for a drink, a suggestion he acquiesced to amiably.

To her intense relief when the orchestra took a break a few minutes later, Solange tripped lightly over, her high spirits apparently unsubdued.

'Are you having a good time?' she asked gaily, drawing Lisa to one side.

'Wonderful,' said Lisa, not altogether truthfully.

'You look a little flushed – are you feeling quite well?'

It was true that she was very warm and when she laid the back of her hand on her forehead, it felt red-hot.

'I'm not used to dancing the night away,' Lisa replied lightly. 'But I feel fine.' Then unable to keep it to herself any longer she burst out, 'Solange, Alex keeps glaring at me. Do you think I should go and talk to him?'

Solange tossed her head so that the feathers tucked in her hair bobbed friskily.

'On no account must you do that, *chérie*. If Alex is determined to behave like an oaf then let him do so alone. If he wishes to keep your interest he must be *amusant* and *charmant*. Now, let us sit this dance out together and have another glass of champagne.'

The rest of the evening passed in a giddy whirl until Solange told Lisa she was returning to their suite.

'I'll come with you,' decided Lisa. After her early start that morning she found herself having to suppress yawns with increasing frequency.

'Do you wish to invite someone back to pleasure you for a while?' asked Solange solicitously. But the only person Lisa wanted was Alex, who'd ostentatiously turned his back on her and was talking to an army officer.

'No, I'm very tired.'

Roland, who'd just been dancing with Solange, offered to escort them. When they arrived at the door to the suite Solange said goodnight to him to his obvious disappointment and then shepherded Lisa inside.

'Madame, something was delivered for you from the Maharajah.' Celeste came bustling excitedly forward.

'And what is this something?' queried Solange, putting her bag down and sinking gracefully onto the sofa. Reverently, Celeste laid a large leather box on the table in front of her mistress.

Solange flipped it open to find a massive, gleaming emerald nestling in solitary splendour on white velvet. It reflected the light so brilliantly that Lisa was briefly dazzled.

'Celeste – fetch my glass please,' directed Solange. Celeste went into Solange's bedroom and to Lisa's astonishment returned a few moments later holding a jeweller's eye-glass. Solange put it to her eye and examined the stone through it for a couple of minutes.

'Very pretty,' she conceded eventually. 'But not of the finest quality. Celeste, have a steward return it to the Maharajah with my regrets that I cannot accept it.'

Lisa had been watching in amazement. 'Wh... why do you have one of those?' she asked, indicating the eye-glass.

'So I may see for myself what are the quality of the gifts I am presented with. Would you believe it, *chérie*, one of my admirers once had the temerity to make me a gift of what he claimed was a sapphire bracelet, but which was nothing but paste.'

'What did you do?' Lisa wanted to know.

'I punished him.'

'How?'

'I will tell you some other time. Now I must prepare myself for my rendezvous.'

'Whom do you have a rendezvous with?'

'I forget his name. The big handsome one with the oh-so-beautiful hands.' She went into her bedroom and began to powder her nose. Lisa followed her and watched while Solange re-applied her lipstick and then sprayed herself with her alluring jasmine and orange flower perfume. The Frenchwoman turned to face her.

'*Chérie*, are you sure that you wouldn't like me to send for Roland to . . . entertain you?'

'No, thank you. I think I'll retire to bed now. Goodnight.'

She bent to kiss Solange's soft cheek and then went into her bedroom, relieved to have it confirmed that her companion didn't consider Roland to be personal property.

She heard her leave as she prepared for bed and was just throwing back the bedcovers prior to getting in and snuggling down under the downy quilt, when there came the sound of raised voices from the sitting room.

She was reaching for her robe, wondering if perhaps the Maharajah had come in search of Solange, when the door to her bedroom was thrown violently open and Alex stood on the threshold, Celeste just behind him.

'I'm sorry, *Mademoiselle*, he forced his way in,' said Celeste agitatedly. 'Shall I ring for the steward?'

Alex's hair was untidy, his bow-tie askew and there was a wild glitter in his eyes which half-frightened her, even as she felt a lascivious kick of lust in her groin.

'No – it's alright, Celeste. I'll call if I need you.' Celeste backed out and Alex stepped into the room, slamming the door to behind him.

'What do you want?' she asked coolly.

'You.'

He walked towards her with the feline grace of a jungle cat stalking its prey. The air in the room suddenly felt electrically charged as he shed his dinner jacket and wrenched his tie off. Lisa tried to stand her ground but the raw carnality of his gaze alarmed her and she backed away until she felt the bed behind her and could go no further.

She was wearing a fragile, lace-trimmed silk nightgown in the palest blue. He reached out and laid a hand on her breast over the diaphanous silk. She could feel the heat of his palm and her nipple hardened in eager response.

She found herself unable to move, hypnotised by the sheer power of his will. Slowly, he caressed her breasts while she felt a flickering tongue of fire licking at her from deep within her sex.

He lifted one of the ribbons holding her nightgown closed over her breasts, his intention plain. She caught his wrist, suddenly angry that he'd dared to burst into her bedroom without an invitation.

'I think you should leave now,' she told him.

His answer was to hook his fingers into the low neckline of the flimsy garment and rip it down to the hem in one rough, violent movement. It fluttered to the floor in a reproachful whisper of silk, leaving her naked before him.

Before she had time to protest, he swung her into his arms, lowered her onto the bed and covered her body with his own.

He tried to kiss her but she hit him furiously on the side of his head, as hard as she could. With lightning reflexes and despite his obviously inebriated state, he rolled the punch and grabbed her wrists, holding them over her head with one hand.

She managed to knee him hard on the leg, but he thrust a thigh between hers and kept her legs immobile with the weight of his own. She struggled wildly, writhing and bucking beneath him and trying to throw him off.

Although he was much stronger than she was, fury lent Lisa strength and briefly she managed to roll out from under him, before he overpowered her again. Strangely, she didn't think of calling for Celeste. This was a struggle for domination between them and she didn't want to involve anyone else.

He held her immobile and began to caress her determinedly, stroking her breasts, hips and belly while she glared up at him, breathing hard.

Despite the barely suppressed violence she could sense simmering just below the surface, his caresses were gentle and arousing. She could feel the warm moisture gathering in her sex, dampening the soft fronds of her russet fleece.

He took one nipple in his mouth, sucking on it and flicking the tip of his tongue around it in a way that made her find it hard to breathe.

His hand grazed over her belly to find her pubic floss and then covered her mound, massaging it with an insidious circular movement. Every nerve ending in her groin responded to the stimulation and her sex-flesh felt hot, engorged and more than ready for his entry.

He shifted his weight and his hand slid between her thighs, coaxing them open and gliding smoothly over her outer labia. She cried out when he made contact with the aching kernel of her clitoris and rubbed it with licentious expertise.

Her pelvis pressed upwards and she parted her thighs for him as he manipulated the swollen little sliver of flesh. She felt herself fizzing internally and moaned, then for an agonising few seconds she trembled on the brink of release before crying out and convulsing into a climax so intense it was almost painful.

She was only dimly aware that he'd moved away from her and was tearing off his own clothes. The bed dipped as he mounted her and she felt the hot, smooth end of his penis poised against the inner petals guarding the entrance to her honey-slick inner-chamber.

He bent his head to cover her mouth with his own and she caught a glimpse of his triumphant smile in the light from the bedside lamp. Without considering the consequences she sank her teeth into his lower lip and heard his shocked grunt of pain.

His shaft felt like velvet-sheathed steel as he thrust inside her and set up a fierce, undulating rhythm. Her internal muscles closed around his manhood in urgent response to the relentless stimulation and she felt burningly, arousedly distended.

The heat from their bodies fanned the flames of each other's need as he pistoned in and out of her with insatiable ferocity. She found her hips rising to meet each powerful thrust and she dug her nails into the hard, muscular planes of his back.

It was a bitter-sweet coupling which nevertheless took her to realms of ecstasy she'd never experienced before. She felt a great wash of heat which indicated another climax was imminent and clutched his shoulders as she spasmed into orgasm.

Alex's movements quickened and then he made several last, frenzied thrusts and came inside her in a volcanic release that left her overflowing with their mingled juices.

He slumped to one side of her breathing hard and they lay

in silence except for the distant throbbing of the ship's engines.

Suddenly aware she had a raging thirst, Lisa eased herself away from him and went into her en-suite bathroom.

She glanced in the mirror and saw her eyes looked unfocused, her red-gold hair lay tumbled around her shoulders and in their current swollen state, the hard points of her nipples looked like autumn berries. She felt dizzy and lightheaded and had to hold onto the side of the basin for a few moments thinking she must have had more champagne than she'd realised.

Her entire body seemed to be burning up. She drank some water and splashed some on her face and breasts, marvelling at the effect Alex had on her. There was still a demanding ache in her sex as she returned to the bedroom.

He lay on his back with his eyes closed, his manhood now detumescent between his thighs. She knelt next to him, taking his shaft in her hand. His eyes flickered open as she began to manipulate it determinedly.

'I hope you don't think we've finished,' she said sweetly. He folded his arms behind his head and watched the bobbing of her breasts as she squeezed his rod and moved her hand up and down it. He was hard again within a few moments, the heavily knobbed end of his penis shiny and plum-like.

She straddled him and used the glans to stimulate her clitoris. She drew it backwards and forwards, enjoying the lewd stimulation, her pelvis moving as she used him to pleasure herself. His hands closed on her hips with the obvious intention of lifting her onto his burgeoning member, but she evaded him and squeezed his shaft warningly.

'You've had what you came for,' she told him softly. 'Now it's my turn.'

She felt the heady sensation of being in control as she rubbed herself faster and faster, her pleasure mounting by the moment. Seeing how his eyes lingered on her breasts she began to caress them herself and saw that watching her behaving so wantonly was driving him to distraction.

She felt the first ripple of her climax and pushed the drenched head of his member against the furled entrance to her sex. As she exploded into release she impaled herself on him, crying out as she felt him searing into her pulsing depths.

His hands closed on her waist as she rode him, urging her onto greater efforts. It was a hot and desperate coupling which seemed to go on for half the night.

But eventually he revved himself up for three last vigorous thrusts then pumped into her with shuddering intensity, leaving them both drenched in perspiration and totally drained.

As she came for the final time, Lisa felt a great wave of dizziness and collapsed onto him, wondering why she could suddenly see two of him lying on her bed.

Chapter Eleven

Lisa had only confused memories of the next couple of weeks. She could just about recall waking beside Alex feeling as though she was burning up and then Solange and Celeste bending over her, talking in hushed voices.

She was vaguely aware that she was ill, that someone kept sponging her perspiring body with blissfully cool water and that she had frequent visits from the ship's doctor, but everything else passed her by unheeded.

The ceiling fan turned constantly, stirring the air and making her feel even dizzier whenever she opened her eyes. She was assailed by feverish dreams in which Alex and Roland appeared, as did many of the people she'd met on the *S.S. Orient* and a shadowy figure whom she knew to be her guardian.

She dreamt she was disturbed by a noise and became convinced that her guardian was in the suite. She half-fell out of bed and stumbled to the door. When she wrenched it open she found not her guardian, but Mark Channing in their sitting room.

He had his dinner jacket under one arm and was struggling to fasten his bow-tie in front of the etched mirror on the wall.

He looked startled to see her and then Solange came out of her bedroom, holding a *peignoir* of gentian-blue satin closed over her naked breasts. She hurried towards Lisa, her *peignoir* fluttering out behind her, and then everything dissolved into darkness.

In another dream, Lisa saw herself naked on a beach of white sand, lying in the shade of mop-headed palm trees, some of which grew almost horizontally towards the sea. She was surrounded by other naked people, many of whom were openly copulating and others touching each other lewdly.

Someone shouted a warning and they all looked out to sea where a massive white-crested wave at least twelve feet high swept inexorably and terrifyingly towards them. She jerked awake just as it broke over them to find Celeste sponging her face and the water trickling down her neck and onto the pillow.

She also dreamt she was in the forest near to the Scottish castle and that she came across a clearing she'd never seen before. Women in gauzy draperies were lying in groups on the mossy banks of a pool, combing each other's flowing hair and stroking each other languidly.

Some of the women disrobed, waded into the pool and bathed, sluicing their naked, creamy limbs with the crystal-clear water, their nipples becoming puckered and hard. But then the water began to form a whirlpool and one by one the women were plucked from the surface and vanished into the depths.

Then there came a day when Lisa woke up feeling weak but clear-headed and struggled to prop herself against the pillows, wondering how long she'd been sick. She noticed immediately that it was very warm in her bedroom, despite the fan and the fact that the door onto their private deck was ajar. Did that mean they'd reached the tropics?

The room seemed to be filled with flowers which hadn't been there before she'd been taken ill. Where had they all come from?

The door opened and Celeste came in carrying a jug of water covered in a muslin cloth.

'Hello, Celeste,' Lisa murmured weakly.

'*Mademoiselle* – you're awake!' exclaimed Celeste. '*Madame* Valois – *Mademoiselle* has awakened.'

Solange undulated into the room, a vision in a grape-green silk chiffon tea gown with scalloped edges lavishly embroidered in darker green.

'*Chérie*, you are back with us. How do you feel?'

'Tired,' said Lisa ruefully. 'Tired and confused. What's been the matter with me?'

'You've had a high fever, we were all most concerned about you.'

'How long have I been ill?'

'Just over two weeks.'

'Where are we? The ship, I mean.'

'We're crossing the Indian Ocean heading for Bombay.'

'No wonder it's so hot,' said Lisa, gratefully accepting the glass of ice-cooled water Celeste passed to her. She drank half of it and put it on the bedside table next to a vase of velvety cream roses, sinking back against the pillows, exhausted by even that small effort.

'Not as hot as it was while we were sailing through the Suez canal. Be glad that our suite is on the port side of the ship so the sun doesn't shine directly onto it. The unfortunate ones on the starboard side say their cabins are unbearable with the sun beating down all day. Several of the army officers have taken to sleeping on deck.'

'What have I missed?'

'Nothing of any import. Many people have enquired after you and as you can see you have been sent lots of flowers. Now you must eat something so that you may recover your strength and make the most of the last weeks on board. Celeste, ring and ask the stewardess for some beef tea.'

When Lisa caught sight of herself in the mirror later that day she let out a shriek. Her face was pale and drawn, her hair dull and matted and her collar bones seemed to be jutting out at a prominent angle.

For the next three days she submitted to the attentions of the hairdresser, masseuse and beautician in an attempt to repair the damage her illness had wrought. She found she was ravenously hungry and ate every meal with the utmost relish, soon putting back the few pounds she'd lost.

She spent the rest of her time lying on a rattan sunlounger on their private deck so the balmy sea air could whip some colour back in her cheeks. Solange refused point blank to let her have any male visitors except the doctor.

'No woman should allow herself to be seen by her lovers looking anything except her best,' was her advice. 'When the roses are back in your cheeks, it will be time enough. Alex is most impatient to see you – he likes his own way too much that one – but I have told him you're still indisposed.'

Lisa particularly regretted not having been able to visit

Gibralter, Malta, Port Said, Suez and Aden all of which had been ports of call. Solange had been ashore each time, but maintained that Lisa hadn't really missed anything.

'Gibralter was ugly, Malta hot and dusty, Suez and Aden like a furnace and Port Said particularly unpleasant,' was her opinion. 'Bombay, however, should be most interesting and we shall explore it together.'

She brought Lisa a pile of books to while away the languid days of her convalescence. To Lisa's surprise they weren't novels, but weighty tomes about Malaya, its history, people and customs. There were also a couple of volumes on rubber planting and one on the flora and fauna of the country.

'Where on earth did you get all these?' asked Lisa, flicking through one.

'Some I bought in London before we left, others are from the ship's library.'

'But what do you need to know all this for?'

'Because I have inherited a rubber plantation which I wish to sell and get the best possible price for. The more I know, the less likely I am to be cheated. As you are about to make a long sojourn there, it would be in your interests to learn as much as possible too.'

Recognising the wisdom of Solange's words, Lisa ploughed through them as best she could and then found herself fascinated. She couldn't wait to arrive at their destination and see for herself.

Young and healthy as she was, Lisa made a swift recovery and Solange at last decreed she could have a visitor. To Lisa's intense disappointment it wasn't Alex, although he had sent her several bouquets of flowers. It was Roland who came bringing an elaborate fruit basket and entertaining tales of shipboard life.

It was from Celeste that Lisa discovered that the Maharajah's courtship of Solange had escalated to the extent that every day brought some new gift, each more extravagant than the last.

The tributes included jewels, two singing birds, bolts of gorgeous fabric, perfumed oils and a pet monkey, all of which Solange had returned.

'Why didn't you accept any of them?' Lisa wanted to know.

'They didn't please me,' was Solange's serene reply. 'And the Maharajah, although most rich and powerful, is not to my taste. He sends me presents and thinks to buy me with them, but he is very much mistaken.'

'I would have loved to have seen the monkey,' said Lisa with some regret. 'Was it sweet?'

'Assuredly not, it excreted in the Lalique bowl in our sitting room,' Solange told her. 'Also it threw my box of talcum powder over everything and bit Captain Saville when he tried to catch it. He was most displeased.'

'Captain Saville was here?' Lisa enquired, surprised.

'Yes, several times, he is a most virile and attentive lover.' Solange looked so pleased with herself that Lisa laughed.

'It looks like I have a lot of catching up to do,' she commented. 'I feel much better today. I think I'll join you for dinner – I'm tired of being cooped up in here.'

'Are you sure, *chérie*? It is true you are in good looks again, but you are still a little pale and you may find it too fatiguing.'

'No, I won't,' said Lisa, determination in her voice. 'And

I'm going for a walk around the deck this afternoon.'

She felt much better for the exercise and the early evening found her dressing for dinner in a primrose-yellow gown of finely pleated georgette flecked with gold lamé. It had a low décolletage and buttoned down the front to just above her knees where it split to show off her legs in their silk stockings as she walked, the skirt swirling around her like yellow foam.

She slipped her feet into a pair of gold brocade evening slippers and clasped an old-gold choker with a large topaz in the centre around her neck.

Solange had chosen a dress in off-white silk faille with a draped hip yoke. It left her back bare to the waist and she'd wound a string of black pearls twice around her slender throat and then let them trail down her spine. She carried a jet-beaded bag and a paper fan with an onyx handle. Elbow-length black gloves with several rings and bracelets worn over them completed the ensemble.

The heat had permeated the entire ship despite the constantly whirring fans and the doors and windows wedged open to let a breeze waft through. The ship's officers were all in tropical uniform and the women had put away their tweeds and cashmeres in favour of silk, linen and cotton voile.

When they walked into the cocktail bar the first person Lisa spotted was Alex, his arm draped over the back of the chair in which Phyllis Templeton was sitting. He was leaning towards her as she spoke and Lisa felt her stomach do a back flip as she saw the intimacy of their pose. She immediately suspected that the two of them had become lovers and cursed her illness for keeping her confined to her cabin.

She was tempted to turn round and flee back to their suite.

It had, after all, been Alex she'd most wanted to see. The memory of their last night of passion had tormented her as her health had returned and with it her libido. He'd obviously found someone else to occupy himself with while she was out of circulation and it didn't please her one bit.

She wondered what Stephen Templeton thought about it. He was sitting on the other side of the table talking to a colonial civil servant and his wife, a brittle bleached-blonde in her forties.

But Lisa had no real alternative but to behave as though she didn't suspect anything and she greeted Alex with the same cool friendliness that she did everyone else. She was gratified when he moved seats to come and sit by her, but told herself not to read anything into it.

Her first glass of champagne tasted like nectar, sliding down her throat in an effervescent stream of icy liquid.

'Are you feeling better?' Alex asked, his eyes flickering over her décolletage.

'Yes – much better. Thank you for the flowers by the way.'

He lowered his voice. 'You look very lovely and very desirable. I've missed you on these long, hot nights with only the memory of how it was between us to sustain me.'

Glancing at Phyllis Templeton, who looked as though she was straining to hear what was being said, Lisa replied brightly, 'How was it between us? I'm afraid I don't remember.'

He shot her an appraising look from between his thick lashes. 'I can see I'm going to have to remind you . . . again.'

'Aren't there rather too many people around?' she said innocently.

He raised his dark brows. 'Then we'd better find somewhere we can be alone.'

'Thank you but I've just emerged from almost solitary confinement and I'm enjoying being surrounded by people and gaiety.'

His hand closed on her arm, but at that moment they were joined by Captain Saville who kissed Lisa's hand with old world gallantry and said, 'Delighted to see you on your feet again, Miss Cavendish. Madame Valois was very concerned about you.'

With obvious reluctance Alex released her as she replied, 'I'm only sorry I've missed so much of the voyage. I'll have to make the most of the last couple of weeks.'

The captain invited them to dine at his table, but Solange decided that she and Lisa would eat with Roland and Alex on their table on the balcony.

Captain Saville looked disconsolate and drew Solange to one side. Lisa couldn't hear what was said, but she saw Solange tapping him playfully on the arm with her fan and shaking her head. He went away but it was obvious he left her side with regret.

'What did you say to him?' enquired Lisa, accepting a refill of her champagne glass. 'He looked really crestfallen.'

'He wanted to visit me late tonight, but I told him it was not possible. He is becoming a little possessive and I have neglected both Roland and Alex recently. Shall we celebrate your return to health by spending the evening with them?'

Lisa wondered whether to ask Solange if she knew for certain that Alex was having an affair with Phyllis Templeton, but she decided it would be better to remain in ignorance.

'Yes, let's do that,' she agreed nonchalantly.

An atmosphere of revelry seemed to hang in the humid air. In the time since the ship had left England many of the passengers had got to know one another and made new friends. There was a general awareness that soon they would be leaving behind the luxury of the liner for more primitive living conditions and in some cases, virtual isolation from society. Every night was party night as the majority of people made the most of it.

Most people seemed to be drinking feverishly and Lisa consumed several glasses of champagne before they even went into dinner.

She dined off stuffed avocados followed by mallard in juniper and sherry sauce served with petit pois, green beans and roasted potatoes the size of marbles.

Throughout the meal she was aware of Alex's eyes constantly on her and felt weak with desire at the thought that soon she would renew her acquaintance with his lean, virile body. Roland too, seemed to be in a highly aroused state and amused them by commenting on the infinite desirability of the women he could see dining below them.

He was particularly taken by a voluptuous brunette. A woman of ample charms, she had a cleavage of stunning dimensions and they had a bird's eye view of it.

'I'll have to have her before the voyage is over,' he decided. 'But she has such a fearsome husband – the major with the outsize moustache sitting opposite her. The trouble is he's always with her, gloating over her like a miser with his money. I say, Solange, you wouldn't do a chap a favour and distract him for me – just for a few hours.'

'Possibly. Or perhaps Alex could challenge him to some manly sport, or maybe a game of cards.'

'I've got a better idea,' said Alex. 'You distract the husband while I have a crack at his gorgeous wife.'

Lisa was on fire because he kept touching her, keeping her in a state of anticipatory excitement. His hand would brush hers for a moment, then stroke her bare arm, or rest briefly on her knee under the cover of the mint-green table cloth. When he leant across to murmur something she could feel his warm breath on her cheek and ached for the moment when his lips would cover hers.

They had been among the last people into dinner and gradually the tables on the balcony emptied as people finished eating and drifted away to the various entertainments on offer. It was very warm in the dining salon and Lisa decided to suggest a stroll on deck when they left it.

Roland, who was sitting directly opposite her, admired her gown, complimenting her on the way the primrose-yellow set off her red-gold hair and pale skin.

'There's just one thing you could do that would make it look even more stunning,' he observed, draping his arm over Solange's shoulders and caressing her satin-skinned arm.

'What's that?' she enquired, aware that Roland had impeccable taste in clothes and was himself always immaculately turned out, unlike Alex who had a more careless attitude towards his appearance and had been known to turn up with his tie askew and his hair untidy.

'Undo the buttons to the waist.'

Solange rapped him smartly on the knee with her fan.

'For shame, Roland, suggesting that Lisa should exhibit

herself in public. What can you be thinking of?'

'Of how much I'd like to sit and look at her,' he said frankly.

'What do you think, *chérie*? Do you wish to allow Roland this pleasure?'

'Other people would see me too,' said Lisa, feeling a small squib of lust beginning to smoulder in her sex at the idea. Solange glanced around the deserted balcony and then down over the parapet to the diners below.

'There's no-one up here but us,' she pointed out. 'Those below can only see your head and perhaps your shoulders and if anyone ascends the stairs we'll notice them well before they reach us. You have your back to the upper entrance, so if someone approaches from that direction we'll see them and you'll have plenty of time to cover yourself.'

'In fact the steward is coming now,' added Roland. 'He's just walked through the doors.'

Mentally, Lisa estimated how long it would take her to fasten the three buttons holding her gown closed over her breasts and decided she would have time to spare.

They all ordered puddings and then watched the steward hurry off to fetch them.

'You see,' Roland observed. 'It would be quite safe.' As soon as their desserts had been served he sat back in his chair, eyes gleaming with anticipation. Somehow, Lisa found her hand going to her breasts and then slowly, she undid the top button. Alex turned sideways to get a better view and Solange fanned herself gently, her eyes never leaving Lisa's décolletage.

Lisa undid the second button, revealing the upper slopes of

her firm, high breasts and then after a pause, the third to expose them completely. She flushed as she felt their eyes on her and the squib of lust in her sex began to fizz. She could feel her coral nipples hardening in response to their avid attention and tried to sit casually back in her chair, reaching for her wine glass.

'So beautiful,' breathed Solange. 'So sweetly round and pert.'

'I'll say,' agreed Roland. 'Is it just me or has the temperature just shot up about ten degrees?'

'The temperature isn't the only thing that has shot up,' marvelled Solange, her hand gliding down to fondle Roland's erect member.

Alex pushed his chair back from the table saying, 'Warn me if anyone comes towards us.'

To Lisa's surprise he lifted the tablecloth and slid under the table. For a few moments she wondered if he'd had too much to drink and succumbed to the force of gravity, but then she felt his hands on her legs.

He slid them caressingly up her silk-clad calves and eased her thighs apart. Lisa found it difficult to breathe and she was certain that two spots of high colour were burning on her pale cheeks.

Deftly, he undid the two lowest buttons so her dress was completely open at the front and then she felt the heat of his mouth on the smooth skin above her stocking tops. It was a deliriously erotic sensation to have an unseen lover kiss, lick and nibble her thighs from beneath the table while the two other diners, aware what was happening, admired her naked breasts.

Beneath her gown Lisa was wearing a pair of champagne

silk camiknickers which buttoned over her crotch with two tiny crystal buttons. She felt Alex delicately stroking the strip of silk between her legs and gasped, opening them even wider to facilitate his movements.

He caressed her through the fine material until gradually it became soaked with her honeyed juices. She had to suppress an urge to wriggle around on her chair, but mindful that her head and shoulders were in view, she tried to keep still and give no indication by the expression on her face of what was happening.

She felt him fumbling with the crystal buttons and then the strip of silk that covered her sex fell open, leaving her exposed to his ministrations.

She gasped as she felt his muscular tongue sliding along the rim of her outer labia and then hastily closed her mouth and tried not to moan aloud as he plunged it into her dripping delta and lapped at her female honey.

She eased herself forward on her chair so he had greater access to her throbbing private parts, digging her nails into the palm of her hand to stop herself sighing with pleasure.

He strummed the shaft of her clitoris and then stabbed the head rhythmically, making her horribly aware that she was being swept along on a wave of sheer carnal sensation.

She glanced frantically over her shoulder, afraid someone might be coming and Roland and Solange hadn't noticed, but there was no-one there.

Alex's tongue became even more active and she realised that unless she stopped him now, in all probability she was going to climax in full view of two other people and anyone who happened to glance up.

But after a couple of weeks of enforced celibacy, the desire for release was too strong and she clutched the arms of her chair feverishly.

'*Aaaaaaah*,' she breathed a few moments later in a long-drawn-out sigh as, with a last knowing flick of his tongue, Alex sent her toppling over the brink into sheer ecstasy.

Her eyes fluttered closed, but they shot open a moment later when Solange hissed, 'Captain Saville – he comes this way. Stay there, Alex! It's too late to come out now.'

Hastily, Lisa struggled to fasten her buttons, but her fingers wouldn't obey the dictates of her brain and she only just made it in time as he came up to their table.

She was uncomfortably aware of the empty chair next to her and prayed the captain wouldn't take it into his head to sit down. He would be bound to realise there was someone under the table as soon as he stretched out his legs.

'I'm sorry to interrupt your meal,' he greeted them nodding at their untouched desserts, 'I wondered if you'd all care to join me for brandy and coffee at my table.'

It was obvious to everyone that it was only Solange he really wanted to join him and Lisa felt almost sorry for him for being so besotted by her he was risking rejection a second time that evening.

'Thank you for your kind invitation,' began Solange and then Lisa saw her eyes widen and her mouth formed a round 'ooh' of surprise. She recovered herself so swiftly that Lisa doubted if the captain had noticed as she continued, 'But I'm afraid we're already promised to some other people. Perhaps we could have a drink together tomorrow.'

Lisa realised instantly what was going on. Alex was taking

unfair advantage of his hidden position to touch Solange intimately. It was very unfair of him and she was tempted to kick him, but didn't dare to for fear of making him cry out.

The captain cast an unfriendly glance in Roland's direction before saying, 'I'll look forward to it.' He bowed towards Solange, then Lisa, nodded curtly at Roland, turned on his heel and marched away.

As soon as he'd begun his descent of the steps Solange made a violent movement under the table and they all heard Alex's grunt of pain, then another as he banged his head on the table.

'*Bâtard*!' she hissed. 'Come out from under there immediately.' He emerged, rubbing his head.

'I'm sorry, Solange,' he said, sinking into his chair. 'I just couldn't resist it. I thought you'd enjoy it.'

'I should have let the brave captain discover you and have you keel-hauled,' she declared. 'I shall revenge myself on you for this.' Her dark eyes flashed threateningly as she reached for a chocolate truffle finger and bit it decisively in half with her small white teeth.

'I'll look forward to it,' he returned, unruffled, reaching for his wine glass.

After dinner they went for a walk on deck and paused to admire the lemon-coloured half-moon rising over the inky ocean and washing the surface in silvery light.

'I'd like to see you naked by moonlight,' Roland told Solange, one hand straying over her bare back. 'I'd like to see your breasts gleaming like marble as if you were a statue which had been carved for my pleasure.'

'I wouldn't be much fun to couple with if I were a cold, unyielding statue,' pointed out Solange. 'And marble would undoubtedly chafe your virile manhood.'

Roland winced. 'Sometimes, my sweet,' he remarked, 'your practicality borders on the unromantic and my sensitive soul is wasted on you.'

'Happily your virile manhood is not,' retorted Solange. 'Lisa, shall we take these two men back to our suite and make them pleasure us to the point of exhaustion?'

Lisa's mouth went dry and she had to swallow before replying, 'That sounds like an interesting idea.'

Chapter Twelve

'Celeste, ring for a bottle of champagne,' Solange directed. 'And then you may go.'

'*Oui, Madame*,' replied the maid, going to the telephone.

'Make yourselves comfortable,' Solange invited their guests. 'Lisa, *ma petite*, may I speak to you for a moment, please.'

Lisa led the way into her bedroom and perched on the bed while the Frenchwoman examined her reflection in the dressing table mirror, smoothed her hair and rearranged her black pearls.

'I have something special in mind for our guests,' she said, smiling enigmatically.

'What?' asked Lisa, intrigued. Solange turned around on the stool in front of the dressing table and leant towards her. In a low voice she outlined her intentions.

'We can't!' exclaimed Lisa, shocked.

'Certainly we can, *chérie*, but I need your cooperation if it is to be effective.' She took one of Lisa's hands and squeezed it conspiratorially. 'And think how much we will enjoy ourselves.'

Lisa thought about it for a few moments and her mouth went dry with renewed desire.

'Very well,' she said at last. Solange kissed her on the lips and rose sinuously to her feet.

'Then let us rejoin them.'

They found Roland deftly removing the cork from a bottle of champagne. He poured them each a glass and sank onto the sofa, stretching out his long legs in front of him. Alex sat on the arm of an armchair, his hands in his pockets.

'Solange darling, that's a stunning gown,' commented Roland, 'but all night I've been picturing you out of it, in just your pearls and underwear. Why don't you take it off for us?'

'Certainly it is a little warm in here,' purred Solange. She sashayed over to Alex. 'Just undo the hooks for me, would you, please.' He obeyed with alacrity. She moved to the centre of the room and crossed her arms so she had a hand at each shoulder. Slowly, an inch at a time, she slid the straps from her creamy shoulders and then let the white gown slip to the floor to fall around her feet in a pale shimmer of silk.

Under it she was wearing a pearl-white lace camisole and camiknickers over a matching suspender belt holding up white silk stockings. The finely-worked lace revealed more than it concealed of the lush fullness of her breasts and the sable triangle of her pubic fleece which formed a dark shadow at the top of her thighs.

She stood with a hand on her hip, one knee bent and thrust slightly forward in a naturally seductive posture. She reached behind her and rearranged the black pearls so they hung down her cleavage rather than her back. Her breasts were the most beautiful Lisa had ever seen. High and firm with coffee-coloured nipples, they seemed to beg to be touched.

'Do let me urge you to remove your dress too,' Solange said

to Lisa. 'You will be much cooler and more comfortable without it.'

Trying to look as though she did this sort of thing all the time, Lisa slowly undid the buttons down the front of her yellow georgette gown. As she'd already exposed herself to the waist that evening it wasn't as difficult as she expected and she was able to stand in front of the others in only her champagne satin camiknickers, suspender belt and stockings, without too much embarrassment.

'Aren't they a sight worth dying for?' commented Roland to Alex. 'Two of the most beautiful women I've ever seen, both half-naked.'

'Worth dying for is all very well,' observed Solange, idly stroking her own breasts over their delicate lace covering. 'But are we worth killing for?'

As she asked the provocative question she let one strap of the camisole fall down her arm to reveal her right breast in all its buttermilk perfection.

'I'll say,' breathed Roland, obviously mesmerised by the sight of the two of them in their different states of undress. His eyes caressed Solange and then wandered over Lisa, before returning to Solange. 'What do you think, Alex?'

'Undoubtedly,' agreed Alex, his voice thick with desire.

'Now you must disrobe too while we watch and then we'll all repair to the bedroom,' Solange suggested.

She perched on the arm of a chair while Lisa sank into its depths. Solange slid her arm around Lisa's shoulder and leant against her. Lisa could see their reflection in the fancifully bevelled mirror on the opposite wall.

She had to admit that they made a pleasing sight. Solange's

dark loveliness and voluptuous body made a striking contrast to her own red-gold hair and pale slenderness.

The close proximity of Solange and the light touch of her arm was arousing Lisa. So was watching Alex and Roland removing their clothes. They both had athletic physiques without having over-developed muscles, which she rather disliked.

The sight of Alex's flat stomach and lean flanks made her swallow and shift on her seat. His member was already hugely erect, slapping against his belly as he bent to discard his underwear.

Virile dark hair curled on his chest and long legs, making her yearn to run her hands over him and savour the uncompromising maleness of his broad-shouldered frame.

Roland too was tall and in excellent physical condition, but he was slimmer and his movements were more languid. His strong, thick penis was twitching with anticipation as he swiftly divested himself of his clothing.

Lisa was glad she didn't have to wear a dinner jacket and starched shirt in such a hot climate. Even in her flimsy georgette gown she'd felt she was wearing too many clothes for the temperature.

When both men were naked, Solange took Lisa's hand and led the way into the bedroom. She reclined gracefully on the bed while Lisa arranged herself next to her. Roland made a movement to join them, but Solange waved him into a chair.

'First, you will watch,' she told him. Obediently he sat on the dressing table stool, while Alex took an upright chair by the door.

Solange turned to Lisa and deftly removed the pins holding

her hair in a loose coil so that it tumbled around her white shoulders in gleaming tendrils.

Solange moved closer to her on the bed and laid one hand over her breast, delicately circling the nipple and then cupping the firm orb. Lisa heard Alex inhale sharply at the sight and she slipped one arm around her companion's hips. Tentatively, while Solange stroked her breasts, Lisa enjoyed caressing the luscious globes of the other woman's *derrière*.

They were fuller and more voluptuous than her own and it was an exciting feeling to be touching them so intimately. She continued to explore them while Solange kissed and licked her breasts, intoxicating Lisa with the scent of her alluring perfume and the sexual heat of her body.

Solange turned and lay on her back propped up against the pillows. Slowly, barely able to breathe, Lisa undid the tiny buttons holding the other woman's camisole closed and then drew it fully open to expose the delectable ripeness of Solange's breasts.

They felt wonderful, firm yet yielding like fruit at its best. She brushed them with her fingertips and felt a tremor of lust when the nipples became even harder and more prominent. She bent her head and kissed one, then took it between her lips and sucked, gently at first and then exerting more pressure as Solange began to move her bottom in sinuous circles on the satin-quilted bed covering.

Solange took her hand and laid it on her lace-covered belly. Lisa stroked it, wanting to let her fingers slip lower between Solange's legs, but not quite daring to do so.

Solange sat up and gently pushed Lisa back against the pillows and then slowly drew her silk camiknickers down her stomach. Lisa raised her bottom to enable the other woman to pull them to the tops of her thighs, exposing her damp russet fleece.

The tension in the room was so strong that Lisa could almost smell it.

She could see the two men gazing raptly at her private parts as Solange eased her thighs apart so her glistening sex-flesh was displayed to them. Roland let out a small appreciative sound and leant further forward, while Alex reached out and moved a lamp so the light fell directly on the bed, providing better illumination for the erotic tableau.

Lisa could feel the sultry air wafting in from the open window and being stirred by the overhead fan so it caressed her semi-naked body intimately. She felt Solange's fingers winding themselves in the silken fronds of her pubic floss and parted her thighs further, aching to feel her friend's touch on her sex-flesh.

But first Solange stroked the smooth skin above Lisa's stocking tops, making her shiver with delight. Then at last she lightly traced the rim of her outer labia with the tip of her finger, so that Lisa moaned and made a small demanding upward movement with her pelvis.

Softly, delicately, Solange ran her fingertip in and out of the intricate grooves of Lisa's vulva, circling the quivering tip of her clitoris and then gliding smoothly into her sex-sheath. Lisa's internal muscles clutched at it convulsively, unbearably stimulated by the pressure as Solange explored her, pressing arousingly against her inner walls.

Solange slipped another slender finger inside her and began to move them rhythmically in and out until Lisa was gasping with pleasure. Alex rose from his seat and advanced on them, his member hugely erect, a single drop of pearly liquid poised on the glans.

'Not yet!' Solange's voice held a note of authority and reluctantly he resumed his seat. Her fingers wet with Lisa's honeyed juices, Solange began to rub the younger woman's aching bud, her sureness of touch indicating her expertise at giving pleasure.

Lisa began to writhe on the bed as a smouldering heat grew deep in her belly, a heat which threatened to consume her totally. She could feel the intensity of Alex and Roland's attention and see their eyes fixed on the two of them as Solange worked her towards a breathless climax.

The heat grew unbearable and she felt perspiration trickling down her cleavage and inner thighs. Suddenly she exploded into a climax which washed over her in wave after wave of sheer carnal pleasure, leaving her weak and trembling. Solange stroked her hair and kissed her, murmuring endearments until Lisa opened her eyes and smiled tremulously.

Solange slid gracefully from the bed and picked up several silk scarves from where they'd been draped over the corner of the dressing table mirror. She went over to Alex and drew one over his chest, before allowing it to flutter into his lap to form an incongruous veil for his rampant member.

'Put your arms behind you, please,' she directed him. Instead he tried to pull her onto his lap but she eluded him.

'Your role is to obey, or you will be punished,' she told him severely.

Lisa almost protested. She wanted Alex to join her on the

bed, cover her body with his own and thrust inside her, filling her completely with his iron-hard manhood. But Solange was in control so she remained silent while the other woman tied Alex's wrists to the back of the chair.

Next she secured his ankles so he was effectively immobilised. Lisa was surprised that he allowed it, but he'd obviously played such games before because he submitted, albeit reluctantly.

Solange took Roland's hand and led him to the bed. He lay between them on his back while she knelt to one side of him. At a gesture from the Frenchwoman, Lisa helped her out of her lacy camiknickers, leaving her clad in just her suspender belt, white silk stockings and unbuttoned camisole.

In a lithe movement, Solange straddled Roland with her back to him and Lisa saw immediately that the blunt, crimson triangle of Solange's clitoris was already protruding beyond her inner labia. It was slick with dewy fluid, as were the surrounding tissues of her vulva.

Alex's eyes were riveted to it and when Solange slipped her hand between her own legs and touched it, he tried to rise from his seat and then yanked at his bonds with frustration when they held him fast to his chair.

Taking Roland's engorged member in her hand, Solange knelt over it and then slowly lowered herself until the swollen tip vanished an inch at a time into her moist depths. Her eyes widened as if she couldn't quite believe how much pleasure it was giving her and then she began to move up and down, giving a corkscrew twist on each downward movement.

Lisa climbed astride Roland, facing Solange and the two women began to embrace, exchanging kisses and caressing each other's breasts. Roland had his hands on Solange's hips, helping guide her movements as she rode him like a hobby horse.

Lisa discovered that if she clasped one of Roland's thighs between her own and rubbed herself on it, the delicious friction sent darts of tingling, salacious sensation coursing through her body.

A grunt from the other side of the room made her look round to see Alex, sweat beading his forehead, straining to free himself. His struggles had dislodged the scarf which had fluttered onto his manhood and his member was so swollen and purple that it looked about to erupt.

He was obviously dissatisfied at the way the evening was going, but strangely he didn't ask them to release him, just continued to pull at the silken bonds which held him so firmly in position.

Intuitively, Lisa sensed that pride prevented him from begging them to free him so he could join in. His jaw was set and his face contorted into grim determination as he strained.

An ominous cracking noise indicated that the chair might be coming off worst, but still the scarves held firm.

Solange glanced at him and then at Lisa, her lips curving beguilingly upwards, a wickedly triumphant expression on her face.

So this was to be Alex's punishment for his earlier transgression. Lisa couldn't help but feel for him, able to witness such a licentious scenario, but not be part of it.

She was tempted to slide off the bed and release him herself, but didn't want to spoil Solange's enjoyment of his frustration.

Solange, meanwhile, was riding Roland with increasing vigour and her moans of delight were becoming louder. Lisa knew that she herself was getting close to a climax and rubbed her vulva harder and harder on Roland's thigh until it was slippery with her nectar.

Solange suddenly arched her back and went rigid, her head falling back on her shoulders, her pliant body even more luscious as she convulsed into a climax. Roland's satisfaction was swift to follow, his deep groans of release sounding as though they'd been dragged from him by force.

It took Lisa a little longer, but then she too was overcome by a wave of pleasure which enveloped her completely, followed by several of receding strength.

Solange raised herself and allowed Roland's penis, fast losing its rigidity, to slip from her. She lay down beside him and beckoned to Lisa to do the same. Lisa hardly dared look at Alex, so deep was her sympathy for him.

She cast an appealing glance at Solange and her companion murmured, 'If you wish, but keep him tied to the chair.'

Leaving the bed, her vulva still tingling from her recent climax, Lisa crossed the room. She sensed that Solange would prefer it if she tormented Alex further, but not only did Lisa not wish to prolong his suffering, she ached to have his shaft deep inside her.

His eyes were glazed and wary as she stood between his thighs and then took his organ in her hand. It twitched and felt red-hot as she positioned it at the glistening entrance to her sex-core. Holding onto his shoulders for support, she climbed astride him in one lithe movement and cried out as she took his manhood all the way inside her.

Immediately he began to thrust his hips upwards, rocking her in a powerful and arousing rhythm. Clutching at his shoulders she bore down with answering urgency and the chair bounced around the floor as they both strove for their identical goals.

It was a hot and desperate coupling. Alex was too far gone to last long, his face was a harsh mask as with one final anguished thrust he erupted into a boiling climax which overflowed Lisa's drenched inner-chamber and ran out of her.

As Lisa clung weakly on, she became aware that Solange must have released Alex because he was suddenly free. His arms closed around her and he rocked her up and down, still impaled on his member, until she too came.

As she leant against him he lifted her from him, carried her over to the bed and deposited her there. He sank down beside her rubbing his wrists, where Lisa was horrified to see angry red marks.

She half expected him to seize Solange and do her some bodily harm, but instead he said to her in a wry tone, 'The least you could do is pour me a drink. I thought I was going to come just watching you.'

Solange took one of his wrists and kissed the red marks solicitously.

'You should not have struggled so. You should have accepted your fate philosophically and enjoyed the spectacle we presented you with. Many men would pay much money to witness such a thing.'

He shot her a sardonic glance. 'I'm not really one of life's spectators, Solange. Now get me a drink or put your beautiful mouth to better use.'

He indicated his detumescent member, but Solange appeared to decline his second suggestion and poured some champagne into his glass. He was just raising it to his lips when she tipped a foaming surge of the icy wine over his groin.

He swore and spilt the champagne in his own glass down himself. Immediately Solange began to lap it up like a cat, her pink tongue visible as she worked her way down his chest and then his belly. Alex groaned as the tip of her tongue made contact with his member, winding itself around his glans until he was hard again.

His hands closed on her full breasts and he fondled them while Lisa and Roland watched. Then Roland shifted position to kneel behind Solange and part her thighs so he could plunge his tongue into the crimson depths of her vulva.

She wriggled ecstatically, pushing her bottom against his face while Lisa decided she needed to use the bathroom and left the three of them to their wanton play.

When she returned, Roland had penetrated Solange from behind, effectively distracting her from her stimulation of Alex's member.

Alex's eyes gleamed when Lisa reappeared. He picked up his clothes, took her by the hand and led her out of her own bedroom and into Solange's, where they could be alone.

Lisa awoke before dawn to find him gone, leaving behind rumpled sheets and a memory of more dark, heady pleasure during the long humid night. She felt hot and sticky, her body bathed in a combination of perspiration and their juices.

She tried to go back to sleep, but she was wide awake and

uncomfortably warm. She switched on the lamp, went into the bathroom and turned on the shower. She stood for a while under a stinging spray of tepid water and when she emerged she felt much cooler.

Solange's bedroom was a mirror image of her own and she sat at the dressing table to tidy her hair. Her eyes fell on a bottle of jasmine and orange flower perfume and she thought how refreshing it would be to use some. Knowing the other woman wouldn't mind, Lisa splashed some on her throat and wrists.

Winding the sheet around her she stepped out onto the verandah and stared up at the sky, still soot-dark except in the east where it was lightening to cobalt-blue. She went back inside, tidied the bed in a cursory fashion and crawled in, suddenly sleepy.

She was just dozing off when something jerked her back to consciousness. She sat up, holding the sheet to her breasts, and could just make out a shadowy figure standing inside the open door leading to the verandah, the curtain billowing around him like a stage backdrop. He appeared to be in the act of shedding his clothes.

'Alex?' she murmured, then the dark figure crossed the room and she felt the bed dip under his weight.

'No, it's damn well not Alex – it's Mark,' growled a deep voice.

Mark? Mark Channing? What on earth was he doing slipping into Solange's bedroom at this time as if he had every right to be there?

She opened her mouth to protest, but he put his hand over it and muttered, 'Not a word. You've been avoiding me,

Solange, and I'm not prepared to wait a moment longer for you to stop playing games.'

She could smell the brandy on his breath which indicated, together with an almost imperceptible slurring of his words, that he was very drunk. She reached out a hand to switch on the bedside lamp, but he seized her wrist, turned her hand palm-upwards and pressed a burning kiss onto it.

'Last time was so good,' he told her. 'But this time will be even better.'

To Lisa's confusion, he pulled her down on the bed and she felt him covering her bare shoulder with hungry kisses. He took his hand away from her mouth and she opened it to tell him in no uncertain terms that he was making a mistake.

But his own mouth came down on it in a hard, demanding kiss and effectively prevented her from speaking. She struggled to push him away, but he nipped her lower lip between his teeth, murmuring, 'No more games.'

A hand glided over her hip and caressed the soft skin of her belly, then toyed with the silken fronds of her fleece. Suddenly, despite her annoyance at his intrusion and the awkward situation it had created, Lisa felt a surge of arousal flooding her body, making her stop struggling and lie quiescently beneath him, bewildered and nonplussed by this unexpected turn of events.

His hand dipped between her thighs and she felt a warm rush of sticky moisture as, with electrifying results, he touched her sex-flesh. The blood seemed to be roaring through her veins and her clitoris quivered with expectation. Just at that moment it ceased to matter that this was a case of mistaken identity. The only thing on her mind was having him assuage this urgent need he'd awakened in her.

He played with the soft folds of her labia, easing them gently apart until he found her engorged, aching kernel. She parted her legs for him and felt him take the plump sliver of flesh between his fingers and thumb and rub it until she moaned out loud.

She reached out and stroked the throbbing column of his manhood which was digging into her hip. She heard him grunt with satisfaction, then his hand closed on her breast. There was a long-drawn-out pause and then he went rigid and snatched his hand away.

The stimulation of her clit ceased abruptly and he groped for the lamp, switching it on and flooding the bed with pale lemon light.

'What the hell!' he exclaimed looking down into her desire-glazed eyes, and at her red hair spread out around her shoulders on the pillow. 'Where's Solange?'

But Lisa wasn't interested in discussing the situation and she continued to fondle his member with amorous intent.

'I'm sorry!' he gasped. 'I thought . . . I'll leave right away.' He tried to disengage himself but she kept her hand firmly around his shaft, squeezing it gently and rubbing her thumb over the glans.

He looked confused and disoriented, as well he might.

'You aren't going anywhere,' she told him huskily. 'Not until you've finished what you started.' She took his hand and guided it back between her thighs.

Chapter Thirteen

When Lisa awoke in the late morning it was to find Mark Channing still stretched out by her side deeply asleep, one hand clasping her breast.

It was very warm in the room, even with the fan creaking as it stirred the sultry air. She watched it turning while she mentally reviewed the bizarre and potentially awkward situation in which she found herself.

How long had Solange been sleeping with Mark? She'd seemed anything but glad to see him when he'd first approached her. But the indications were that she'd been enjoying some sort of liaison with him if he'd felt free to enter her room late at night and join her in bed.

She remembered her dream about finding him in the sitting room when she'd been ill. Perhaps it hadn't been a dream, maybe it really had been him.

It was mildly embarrassing to remember that he'd been about to leave as soon as he'd discovered that it wasn't Solange in the bed and that she'd virtually forced him to stay and make love to her. Not that he'd needed much persuasion, but then he was a man and he had been both drunk and aroused.

Lisa gave a little moan of shame as she recalled her own brazen behaviour. And that was after Alex had pleasured her time and time again. She was becoming insatiable. Was that because of the relentless heat through which the ship was sailing now it had reached the tropics, or was it because she'd been ill and felt she had a lot to catch up with?

And what on earth was Solange going to say about it? Lisa was intrigued to know.

Mark shifted in the bed and then his eyes flickered open. He stared at her for a few moments, closed his eyes, then opened them again. He sat up in bed and groaned, but whether from the shock of finding himself in bed with the wrong woman, or because he had a hangover, it was impossible to tell.

'Good morning,' she greeted him with what composure she could muster.

'Good morning,' he muttered. There was a silence and then he continued, 'I really can't apologise enough for my intrusion last night.'

His own embarrassment made Lisa feel better.

'That's perfectly alright,' she reassured him. He looked around the room and saw his clothes littering the floor by the door leading to the verandah. He'd obviously hoped to find something near enough to wrap around him before he left the bed, but there was nothing to hand.

He got out and walked naked across the carpet while Lisa admired the taut muscles of his back, buttocks and thighs. He really was a splendid male animal, she thought idly, as he bent to pick up his crumpled shirt. He'd been a splendid lover too, leaving her aching, exhausted but very, very satisfied.

He was just fastening his shirt when the door leading to the verandah was pushed open and Solange stood there wearing Lisa's shell-pink robe, her eyes hidden by a pair of round, tortoise-shell dark glasses.

'What is the meaning of this?' she demanded, her voice quivering with outrage and indignation. She removed her dark glasses and stood with her hands on her hips, glaring threateningly at Mark, who obviously felt at a disadvantage as he was naked from the waist down.

'I . . . I came to see you last night.' he explained.

'Indeed?' Solange's voice was dangerously quiet. 'Then as you obviously didn't find me, why are you still here?'

There was a silence and Lisa realised that Mark was obviously too much of a gentleman to tell Solange the truth that her companion had insisted upon.

'So,' said Solange advancing upon him, her eyes glinting. 'You didn't find me, but you found an innocent young girl and decided that she would do to vent your bestial lusts on.'

Mark looked completely nonplussed at the unexpected turn events had taken. 'I wasn't to know that you'd swapped rooms,' he protested.

'You would have known if you'd waited for an invitation rather than barging in so rudely,' she pointed out. 'Did he hurt you, *chérie*?' she asked Lisa solicitously. 'Shall I send for the captain and ask what he plans to do about this debauched creature who roams the ship at night looking for unsuspecting girls to prey on?'

Mark began to pull on the rest of his clothes, apparently unwilling to be at a psychological disadvantage any longer. Solange looked magnificent. Her dark eyes were flashing and her robe had fallen open just enough to give a hint of her impressive cleavage.

She shot a brief, collusive glance at Lisa, which unfortunately Mark intercepted because his expression became grim as he fastened his trousers and thrust his feet into his shoes.

He caught Solange by the wrist and looked broodingly at her beautiful face before saying from between clenched teeth, 'You have no more heart than that statue.'

He nodded tersely in the direction of a sculpted figure of a naked girl on the bureau, her body arched so her small, perfect breasts were thrust out in a provocative manner. 'But then you never did have,' he continued. 'Even your husband's death hasn't stopped you from putting your own selfish pleasure above everything.'

He kissed her hard on the mouth and left the room saying over his shoulder, 'It isn't me playing fast and loose with most of the passengers on this ship. Have you worked your way through *all* the men yet, Solange, or haven't there been enough hours in the days and nights?'

As soon as he'd gone Solange sank onto the stool in front of her dressing table and Lisa could see she was trembling.

'That poor man, you really made him squirm,' said Lisa at last.

'It's no more than he deserves,' replied Solange, picking up her powder puff and dusting her nose with translucent powder, her hand shaking slightly. 'You may already have noticed, *ma petite*, that men are very possessive and always believe that they have exclusive rights. Why they should think this I do not know. So, did you enjoy yourself with the dashing Mr

Channing?' She tried to ask the question lightly, but Lisa could tell his words had upset her.

'Very much,' replied Lisa. 'I really behaved very badly. As soon as he realised it wasn't you he was ready to leave, but I insisted he stay.'

'Your prerogative when he'd behaved with such a lack of *savoir faire*.'

'I . . . I didn't realise that you and he were so friendly,' ventured Lisa. There was no reply as Solange drew a brush through her glossy, dark hair, seemingly preoccupied by smoothing it into a burnished bell. 'In fact I'd got the impression that you didn't like him,' she added, thinking that if Solange didn't say something soon, she'd have no alternative but to drop the subject.

In the mirror she could see the other woman's face and her expression was sombre.

'I don't,' said Solange after a long pause. 'And he doesn't like me, but sometimes liking doesn't come into it. I'm sorry you were unable to have your own room last night, *chérie*, but it is now restored to order and has clean linens.'

Taking the hint, Lisa left the bed and looked around for something to wear. Solange let the shell-pink robe slip from her shoulders and handed it to Lisa.

'As you can see, I availed myself of your robe. Tonight we are invited to a party by the Maharajah who leaves the ship tomorrow at Bombay.'

Lisa slipped into the robe and left the room, saying over her shoulder, 'I'll look forward to it.'

As she dressed for dinner that night Lisa pondered the strange situation. Why was Solange having an affair with a man she didn't like? And why was he having an affair with her if the feeling was mutual? His mention of her husband's death had obviously upset her, as well it might.

She changed into a backless gown of almond-green shot silk. It fell from a gathered waist to diamond points around her ankles and had a matching tunic jacket. She was just clipping emerald earrings into place when there was a tap at the door.

'Come in,' she called. Celeste stood on the threshold.

'*Monsieur* asks if he may enter,' she said, indicating Alex who was standing just inside the door of the suite's sitting room.

'Yes, come in, Alex,' she greeted him. He handed her a corsage from the ship's flower shop where they were kept in a huge refrigerator. At every port of call they took on board freshly cut flowers packed in ice to extend their life as long as possible.

Shutting the door behind him, he took her in his arms and kissed her so passionately that she was instantly on fire.

He backed her against the door and scooped her breasts from her low-cut gown, caressing them avidly while he continued to kiss her. He pressed his pelvis into her so she could feel the bone-hardness of his erection against her hip.

As she felt a hungry tongue of flame licking at her core, Lisa forgot that she'd just spent over an hour on her make-up and hair, that Celeste had only just pressed her gown and that they were due at a party.

None of that seemed to matter as her hand found Alex's member and caressed it through the stuff of his trousers, feeling it straining at the constricting material. She heard him exhale sharply as she pulled his zip down and slipped her hand into the aperture.

The hungry tongue of flame roared into an inferno, threatening to consume her with lust as his hands roamed over her body, kneading her buttocks and stroking her mound.

He moved away from her and dragged her skirt up around her waist, at the same time wrenching her jade silk camiknickers around her thighs so roughly that the pearl button that fastened them over the hip shot off and they fell unheeded to the floor.

Lisa parted her thighs and felt him pushing his hand between her legs to massage her vulva, palm-upwards making his skin instantly sticky with her warm juices. She bore down against him, squeezing his shaft as he slipped two fingers inside her and moved them up and down until she felt as though she was running like a tap that had been left on.

They were both breathing hard and she could hear a sound like surf crashing on a beach thundering in her ears. She was only dimly aware that it was the hectic beating of her heart and the blood roaring hotly through her veins.

She guided his shaft to the bubbling entrance of her sex and gasped as he drove straight into her, almost lifting her off her feet and jamming her back against the door.

She came immediately, moaning as the waves broke around her into a million fragments of pleasure which then became a composite whole as he drove relentlessly in and out of her, making the door bang with each urgent thrust.

She worked her hips to meet him, squeezing his rod with her internal muscles, goading him on to move faster and faster.

She came again, crying out as another dizzying climax swept over her.

She felt Alex's hand's close on the pert mounds of her *derrière* and then he held her tightly against him as he came in a great surge of release.

They both slipped to the floor and lay panting against the door, perspiration bedewing their bodies. Lisa was the first to move, detaching herself and getting awkwardly to her feet, her gown crumpled around her legs.

She moaned when she caught sight of her reflection in the mirror and saw that her dress was wrinkled and creased and that it now had a large, rapidly spreading damp stain down the front. Her red hair too was in disarray and Alex had kissed her lipstick off.

'I'm going to have to take a shower,' she told him weakly, 'Would you tell Solange to go on without me – I'll meet her there.'

In the bathroom she stripped off and stood for a couple of minutes under the cool water, then wrapped a large, fluffy towel around her waist and returned to the bedroom. Alex was engaged in mixing gin fizzes and passed her one after agitating the silver cocktail shaker vigorously.

He took his glass into the bathroom with him and she heard the sound of the shower going as she selected fresh underwear from the bureau. She was just struggling to fasten a gown of vieux-rose slipper satin with two narrow shoulder straps which crossed over her shoulder blades, when he emerged.

'Allow me,' he murmured, kissing her neck and then deftly doing up the tiny hooks and eyes. The dress had a silk rose of deeper pink at the bosom, the petals of which half-hid the indecent amount of cleavage the dress would have otherwise revealed. She slipped her feet into a pair of cream brocade shoes and picked up a small matching bag.

She repaired the damage to her hair and make-up and then stepped out onto the verandah, hoping to catch a cooling sea breeze.

But the air was still warm and humid although the tropical night had already descended with its usual speed. She sipped the gin fizz absently, enjoying the cool effervescence of the lemonade and the tart, scented bite of gin against the back of her tongue.

'Have you seen much of the Maharajah on the voyage?' she asked Alex when he came to join her.

'A few times. He seems to keep pretty much to his suite but I saw him in the pool room yesterday. His guards had ordered everyone out of the water so his highness could enjoy it alone and I think a couple of passengers later complained to the captain.'

'Didn't they complain at the time?' Lisa wanted to know.

'Absolutely not. Those guards are armed to the teeth and look more than prepared to use their various weapons. I was just leaving when they arrived so I hung around to watch the fun for a couple of minutes.' He caressed Lisa's waist as he spoke, his hand moving seductively over the polished sheen of the satin.

'Solange said that the party's in the Oriental room. I don't remember seeing that. Do you know where it is?' she asked.

'On "A" deck. Apparently the Maharajah took it over as soon as he boarded the liner. His suite and all the staterooms on his corridor weren't adequate accommodation. I've been told that his palace makes Buckingham Palace look like an artisan's cottage.'

'Solange said that he'd invited her to leave the ship at Bombay and be his guest for an indefinite length of time,' said Lisa with a giggle. 'I suspect he still thinks he can persuade her to become his mistress.'

'I'm surprised she's not tempted,' observed Alex, turning to lean against the verandah's rail. 'His wealth is supposed to be beyond the dreams of avarice, but I suppose he'd take a dim view of her bestowing her favours on whichever of his retinue took her fancy. There's a rumour going around the ship that he's determined to have her before he disembarks.'

Lisa suddenly shivered at the thought and hoped fervently that Solange would remain firm in her determination to refuse the Maharajah's blandishments. He might have her killed if she became his mistress and then was unfaithful to him.

'Shall we go?' she asked. 'I'm dying to see the Oriental room.'

It turned out to be well worth seeing. Richly decorated in crimson and gold, it had a double row of embossed ebony pillars supporting the ceiling. Brass chandeliers glowed with hundreds of tiny lights and the honey-coloured parquet flooring was strewn with thick Chinese rugs in crimson, gold and royal-blue.

At one end of the room a fountain played in an oblong marble pool a couple of feet deep, the tinkling noise it made just audible over the hubbub of conversation. Rattan furniture and leather pouffes were grouped at intervals and exotically carved statues stood on plinths in arched niches along the walls. The Maharajah's guards were standing to attention around the room, their backs ramrod straight, their eyes watching for any hint of danger threatening their monarch.

'Goodness,' murmured Lisa to Alex, 'it's like something out of a film.'

She immediately spotted Solange, her arm linked in that of Captain Saville and thought her friend very wise to have claimed his protection. If the Maharajah was indeed desperate to have the Frenchwoman before he disembarked tomorrow, he might be difficult to fob off.

Beautiful dark-skinned Indian girls in saris were circulating, carrying trays of Indian nibbles. Lisa accepted a plate and took several different types to try.

'Uum, this is delicious,' she exclaimed, after eating half a small battered ball which was filled with pieces of fried onion. She'd still not tried any of the curries on offer in the dining salon and decided that tonight she would do so at last. She enjoyed everything she ate, marvelling at the array of spicy aperitifs.

The other first-class passengers who'd been invited were milling around and Stephen Templeton came to talk to her while Alex was claimed by Phyllis Templeton who drew him to one side and began to whisper in his ear.

'What do you think of the food?' Stephen asked her, refilling his plate from a tray held out by a particularly lovely Indian girl and giving her slender, pliant form an approving glance.

'Marvellous,' said Lisa enthusiastically. 'I hope the food in Malaya is as good.'

'It's a bit of a mish-mash from different cultures,' he explained, 'but you get addicted to it. I didn't manage to eat a decent curry all the time we were back in England. I thought I'd want to eat roast beef and Yorkshire pud every day, but before we'd been there a week I was dragging Phyllis around London looking for a passable Indian restaurant, which is about as near to Malayan food as you can get back in Blighty.'

'How do they differ?' she wanted to know.

'Malayan cooking is strongly Indian influenced, but it also has aspects of Chinese and other Eastern countries. I hope you like coconut milk because they put it in practically everything.'

'I've never had it,' replied Lisa, suppressing a smile at the thought of something so exotic being served at her boarding school.

'Rice cooked in coconut milk has to be tasted to be believed,' he said affably. 'So does satay. We must have dinner together when we've arrived in Penang and I'll take you through the menu.'

'We'd love to,' she said, glancing at where Alex and Phyllis were deep in conversation. She wished the other woman wasn't clinging to his arm quite so tightly. Didn't her husband mind? It seemed not because he didn't look in their direction once.

Lisa noticed that the Maharajah had managed to get Solange on her own and that he was talking to her persuasively. Lisa saw Solange laugh and tap him on the arm with her fan, but when she tried to move away he looked angry and spoke to her sharply.

Solange's bearing immediately took on an imperious air. She stared at him haughtily, then turned on her heel and walked away.

'Shall we go to dinner, *ma petite*?' she asked Lisa, joining her. 'I'm hungry and I do not care for this spicy food.'

'Certainly – I'll just get Alex.'

They found Roland at their table in the dining salon. He was exchanging flirtatious glances with the woman at the table below and Lisa wondered if their relationship had advanced beyond that yet.

Lisa ordered pappadams with lime pickle and then a mild chicken curry served with a spicy vegetable side dish and rice. For her last course she chose vanilla ice cream with mango sauce which she declared to be sublime.

Alex too ordered Indian food and Lisa felt sorry for Roland who would obviously have liked to do the same but didn't because it would have meant banishment from Solange's bed.

Solange complained several times about the smell.

'It will be too horrible in Malaya,' she told them. 'Everyone will stink of this vile spicy food and I shall have to walk around with my nose buried in a scented handkerchief.'

'The smell of curry will be the least of your worries,' Roland informed her cheerfully. 'It will seem like the scent of attar of roses compared to the stench of the open sewers.'

Solange shuddered dramatically.

'Then let us hope I can complete my business very swiftly and then return to Paris where I may live like a civilised person,' she announced.

At the end of the meal Lisa reached for her bag, intending to go and powder her nose, only to find she no longer had it with her. She wrinkled her smooth brow and tried to remember when she'd last seen it. It must have been when she'd laid it down on the plinth of one of the statues standing in the arched niches in the Oriental room. She'd wanted to free her hands so she could eat the spicy nibbles.

She excused herself and hurried back there, hoping the party was still in full swing and she could retrieve her bag unobtrusively. But the room, when she reached it, was deserted. Nervously she pushed the door open, uncomfortably aware that she was trespassing on the Maharajah's territory and hoping she wouldn't be discovered by any of the fearsome guards.

Luckily her bag was still there, but as she picked it up she heard the sound of the door at the other end of the room opening and ducked behind the plinth.

She was glad she had when one of the guards strode into the room, his turquoise silk trousers billowing around his thighs and calves before being caught around the ankles by bands of the same fabric. He was only young and very attractive in a ferocious kind of way with liquid dark eyes, a carefully trimmed moustache and high cheekbones.

He lounged on one of the leather pouffes near the fountain, toying with the handle of his knife in a way that made Lisa pray that he wouldn't discover her. She wished fervently he would go away so she could slip out of the room, but she prayed in vain.

After about ten minutes the door opened again and one of the beautiful dark-skinned girls glided gracefully into the room, her eyes lowered.

She was wearing a sari of bright amethyst with a gold border and her feet were bare. The guard leapt to his feet when he saw her and held out his arms. Moments later they were embracing with a passion that made Lisa look away, before curiosity got the better of her and she began to watch them again.

The guard obviously understood the secrets of the sari because his hands kept vanishing into the diaphanous folds and his caresses were making the girl moan ecstatically. He made her kneel on one of the high leather pouffes and then drew her sari up around her waist, revealing her perfect, heart-shaped bottom.

The guard caressed it fondly, slipping his fingers into the cleft between her buttocks and then lower to toy with the damp fronds of her fleece. From her hidden vantage point Lisa forgot her fear of discovery as the lewd scenario unfolded before her.

It reminded her of the time she'd inadvertently come across Solange and Roland making love in the gentleman's club in London and like that time she found it exciting in the extreme.

The guard explored the girl's private parts with his hand and then bent to lick and nibble her buttocks, making her wriggle and push her bottom back against his face.

When he'd explored her thoroughly he parted her thighs and pushed her forward on her hands and knees. Lisa could see the girl's sex, the crimson folds swollen and dripping, her sable fleece curling in damp tendrils around it.

Her clitoris was a prominent triangle like the sail of a yacht and when the man flicked it gently with his finger she cried out and opened her thighs even wider.

He unbuckled his belt, dropped it to the floor and then pulled open the front of his baggy trousers to reveal a long, slim penis. He stood behind his lover, grasping her by the hips to pull her a little further back and then positioned his member at the whorled entrance to her sex.

He slid it in an inch at a time and Lisa felt her own core contracting in aroused empathy for the other girl who obviously wanted more than he was giving her. When he'd buried his shaft in her all the way to the hilt he began to move it in and out at a maddeningly slow rate.

He leant forward and freed her breasts so they hung down like apples from a tree. He squeezed and caressed them as he eventually increased the pace of his movements, pistoning in and out at a steady rate.

The girl rolled her hips sinuously, obviously trying to goad him into pumping faster, but he wasn't to be hurried.

Lisa felt her own sex-flesh practically sizzling with desire as she watched the couple, wishing Alex was with her and taking her in the same way.

She ground her mound against the plinth and continued with her covert scrutiny. After what seemed like a long period of time the guard suddenly increased his rate of movement and began to thrust more rapidly. His last dozen strokes would have sent the girl skidding off the other side of the pouffe if he hadn't held her by the waist.

His cry as he came was long and loud – more like a wail in fact – reminding Lisa of the cries of animals in the Scottish forest at night.

When it was over he pulled out of his companion and then they both bathed in the pool before dressing and coming together in one last kiss. She slipped from the room and after a couple of minutes he followed her, leaving Lisa alone and on fire with frustrated desire.

Chapter Fourteen

Lisa stood on deck leaning against the brass rail feeling elated and nervous at the same time as the liner approached Penang. The lengthy voyage had at last come to an end and her destiny lay before her.

From her reading about Malaya, Lisa now knew that Penang was in fact an island fifteen miles long, and that the Malayan mainland lay on the other side of a flat stretch of water usually crossed by ferry.

The ocean which had been a clear turquoise became increasingly opaque as they drew near to the harbour, until it was the colour of dark jade. The docks were lined by solid, substantial looking buildings, one of which had a square tower topped by a dome.

They were all dazzlingly white in the brilliant sunshine, a stark contrast to the grey stone walls of Fort Wallis with its cannons pointing out to sea, reminding Lisa that this was part of the British Empire, however foreign it might appear.

Chinese shacks on stilts straddled the water and as the liner sailed into the harbour a flotilla of small boats came to meet it, full of hawkers selling food, souvenirs and flowers.

Lisa became aware of a strange, unfamiliar smell. It was a

damp, smoky, spicy smell overlaid by the faint fragrance of blossoms. She sniffed doubtfully, not sure whether she liked it or not.

Solange joined her, holding a white parasol to protect her creamy skin from the strong sunshine. Her companion looked as serenely untroubled as always, despite the fact that she was about to leave the haven of the ship to embark on what seemed to Lisa to be a hazardous undertaking.

She herself would have the protection of her guardian whom she'd be meeting at long last, but Solange would be a woman alone in an unfamiliar country.

The noise and bustle of the docks seemed overpowering after the relative peace and tranquillity of the ship. Their trunks and valises had been packed and were stacked in the corridor outside their suite ready to be taken ashore and to the hotel where they would be spending the first few days in Penang.

Alex and Roland joined them. Roland was staying on board and would disembark in Singapore to take up his new position, so their parting was imminent. Lisa wondered how much Solange minded, but with the Frenchwoman, it was always difficult to tell.

It seemed like an eternity before they were able to leave the ship and Lisa found herself increasingly nervous about meeting her guardian after all these years. Would he be on the quay to greet her? She wasn't sure and neither was Solange. All the other woman could tell her was that rooms had been booked for them at the Eastern and Oriental Hotel.

When the time came for them to disembark, Lisa hugged Roland fiercely.

'Try to get down to Singapore,' he invited her. 'We'll have a whale of a time.'

'I'll try,' she promised him. 'I'll ask my guardian.'

Solange kissed him and promised to keep in touch, then they were escorted to the gangplank by Captain Saville who seemed reluctant to let Solange leave and kept her talking, holding up the other passengers who were forced to form a long line behind them.

At last they descended to the quay, followed by a nervous Celeste, who looked frightened out of her wits at the sight of so many people of such diverse nationalities gathered on the dockside.

Alex was immediately approached by his agent, an overweight man in white ducks and a solar topi. Alex and his family owned several tin mines in the country, but the profits had been eroded by what he suspected was embezzlement on a grand scale. The agent had been unable to solve the problem and had appealed to Alex to come out himself.

After a minute's conversation with the man, Alex returned to them. He drew Lisa to one side, kissed her hand formally and said, 'It looks like it's time to say goodbye – at least for now.'

But there was nothing formal about his burning gaze which reminded her all too explicitly how they'd spent last night. She'd been so aroused after seeing the couple having sex in the Oriental room that she'd returned to the dining salon, dragged him away from the table and back to her room where they'd spent the night making love over and over again.

'I'll contact you at the hotel within the next couple of days. I'm so hot for you I don't know how I'll manage to keep away, but as you know, I have business to attend to which will take up a lot of my time,' he told her ruefully. 'I'll just wait to see you safely with your guardian.'

But no-one came forward to meet them and after a few minutes they were hailed by Stephen and Phyllis Templeton.

'Can we drop you anywhere, ladies?' Stephen asked them, indicating a chauffeur-driven car which was pulled up a few yards away.

'That would be most kind,' said Solange. 'Could you take us to the Eastern and Oriental Hotel?'

'The E & O? No problem at all – that's where we're staying. It's only a few minutes away, but we'll take a bit of a detour just to give you a quick look at Georgetown.'

Solange turned to Lisa. 'It may be that your guardian is waiting for us at the hotel. If he isn't there, he will surely have left a message.'

Lisa nodded and didn't know whether to be glad or sorry that meeting him was to be delayed. She said goodbye to Alex and he kissed her briefly but hungrily before vanishing into the crowd with the agent.

Lisa looked around her wide-eyed as the car drove slowly through the congested streets of Georgetown. It was more *foreign* than she'd been able to imagine and she listened eagerly as Stephen pointed out Malays, Chinese and Indians among the thronging crowds. She was enchanted by the rickshaws and vowed to take a ride in one as soon as possible.

'Look!' she exclaimed to Solange, 'What an astonishing building!' She indicated a fancifully decorated structure with upswept eaves and two carved gold dragons on the roof.

'That's the Chinese temple,' explained Phyllis. 'And that

one over there – that's a mosque. Penang is a real melting pot of cultures.' Most of the houses which jostled for space had red tiled roofs and many were painted in pastel shades as well as white and cream.

The splendour of the palm-shaded Eastern and Oriental Hotel must have reassured Solange that she wasn't about to go from the high standard of comfort on the ship to considerably inferior accommodation.

'*Bien*,' she commented in satisfaction as the car drew up at the entrance. 'It seems we may be quite comfortable in this primitive country – at least for the next few days.'

'The E & O is owned by two Armenian brothers,' Stephen told them. 'Same chaps who own Raffles in Singapore.'

As they went inside and crossed the chequered marble floor attended by the hotel's respectful porters carrying the valises they'd brought in the car, Lisa thought it was a good thing she'd become accustomed to luxurious surroundings and opulently appointed salons on the *S.S. Orient*, otherwise she'd have been completely intimidated.

'I am Madame Valois and this is Miss Cavendish,' Solange announced to the man behind the reception desk. 'I believe you have rooms for us reserved by Mr Varonne.'

'Of course, Madame Valois – some of our finest rooms have been allocated to you,' he assured her.

'Has Mr Varonne arrived yet?' she asked.

'Not yet, Madame, but your rooms have been ready since the beginning of the week.'

'Is there any message for us?' The clerk shook his head regretfully. 'Then would you please ask him to contact us the moment he arrives.'

'Of course, Madame. Your luggage will be collected from the ship this afternoon. May I wish you a pleasant stay with us.' He bowed and after signing the book, Solange and Lisa were conducted to their adjoining rooms by a red-jacketed porter.

'Not bad,' conceded Solange, looking around her lavishly furnished bedroom with the inevitable fan whirring overhead. The wide, high bed was festooned by white mosquito netting, held back by two satin ties. The room overlooked lush, tropical gardens and even though the windows were all open, the air was thick, sticky and humid.

Lisa had thought it hot on board the ship but the humidity had been considerably less and there had usually been a light sea breeze, particularly at night.

'Is it always like this, do you think?' she asked doubtfully, fanning herself with the hat she'd just removed.

'I believe so. Shall we bathe and change and then have tea on the terrace? After that I think we should take a nap. Perhaps your guardian will arrive soon.'

From the silver tea pot to the tiny cucumber sandwiches, afternoon tea at the E & O was served in just the same way as in Britain. The terrace overlooked the sea and the warm wind was causing a slight chop on the water, fringing the waves with off-white frills of foam.

They sat at a rattan table covered by a starched white cloth and Solange dispensed the tea, casting an approving glance at the bone-china tea service and array of dainty sandwiches and cakes.

'Wh . . . what will we do if my guardian doesn't arrive?'

asked Lisa doubtfully, while Solange tried to decide between a miniature chocolate eclair and an equally small vanilla slice.

'We will make enquiries and find out where he is. Do not worry, *chérie*, he has obviously been delayed and will no doubt soon be with us. I shall not leave you until I have delivered you safely into his keeping. In the meanwhile let us enjoy ourselves as much as we might. You may find that opportunities to do so in the future are limited if he is a strict guardian.'

That very thought had been troubling Lisa. Under Solange's relaxed chaperonage she had done pretty much as she pleased. She was sure she would now find it difficult to return to a more rigid way of life.

'So, what shall we do tonight?' asked Solange. She lowered her eyes and looked a little self-conscious. 'Mark has offered to be our escort if we wish to venture into Georgetown.'

Lisa had wondered whether he'd remain in touch with her friend once the voyage was over, but hadn't liked to ask.

'That would be lovely,' she said enthusiastically. 'Let's try some of the Malay cuisine.' Solange made a little moue of distaste, but then acquiesced gracefully.

'I may as well get used to it, I suppose. Stephen told me that once I go up-country, there will be nothing else, although any cook worthy of the name should be able to make simple French cuisine.'

Lisa was delighted that she would be able to see more of Georgetown that very night – she hadn't left the ship during the entire five week voyage to Malaya. Her illness had prevented her from going ashore at the earlier ports of call and an unfortunate episode involving the Maharajah had rendered sightseeing in Bombay undesirable.

The Maharajah, unable to accept his rejection by Solange, had sent four of his guards to their suite late at night following his cocktail party. Their orders were to bring Solange to him by force.

But Solange had been entertaining Captain Saville in the suite's sitting room and he'd drawn his pistol and held them at bay while Solange used the phone to summon help. The guards had been incarcerated in the hold and the Maharajah and the rest of his retinue kept under armed guard in his quarters until the ship docked in Bombay.

Much to Lisa's disappointment the captain had strongly advised them not to leave the ship when they put into port, as he warned them that their safety could not be guaranteed if the Maharajah decided to try again.

She'd had to content herself with observing the legendary great stone gateway from the deck of the *S.S. Orient*. It had been an awe-inspiring sight, a Roman triumphal arch with four Gujarati domes dominating the harbour promenade.

One of the officers had pointed out the yacht club and the famous Taj Mahal Hotel, an eclectic mix of Oriental and Western styles.

But she'd been very disappointed that she'd travelled halfway around the world and seen nothing as yet. She'd vowed to take every opportunity to explore as much of Malaya as possible while she was there.

It rained while Lisa was stretched out on her bed trying to take a nap. It was unlike any rain she'd ever seen in Britain. One minute the sun was shining brightly and then boiling grey-green clouds rolled overhead and a torrential deluge ensued.

It came down in straight sheets, hitting the ground with such force that on hard surfaces it bounced back several feet in the air.

She left the bed and went over to the open window, expecting the downpour to bring some respite from the thick, sticky heat. But instead the heat seemed to intensify and just the effort of moving from the bed to the window was enough to make beads of perspiration form on her cleavage.

She lay down again, hoping it would have cleared up before Mark took them into Georgetown that evening.

It stopped as suddenly as it had started and so when Mark arrived they went out onto the terrace. They stretched out on long rattan chairs and tried gin pahits – tepid cocktails of gin, water and Angostura bitters.

Lisa grimaced as she sipped hers – in London and on board the *S.S. Orient* she'd become accustomed to her cocktails being shaken over ice and preferred them that way. But she didn't think that even chilling would render this particular drink palatable; it tasted like medicine, but she didn't like to say so.

Solange had no such reservations. 'How dreadful,' she commented, putting down her glass after one sip. 'Order some champagne please, Mark – this is truly horrible.'

Lisa felt somewhat awkward around Mark after the night she'd insisted he make love to her. There was also an intensity in the way he looked at Solange which disturbed her. His gaze was often brooding and he lacked Roland's easy good-humour and Alex's witty conversation.

Although perfectly well-mannered, he appeared less polished than the other two men, possibly because he'd spent most of his adult life in the Far East, often miles away from the nearest European society.

Nevertheless she was glad they had a male escort on their first night in the Orient. She was unsure how safe it would be for two women to go out on their own.

They were waiting in the foyer of the hotel for the doorman to summon two rickshaws, when to her surprise Alex appeared, making her stomach lurch with lust.

'I've been shamefully rude to my host by not dining with him,' he told her, 'but I had to see you. Where's your guardian?' he added, glancing around the foyer.

'He hasn't arrived yet.' Solange had enquired at the desk when they'd descended for cocktails, but no message had been left for them.

Alex's face broke into a lascivious smile at the news.

'Good. Let's go out for dinner. Where do you recommend, Channing?'

'I know just the place. Follow us.' Mark's hard-boned face was difficult to read, but Lisa got the impression he was glad that Alex had turned up, so he could monopolise Solange. He helped the Frenchwoman into the first rickshaw, calling, 'We'll take in a few of the sights on the way.'

Lisa sat gingerly on the rickshaw's oilcloth-covered seat and then Alex climbed lithely in beside her. She revelled in the sensation of his thigh pressing against hers as they were pulled through the teeming streets.

Savoury aromas from the dozens of food stalls hung on the hot, damp night air. There seemed to be any number of dishes on offer, many cooked over charcoal braziers. Hawkers sold green coconuts, mangos and papaya, waving their wares under Lisa's nose whenever the rickshaw slowed down sufficiently.

The streets of Georgetown were narrow and criss-crossed by dozens of alleyways. Each one they passed looked well worthy of exploring and Lisa was determined to come back tomorrow during the day and wander around on foot.

The restaurant Mark took them to was excellent and on his recommendation Lisa tried a coconut milk and fish soup with noodles in it called *laksa*, which she thought tasted odd, but nevertheless enjoyed. For her main course she ordered a dry, spicy beef curry served with rice cooked in coconut milk, which she considered delicious. She could see that Solange was making a heroic effort to eat the food, but left most of it on her plate.

After they'd eaten they went to a club and danced until Lisa was half-delirious with desire from having Alex's lean body pressed against hers, the granite hardness of his erection signalling his own arousal.

'Shall we go back to the hotel?' she breathed as they clung together in the smoky darkness. In answer he disengaged himself, took her hand and led her over to where Solange and Mark were sitting at a small table in the shadows. They said their goodnights and then emerged into the darkness to hail a rickshaw.

Lisa's slender form was tightly sheathed in an oyster-grey silk dress cut on the bias which had a split up the back to midthigh.

As soon as Alex had joined her in the rickshaw he muttered, 'Raise your bottom a moment.' She obeyed him unsteadily, holding onto the side of the rickety vehicle while he swiftly slid the back of her gown upwards so that when she sat down she was sitting on the split.

As they headed back towards the hotel he slipped his hand under her and manoeuvred it up her dress. She obligingly shifted position so he could get it inside her loose-fitting camiknickers and make direct contact with her sex-flesh.

Such was the effect of his touch on her that it felt like a jolt of high voltage electricity and she was aware that her labia were spreading like the petals of a swiftly opening flower. It was a heady and erotic sensation as they were pedalled through the streets passing pedestrians, cars, trishaws and other rickshaws to know that he was secretly caressing her so intimately.

To give him more freedom of movement she leant forward as if anxious to see the sights, while he massaged her vulva with voluptuous tenderness. She felt the heat gathering in her groin as he managed to get one finger inside her and then another. She wriggled slightly and bore down on them, swallowing as her body was suffused by a wave of carnal heat.

What she hadn't realised was that some of the streets were cobbled and as they rode onto the first one she had to bite back a cry of surprise as she was bounced around on the fingers impaling her so pleasurably, increasing the sensation tenfold.

They had gone less than thirty yards over the bumpy surface when she climaxed, sinking her teeth into her lower lip to stop herself making any sound. It was almost a relief when they turned onto a street with a relatively smooth surface because she was convinced that had they stayed on the cobbles, her climax would have continued indefinitely and she would have been unable to hold onto any vestige of self-control.

She'd more or less got a grip on herself when the rickshaw sped across a rutted intersecting road, throwing her up and down on Alex's fingers again – albeit briefly – with the inevitable result.

She could tell Alex was revelling in her uninhibited response to the unexpected stimulation. His hand moved under her and inside her, bringing her back to the brink of orgasm.

'Here we go again,' he said wickedly, as they approached another cobbled street. Lisa hung onto the side of the rickshaw and clenched her teeth, buttocks and internal muscles to no avail; the erotic friction was just too strong.

'*Aaaaah* . . .' she breathed as she spasmed into another heady climax, aware that not only were her warm juices soaking into her camiknickers, but they were also forming a puddle on the seat.

When they arrived at the brightly illuminated entrance to the E & O, as Alex helped her from the vehicle she glanced behind her at the back of her gown. Just as she'd suspected, a damp stain had formed on either side of the split.

'My dress is wet,' she whispered frantically, 'keep close to me.'

Obediently Alex put one hand on her waist and kept right behind her as she retrieved her key from the reception desk and took him up to her room.

Someone had turned back the bed and arranged the mosquito netting over it so it looked like a ghostly tent. Two lamps were burning and the curtains had been closed.

Alex moved around the room, rearranging some of the furniture to suit his own ends. He placed a rattan lounging chair with green silk cushions so it faced an angled mirror. He arranged two lamps on small tables on either side of the chair and bent down to consider whether he'd positioned them correctly for whatever he had in mind.

Feeling hot and sticky, Lisa went into the bathroom, discarded her damp clothing and ran a bath. She went back into the bedroom wrapped in a towel to find Alex stretched out on the rattan chair, smoking.

She opened the enormous wardrobe, wondering what to put on and whether it was worth it before Alex took it off again.

'Just a slip,' he directed her. 'A short one.' She lifted a couple out and held them up for his inspection.

'That one,' he decided, pointing at a diaphanous sliver of shantung silk. 'Nothing else, except your pearls.'

She stepped into it and adjusted it in the mirror. Two triangles of open-work embroidery covered her breasts, offering enticing glimpses of her creamy skin and the darker rose-pink of her nipples whenever she moved. The slip fell to mid-thigh and dipped to the waist at the back.

She left her hair loose so it cascaded around her pale shoulders and looped her pearls around her neck so they hung as a single strand.

Alex led her to the bed, brushing aside the mosquito netting, and laid her against the pillows. He used her pearls to caress her, rolling them over the smooth skin of her shoulders and décolletage, then looping them over her breasts the way he had on the night Roland had held her wrists behind her back.

She sighed and let herself be carried along on a gentle tide of exquisite arousal as he lifted them from her neck and drew them across her belly over the thin silk of her slip.

He indicated he wanted her to turn over and then lifted her slip so he could trail them over the firm globes of her buttocks and dangle them into her cleft. She sighed and wriggled voluptuously, soothed into a state of languorous anticipation by his licentious attentions.

He took the pillows from behind her head and shoulders and piled them up in the middle of the bed. He made her lie flat on her back with her hips and bottom supported by the pillows and her legs widely parted.

He pushed her slip over her belly and drew the pearls over her mound, dipping them between her thighs so they lay against the slick, overheated folds of her vulva.

He swung them gently to and fro so they touched her inner-thighs and then slowly worked his way upwards until they made fleeting contact with her outer-labia. She felt them against her inner sex-lips, before he swung them so they slapped gently into her engorged clitoris. She closed her eyes and focused on the sensation, enjoying the sheer eroticism of what he was doing.

He laid the pearls in a heap on her mound, where they formed a bizarre ornament for her russet fleece. He began to toy with her sex-flesh, pulling softly at each fold, opening her out until she was spread for him, the furled entrance to her hidden core clearly visible.

She inhaled sharply when he slid a finger inside her and moved it from side to side as if trying to increase the circumference of her sex-sheath. He held open her sex with one hand, carefully spreading it with his fingers, and then picked up her pearls again.

She gasped when he began to slide them inside her, one at a time. She watched fascinated, unable to believe how easily they vanished into her. It was a wonderful sensation as he used his long forefinger to position them in her hidden chamber with the utmost delicacy. It took a long time but eventually there was only a loop about six inches long left outside her.

'Get up and walk around,' Alex bade her. 'And hold your slip above your waist.'

She swung her legs to the floor and took a couple of tentative steps, sure that they'd immediately cascade out of her. But they didn't, her internal muscles held them in position as she strolled the length of the room.

She gulped as she felt them moving around inside her, pressing against her channel, exciting and arousing her, the six-inch loop brushing against her inner-thighs.

Alex seated himself in the rattan lounger, his legs stretched out in front of him, placed a small cushion between his thighs and beckoned to her to come and sit on it. Now she saw why he'd arranged the furniture the way he had. She was sitting with her back to him facing the mirror, so they could both see her reflection.

He made her draw up her knees and spread them so the whole of her sex was clearly visible. She could see the swollen kernel of her clitoris, prominent and very, very red.

Alex began to play with her breasts over her slip, squeezing and fondling them while she watched fascinated.

'Touch yourself,' he ordered her softly. 'Make yourself come.' She hesitated, suddenly self-conscious.

'Do it,' he growled, rolling her nipple between his finger and thumb in a way that made her feel invisible threads must run straight from it to her clit which tingled in swift response.

Tentatively, she touched it with the tip of her finger and then slowly stroked it. Alex continued to caress her breasts, sliding her shoulder straps down so her slip fell to her waist. As he coaxed her nipples into swollen points she thought fleetingly that they were almost as intense a crimson as her engorged bud.

All three nubs of flesh were stimulated at the same time and she felt her breathing becoming increasingly erratic as she watched herself.

She looked wanton and abandoned with her thighs splayed and the necklace trailing from her sex. She concentrated on rubbing her clit with two fingers in the way she knew would make her come very quickly. As she climbed higher and higher towards the peak, he took hold of the loop of pearls and began with agonising slowness to pull them out.

They emerged one at a time, glistening with her juices, adding unbearable additional stimulation to her over-sensitised private parts. She felt the wave of heat that preceded her orgasm and cried out as it broke over her in a series of womb-wrenching spasms.

Alex paused, then just as it was coming to an end he jerked the necklace and the rest of the pearls flew out of her, making her come again in another long, liquid climax.

Chapter Fifteen

The morning dawned misty and cool with wisps of vapour wrapping themselves around the trunks of the palm trees in the hotel's gardens.

Lisa leant out of the window enjoying the caress of the fresh air on her bare shoulders. A Malayan gardener came into view and she hastily pulled the curtains together and went into the bathroom.

Alex had slipped out of her room in the early hours to return to his agent's house.

'I wish now I'd insisted on putting up here,' he'd commented as he buttoned his limp evening shirt. 'But Arnold – our agent chap – insisted that his wife had prepared the spare room and would be disappointed if I didn't stay. I can see why she was so keen to have a total stranger in the house – Arnold is easily the most tedious man I've come across in years. She must be bored into a coma over dinner every night, she practically wept when I said I had a previous engagement.'

'I wish you were staying here too,' said Lisa wistfully. 'Although once my guardian gets here it may not be possible for you to come to my room.'

'Don't worry – we'll find some way to be alone,' he

reassured her. 'When I left England I didn't have a clue what the lie of the land would be out here and thought I might as well stay with the chap as not. But it can be damned awkward being a guest in someone else's house.'

He'd left after kissing her and assuring her he'd be in touch very soon.

As Lisa took a bath she decided to have breakfast and then set off on foot to explore. Solange was unlikely to emerge for hours and she herself was impatient to see more of the Orient.

As she left the hotel she hoped she wasn't committing some social solecism by venturing out alone. It was just too bad if she were, if she waited for Solange the day would be half-over.

It was only a short walk to the area they'd passed through last night and as the sun began to break through the mist she found herself in the narrow alleyways and streets which had looked so inviting.

Pastel-coloured shophouses were interspaced by bazaars, coffee houses, temples and mosques. Cloth merchants, goldsmiths and silversmiths offered a stunning array of goods ranging in price from what seemed to be astonishingly cheap, to unbelievably expensive.

Although many traders tried to interest her in their wares, she was treated with the utmost courtesy and didn't at any time feel intimidated. The proprietor of a coffee house may have been surprised to see her when she ventured in attracted by the smell of freshly ground beans, but if he was, he didn't show it.

She bought a guide-book to the island and flicked through it as she drank her coffee, determined to drag Solange to absolutely everywhere of potential interest. Afterwards she purchased a few trinkets thinking she could send them back to

Britain as presents for her school friends.

She lingered over bolts of jewel-coloured silks which merchants unrolled for her approval, but decided to wait until Solange was with her before buying any.

The sun was soon shining strongly enough to make her glad that many of the streets had covered arched pavements, offering shade from the sun and shelter from any sudden shower.

It was late morning before she hailed a rickshaw and returned to the hotel, wondering if her guardian had arrived yet.

His absence seemed very strange considering he'd had her travel thousands of miles to meet him. Whatever the reason for his non-appearance, she couldn't believe he hadn't been able to get a message to the hotel.

It was comforting to think that Solange would stay with her until he did arrive, but her companion had her own business to attend to. The rubber plantation her husband had left her was still being run by the manager Monsieur Valois had appointed, but she must be keen to see it and attend to the sale.

She found Solange in the lounge, drinking coffee with Stephen and Phyllis.

'Rum do, this guardian of yours not turning up,' Stephen greeted her. 'We've just been wondering where he's got to. I think I'd better make some enquiries for you.'

'If it wouldn't be too much trouble,' murmured Lisa, accepting a cup of coffee.

'I thought we might all dine together tonight,' suggested Phyllis. 'The Penang Palace has some of the best food in the area.'

'That would be delightful,' said Solange sweetly. 'But tell me – are there any French restaurants in Georgetown?'

'Not that I know of,' replied Phyllis, 'Although I think there may be one in Kuala Lumpur.'

They ate an early lunch in the hotel and then Phyllis took the other two women for a drive to see Millionaires Row. This turned out to be a a series of mansions on Northam Road on the outskirts of Georgetown.

The road ran parallel to the seafront and was lined by massive angsana trees which almost met overhead to form a shady canopy in the afternoon's heat. The mansions themselves were in different architectural styles, but all fanciful in the extreme.

Turreted roofs, copper domes, Doric columns and plaster curlicues abounded. Each house was balconied and shuttered and had its own carefully tended lawns sloping down to the sea.

'The rubber czars live in some of them,' explained Phyllis, 'and the Straits Chinese.'

Afterwards she dropped them on Pitt Street and Solange threw herself into shopping with tireless zeal until the afternoon downpour began. They took a trishaw back to the hotel, the canvas cover protecting them and their purchases from the deluge.

Lisa felt a warm glow suffuse her body as they passed over the cobbled streets which had caused her so much pleasure the night before. Solange obviously missed the erotic potential of this mode of transport and complained that every bone in her body was being shaken.

When they returned to the hotel, Mark was reading

a newspaper in the foyer and accompanied Solange to her room with what Lisa assumed to be carnal intentions. She wished Alex were here too, but hopefully she'd see him tonight.

She bathed and stretched out on her bed with no real expectation of sleeping. But she soon drifted off and was roused from a confused dream about Alex and her guardian, by the sound of raised voices.

She sat up and rubbed her eyes, registering that some sort of altercation was taking place in Solange's room and the sound was drifting in through the open window. She fastened a robe hastily around her waist.

She heard Solange exclaiming, 'That's no business of yours – I'll behave in any way that pleases me!'

'And I'm telling you that as long as we're together – you won't!'

Lisa hadn't planned to eavesdrop, her intention had been to ascertain whether her friend needed her help – if Mark were behaving violently for example – in which case she would have had no hesitation about rushing next door.

But as she strained to ascertain how far the altercation had gone, she heard Mark say harshly, 'You killed your husband as surely as if you'd held the gun to his head and pulled the trigger – and you know it!'

Lisa clearly heard the sound of a slap and held her breath for a few seconds before Mark snarled, 'You vicious little bitch!'

Relieved that it hadn't been Solange on the receiving end of the slap, but afraid she might be soon, Lisa wondered if she should go and knock on the door anyway. The unmistakable crash of china hitting a hard object followed and then Mark yowled loudly.

'Get out of here before I stick this through your black heart!' were Solange's next blood-chilling words. Deciding things had gone far enough, Lisa hurried to the door and opened it, just in time to see Mark storming off down the corridor.

She tapped on Solange's door calling, 'It's Lisa – may I come in?'

There was no reply and it was with some trepidation she turned the handle and pushed open the door to find her friend stabbing a large hat-pin with an ivory handle into a cushion. The shattered remnants of the rather pretty Chinese vase which had stood on the dresser lay on the floor and Solange was fetchingly attired in only her parchment-coloured camisole, stockings and suspender belt.

Leaving the hat-pin in the cushion she turned to Lisa with her hands on her hips, her voluptuous bosom heaving.

'Please ring room service and ask them to send up a shaker of vodka martinis immediately,' she said, before going into the bathroom, her hips undulating sinuously even in her overwrought state.

The martinis had arrived together with triangular glasses cooling on a bed of ice, before Solange emerged from the bathroom tying her robe and looking considerably more composed.

She poured them both a cocktail and then went over to look out of the window while she tossed her drink down her throat with an accomplished flick of the wrist.

'Are you alright?' asked Lisa diffidently.

'I will be very soon,' replied Solange, refilling her glass.

'I . . . I heard some of what he said,' murmured Lisa. 'Solange – what did he mean by saying you killed your husband?'

For a moment she thought she'd presumed too far as Solange stared at her coldly. But then the Frenchwoman came to sit on the rumpled bed, curling up against the cushions and looking far too vulnerably feminine to have ever inflicted bodily harm on a man Mark's size.

'Come and sit down, *ma petite*,' she invited, patting the bed next to her.

Lisa obediently propped herself up next to her and waited expectantly.

'I loved my husband very much,' began Solange. 'But he was a man with a great many business interests in the Far East and a couple of years after we were married he announced his intention of travelling out here to attend to them. He was to be away for months and I couldn't bear the idea of being separated for so long.'

She took a sip of her drink and adjusted the front of her robe where it fell open over her legs before continuing.

'I assumed I would accompany him and although I was afraid of the hardships such a journey would necessitate, nothing would have stopped me from going.'

Lisa suppressed a smile. Their voyage on the *S.S. Orient* could hardly have been classed as any sort of hardship.

'But then I discovered to my dismay that he did not intend for me to go with him. I was to stay in Paris like a good wife and busy myself doing embroidery or some such nonsense. I put aside my pride and begged him to take me, but he said that a woman such as myself would suffer great discomfort in a foreign country, away from all the comforts of civilisation.'

Solange took another gulp of her drink, but the alcohol had obviously reached her bloodstream because she seemed much calmer.

'He went without me and I was desolate. I'm afraid, *chérie*, that I am a woman who cannot live without a man and while he was with me, attending to my needs, I never strayed. But once he'd gone and I was all alone I could not bear to stay in each night pining for him. Instead I went out with my friends to restaurants and nightclubs and had an amusing time. Of course the inevitable happened and I took a lover.'

She smiled reminiscently. 'After that I bedded who I wished, when I wished. I knew Mark slightly in Paris and he heard that I enjoyed *amours* while my husband was overseas. There is nothing unusual in France about a married woman having lovers, but Mark is a stuffy, disapproving Englishman. All my friends wondered why it had taken me so long – we had after all been married over two years.'

Solange paused as if the next part of the story was almost too painful to recount.

'My husband was found dead in the jungle near to the plantation house – he'd been killed with a single shot from his own revolver. Mark told me that he'd killed himself because he'd heard about my infidelities and couldn't bear it, but I believe his gun must have gone off by accident. A Frenchman would never kill himself because his wife was unfaithful. But even though I believe this to be the case, there is a little part of me that wonders. I continue to mourn him even now.'

'Then why ... why do you sleep with Mark, if he said

something so cruel?' asked Lisa, baffled.

A wry smile curved Solange's luscious mouth.

'Because we cannot always choose whom we're attracted to. I detest Mark Channing – he's a censorious prig – but he has only to look at me in a certain way and immediately I'm on fire. His touch thrills me to my very core and I come constantly when he is making love to me.'

'Goodness,' said Lisa, thinking what an unbelievably complex issue sex could be. 'But is it worth it to have him revile you in such a way?'

'That, my dear Lisa, is a difficult question. He is most troublesome and a lot of the time I would like to kill him. But when he holds me in his arms and does all those delicious things to me, I forget that I detest him.'

'And why does he want to have an affair with you, if he has such a low opinion of you?'

Solange smiled a wicked, cat-like smile. 'Because, most inconveniently for him, he lusts after me in a way which he cannot control. He burns for me and hates himself because he cannot resist my charms and his liaison with me troubles his so-very-upright British conscience. He punishes me therefore for his own incontinent loins.'

Lisa was awed by Solange's instinctive grasp of the situation. 'Do you intend to go on seeing him?' she wanted to know.

Solange stared thoughtfully into her glass.

'He becomes increasingly tiresome. He says I must give him my word that I will go with no other man than him, but this I will not do and it puts him in a great rage.'

Solange placed her glass on the bedside table, stretched and yawned. 'Now if you will excuse me, *ma petite*, I will take my nap.'

But sleep eluded Solange and after tossing and turning for a while she rose, dressed and went down to the bar. She ordered a champagne cocktail and studied the men whiling away the wet late afternoon by drinking.

Several of them kept glancing in her direction and it didn't take her long to decide which one would best serve her purposes.

He was an army officer with a ruddy complexion and large, very-white teeth. He had a virile, well-exercised body and looked as if he'd excel at sports. His movements were all decisive and he had the appearance of a man who'd never had a moment's self-doubt or been troubled by his conscience in his life.

The next time he looked in her direction she smiled a sweet, seductive smile and then lowered her eyes as if in confusion.

Through her long lashes she saw him say something to his companion and then he made his way over to her.

'I say – could I buy you a drink?'

'How very kind.' Solange's lips curved again in a beguiling smile. 'But I really shouldn't accept a drink from a man to whom I have not been introduced.'

He bowed. 'Captain James Chandler at your service, ma'am.'

'Madame Solange Valois.' She extended her hand and he kissed it.

'Now may I buy you a drink?'

'Very well,' she acceded graciously. He snapped his fingers

and a waiter came across to take their order. They chatted for a few minutes and then Solange, after glancing at her watch and realising she didn't have much time before she would have to change for dinner, decided to move things along.

'Captain Chandler . . .'

'Ma'am?'

'Would you like to make love to me?'

The question took him so much by surprise that he had difficulty in swallowing his drink. His already high colour deepened and a brief glance at his groin confirmed that he found the idea extremely arousing.

'Yes,' he said in a strangled voice as soon as he could speak. She rose to her feet, dangled her room key so he could see where to find her and murmured, 'Join me in five minutes.'

When he knocked on the door she'd already undressed and was reclining seductively on the bed in her parchment-coloured camisole, camiknickers, suspender belt and stockings. She said softly, 'Why don't you undress, my brave captain?'

Solange didn't think she'd ever seen a man shed his clothes so fast. Within seconds he was approaching her with his member, a dark brick-red, rearing up against his belly.

She knelt up as he reached the bed and bent her head to take the glans in her mouth. He stood with his hands on his hips while she flickered her tongue around the ridge below the glans, then strummed her way to the base. She licked the soft spherical swellings of his testicles and then kissed her way back up to the head.

She glanced upwards and saw that his face wore an expression of ecstatic bemusement. No doubt he was of that breed of Englishmen who thought only whores ever behaved in such a way. Or perhaps he'd put it down to her being French.

She slid his phallus into her mouth and commenced a seductive sucking, tugging gently with her lips and then sucking harder so that he groaned and moved his hips.

Solange used her considerable expertise to bring him to boiling point and then drew him onto the bed beside her. He tried to mount her, but she twisted away.

'No. You lie on the bed on your back.'

He obeyed her and reached for her with eager hands. He caressed her body over her silk lingerie, weighing her voluptuous breasts in his hands and squeezing and fondling her curvaceous bottom.

She knelt to one side of him and he removed her camiknickers and then her camisole. He still had the dazed air of a man who couldn't quite believe his luck and was afraid he might wake up at any moment.

But when he pushed his hand between her legs it became obvious he had no real knowledge of a woman's anatomy. He just delved briefly into her vulva and then lifted her so she was astride him. Determined that he wouldn't leave her bed until he'd made her come, Solange lowered herself onto his phallus, facing him.

She began to move on his shaft, rotating her pelvis and rocking up and down. She used his member to give herself pleasure, while he caressed her breasts with his large hands.

But he was impatient for release and grasped her by the hips to move her up and down in an increasingly fast tempo. He jammed her down so hard as he came that she winced.

As soon as the throes of his orgasm had died away he dozed off and Solange eased herself free of his rapidly-shrinking phallus. When she pulled his wrists to the top of the bed and lashed them deftly to the headboard with one of her silk stockings, he opened his eyes groggily.

'Eh? What are you doing?' he asked her, bewildered.

'Something you'll enjoy very much,' she assured him.

'I've just done what I enjoy very much,' he pointed out, tugging at his bonds. But Solange's knots held fast and he began to look alarmed, turning his head from side to side, looking for some way of getting free.

'Shh,' murmured Solange, stroking his chest and trailing her fingers over his belly. 'Relax – we still have a little time.'

'I'm due back on duty in an hour,' he told her.

'You may go as soon as you have satisfied me,' she informed him huskily.

'I thought I already had.'

'Partially, but I did not experience a climax and it would not be very gentlemanly of you to leave without taking care of that.'

'I've had what I came for and now I want to leave,' he told her unpleasantly. He yanked at his ties. 'Now let me free, you little French witch, or I'll yell my head off.'

'Go ahead,' Solange invited him. 'It matters nothing to me because I'll be going back to France very soon. But everyone on the island will know that you were found naked in a woman's hotel room, tied to her bed. What would your commanding officer say about that, do you think? And the men you command – what would their reaction be?'

His face went a mottled magenta and he cursed colourfully.

'Those are not nice words to use in front of a lady,' Solange reproved him. 'I think your manners could do with a little improvement, *n'est ce pas*?'

She drew his heavy leather belt from his uniform and walked around the bed flipping it playfully. 'Now apologise for your rudeness,' she ordered. He remained obdurately silent and she flicked him with the belt, catching him a small, stinging blow on the thigh. She hit him again a couple of times, light blows with no force behind them, but he was obviously not about to apologise and after glancing at the clock on the dresser, she decided to get down to business.

She sat astride his chest and toyed with his member, not ceasing her ministrations until it had achieved semi-tumescence. Then she moved up the bed and positioned herself over his face. She parted her sex-lips with her hands and showed him the slippery folds of her vulva and the little point of her bud.

'To make me come you must stimulate me here with your lips and tongue,' she told him.'

'I'm not doing that,' he protested. 'It isn't natural.'

'I think you will,' she said sweetly, lowering herself towards his face.

'Let me go, you little slut!' he exclaimed, yanking at his bonds again. Inexorably, Solange lowered herself until she was astride his face, effectively muffling his cries.

When at last he'd mastered the art of giving a woman pleasure with his mouth, she rewarded him by riding him until he came again.

In the excitement of it she lost track of the time and it was only Lisa tapping at the door calling, 'Solange – are you ready?' that reminded her they were supposed to be meeting the Templetons in the bar.

'Just a moment, *chérie*,' she called, scrambling hastily off the exhausted Captain Chandler.'

She shrugged into her robe and opened the door a crack, just enough for Lisa to catch a glimpse of a naked torso and legs.

'Anyone I know?' she asked.

'I think not. I'm sorry, I became distracted and lost track of time – I will be ready in half an hour. Please apologise to Phyllis and Stephen on my behalf.'

Smiling to herself, Lisa headed downstairs while Solange went back into her room. She rang room service, ignoring the captain as he called her every name under the sun and threatened her with dire consequences if she didn't release him. She ordered a champagne cocktail then loosened the knots on the stockings.

'Room service will be here in less than five minutes,' she warned him. 'I think you will not wish to be here then.' She retreated prudently into the bathroom and locked the door, watching with amusement through the keyhole as he threw on his clothes and left in a hurry.

They had a pleasant evening with the Templetons although neither Alex nor Mark put in an appearance. It was late when they returned to the hotel. As soon as they entered the foyer, the manager appeared and approached Solange.

'May I speak to you for a moment, Madame Valois?'

As she followed him into his office, Solange wondered if

the army officer she'd taken up to her room had been ungallant enough to complain about her. She didn't think so, but couldn't imagine what else the manager might wish to see her about.

Lisa and the Templetons waited in the bar. Five minutes later Solange reappeared pale-faced and sank into a chair.

Turning to Lisa, she said, 'I'm afraid I have some very bad news, *chérie* – your guardian, Mr Varonne, is dead.'

Chapter Sixteen

For Lisa, the next week passed in a blur of confusion. She was told that her guardian, apparently for many years in poor health, had succumbed to a tropical fever a few days previously and had died on the day of their arrival in Malaya.

She was unable to feel sorrow – she had after all never met him – but she did regret the fact that now she'd never have the chance to get to know him. She was grateful for the way in which he'd assumed responsibility for her all these years and would have liked to have had the opportunity to express her gratitude.

She was indebted to Solange who, with Mark's help, took care of all the funeral arrangements. It was also Solange who managed to track down Mr Varonne's solicitor, who came to see them at the hotel and told Lisa that other than for some minor bequests, she was the major beneficiary. She was stunned to discover that she was now a wealthy woman.

'But whatever will I do with all that money?' she asked Solange as they sat on the terrace and sipped gin slings the evening after the funeral.

'Whatever you wish,' said Solange. 'The world has just opened up for you. You are your own mistress now – there is no-one who can tell you what you may or may not do.'

'But I don't know what I want to do,' wailed Lisa.

'You must learn to be practical, *chérie*. I think perhaps your first step must be to decide what you wish to do with the rubber plantation. Do you want to sell it? Do you wish to live there and run it yourself? Do you not want to live there but to have someone run it for you?'

'I . . . I don't know,' confessed Lisa miserably.

'Then I think the best thing will be for us to visit our respective plantations – they're adjoining so we can travel together. Then I shall arrange for the sale of mine and you will have time to decide what to do with yours.'

'That sounds like a good idea.'

Lisa was already dreading the day when her separation from Solange would be inevitable. As soon as the Frenchwoman had finalised her business in Malaya she would return to France and then Lisa didn't know what she herself would do.

There was no particular reason to go back to Scotland, but if she didn't return there, where would she go? She knew Mrs Ross would be glad to see her, but she had her own family and friends and although Lisa had been fond of her, they'd never been particularly close.

But Solange's advice to settle her guardian's affairs in this country before thinking any further ahead, was sound. She needed to get used to the idea that she was a woman of independent means.

Alex had had to go down to Kuala Lumpur on urgent business, but had assured Lisa he'd return as soon as possible and she was hoping to see him the next day.

Mark joined them for dinner in the hotel. He and Solange appeared to have temporarily settled their differences and their tempestuous affair seemed to be back on – at least for the moment – but Solange hadn't confided the details. His local knowledge had been invaluable to them in arranging the funeral, so after dinner Solange asked him the easiest way of travelling up-country to their respective plantations.

'There isn't an easy way,' he informed her. 'But the best way is probably a ferry to the mainland, railway, a boat up the river and then hopefully someone from one of the plantations will be able to meet us in a car – or more likely, a jeep.'

'Us?' queried Solange, her delicately-winged brows drawing together.

'You can't seriously think the two of you will be able to travel alone?' Mark's tone was dismissive in the extreme.

'No – of course not,' returned Solange sweetly. 'I'll be taking my maid.'

'You'll need to take more than your maid,' he said grimly. 'The jungle isn't like the Bois de Boulogne, only hotter. I'll come with you and make sure it's safe for you to stay there. Some of those planters live pretty primitive lives, so don't expect the houses to be of the standard you're used to in Europe. If neither of them is habitable I'll have to bring you back the following day, but at least you'll both have seen what it is you have to sell and you can handle the actual sale from here – or K.L, if you prefer.'

'K.L.?' queried Lisa.

'Sorry – that's how the ex-pats refer to Kuala Lumpur.'

'It's most kind of you to make such an offer,' said Solange.

'But I assure you we'll be perfectly alright on our own – won't we, *chérie*?'

Lisa hesitated. Loyalty dictated that she side with Solange, but common sense indicated that they take Mark up on his offer. She knew from the books Solange had lent her that the jungle was inhabited by elephants, tigers, leopards, panthers, rhinos and honeybears, not to mention any number of monkeys, snakes and insects.

She wasn't quite sure what action it was best to take when confronted by any of them and would really rather be travelling with someone who did know.

She was just wondering how to frame her opinion diplomatically, when Alex strode into the hotel restaurant.

'Here's Campion,' said Mark, 'I'm sure he'll agree with me.'

The waiter brought another chair and Alex sank into it and immediately ordered a whisky. Before he even had the chance to ask them how the funeral had gone, Mark took the offensive.

'Solange and Lisa are planning to travel up-country to visit their plantations as if they were taking a trip from London to Bath. They seem to think they can travel through the jungle with just a maid and a dozen suitcases – stopping for refreshments at various hotels along the way no doubt. I've offered to escort them, but Solange has taken umbrage and decided I'm interfering.'

'And patronising,' added Solange, unperturbed.

'I was planning to go with them anyway,' replied Alex, taking a gulp of his whisky. 'I've never seen a rubber plantation and I'd like to visit one before I go back. But I for one would be glad to have you along, Channing – none of us speaks the lingo or know what the form is.'

Solange glared at him, but he ignored her and took Lisa's hand.

'How are you?' he asked. 'I imagine the funeral was pretty grim and I'm sorry I wasn't here for it. But I've got the most pressing of my business out of the way and I'm at your disposal for a week or so. Shall I come with you?'

'Oh, yes, please,' was Lisa's fervent reply.

'You might as well admit defeat, Solange,' said Mark, shooting her a triumphant look.

'We'll discuss it in my room,' said Solange, rising from her seat. 'We will leave Alex to eat his dinner and Lisa to watch him fondly.'

After Alex had eaten he suggested they go for a walk, so they wandered out into the scented night and strolled hand in hand under the palm trees. Alex paused to pick a waxen frangipani flower from a bush and pushed it behind her ear, so she was enveloped in its sweet fragrance.

In the shadows he took her in his arms and kissed her deeply, his hands sliding up and down her back and caressing her over her thin silk dress, making her go weak with lust.

'Let's go up to your room,' he breathed. They went back inside the hotel but no sooner had the door to Lisa's room closed behind them than there was a knock on it.

It was Solange. 'That man is impossible,' she announced. 'I do not wish him to accompany us. Alex may come if he wishes – at least he is not only always telling me what to do – but I will not travel with such a detestable oaf.'

She sank onto the rattan lounger and looked at them challengingly, daring them to disagree with her. Alex leant against the dresser with his hands in his pockets while Lisa struggled to think of something diplomatic to say.

Her thought processes weren't helped by the fact she was aching with desire and found it difficult to switch her attention to something else.

'Don't you think we might find communication a problem?' she managed to say at last. 'None of us speaks the language and that will probably make things very difficult.'

'Then we shall hire an interpreter,' said Solange, decidedly.

'Solange, my sweet – stop pacing the room,' said Alex. 'It's making me feel tired just watching you. The heat's too intense for such pointless activity.' Taking her by the hand he led her over to the bed. 'Lie down and I'll rub your back until you're less overwrought.'

Her expression still stormy, Solange stretched out on the bed and Alex began to massage her back. Lisa watched, her sex was pulsing furiously and the heat in her groin threatened to consume her.

But Solange appeared to be relaxing as he coaxed the tension from her muscles.

'Why don't you massage her legs?' Alex invited Lisa. It wasn't exactly how she'd envisaged spending the evening, but she perched on the edge of the bed with as good a grace as she could muster and began to stroke Solange's shapely calves.

It wasn't long before the older woman's previously tense body was limp and relaxed and she made a small sound of satisfaction as Alex unzipped her dress so he could continue with his ministrations on her bare skin.

Solange shifted position and her skirt rode up around her thighs, exposing her stocking tops. The soft skin visible between her black stockings and camiknickers looked a pale, milky-white in contrast. Lisa ran her fingers around it, wondering if her own thighs felt as smooth and satin-skinned.

She heard Solange make a small purring sound and the Frenchwoman parted her thighs slightly and wriggled her bottom in the air.

Alex obligingly ran his hand over her curvaceous rump, but it kept getting caught in the folds of her dress.

'Raise your hips a minute,' he directed her, then managed to slip the flimsy garment off and threw it to one side.

Underneath Solange was wearing a black lace bra and a matching suspender belt and camiknickers. It made Lisa catch her breath just to see her like that and one glance told her what sort of effect the alluring sight had had on Alex.

He fondled the firm globes of Solange's bottom, squeezing and kneading them, easing them apart and then pushing them together. The lace had a very open weave and he found a hole large enough to admit one finger which he ran up and down the cleft between her buttocks.

He circled her tiny rear aperture and then pushed his finger far enough down to make contact with the back reaches of her sex-flesh. Solange moaned softly and butted her bottom against his hand.

He drew her camiknickers down her buttocks and she obligingly lifted her hips so he could ease them over her thighs. Lisa took over and pulled them down Solange's slim legs, leaving her bottom and sex completely exposed.

Alex bent over her and began to nibble the smooth cheeks,

kissing and sucking them and driving Solange into a frenzy. The Frenchwoman changed position so she was kneeling on all-fours, her thighs widely parted, displaying the intricate folds of her sex to Lisa.

Lisa could see the crimson point of her bud and the clear honey oozing from her inner-chamber, making her vulva glisten invitingly.

Alex pulled her buttocks apart and said to Lisa, 'Hold her open for me like that.'

Lisa moved to kneel beside her friend and did so. He stripped off his trousers to reveal an arrogantly rampant phallus which twitched as he knelt on the bed behind Solange. He positioned it at the whorled entrance to her inner-chamber and then slid it slowly inside her, an inch at a time. Solange gasped as he sheathed it right up to the hilt and then remained immobile behind her.

'Make her come,' he directed Lisa.

Lisa reached under Solange's belly and found the swollen point of flesh. She stroked it deftly, imagining it was her own, which was throbbing in empathy.

Solange squirmed as Lisa manipulated the slick little bud, undulating her hips around Alex's rock-hard column of flesh which was impaling her so satisfyingly. She rocked backwards and forwards against him, obviously eager for him to use his member to stimulate her further, but he remained determinedly still.

Lisa found that her own breathing was becoming ragged. She could just discern the scent of Solange's arousal overlaid by her familiar jasmine and orange flower perfume.

With a husky cry, Solange came, her back arching and her

body convulsing as waves of pleasure broke over her. As soon as the climax hit her, Alex commenced a vigorous pumping which made Solange cry out over and over again as her orgasm was prolonged almost beyond endurance.

Alex pulled out and rolled to one side of her to lean against the pillows. Lisa joined him and he began to fondle her breasts over the silk chiffon of her gown.

Solange opened her eyes and observed the proceedings with interest before announcing, 'I am so very hot. I think I'll cool down in the bath.'

She slid off the bed and went into the bathroom, her bottom swaying voluptuously, still slightly pink in places where Alex had sucked and nibbled it.

Through the open door they watched her shed her clothes and then pin her hair up. She shook some scented powder into the water and climbed in.

'Most refreshing,' she told them. 'Why don't you join me?'

Lisa did feel very warm and could feel her gown sticking to her damp skin.

'Shall we?' she asked Alex.

'Why not?' was his reply. 'The bath's big enough.' They both undressed and went into the bathroom where Solange was amusing herself by working up a rich soapy lather and covering her breasts with it. Alex sat against the end of the bath with Lisa between his thighs while Solange obligingly slid to the far end.

Alex took a bar of scented soap and began to wash Lisa's back, moving his hands gently down her spine and then massaging her shoulders. She held out one arm to him and then the other while Solange soaped her legs. It was strangely soothing to have two people attending to her like that and Lisa felt wonderfully cosseted as well as sexually aroused.

She could feel Alex's erection growing against the cleft between her buttocks and it excited her. She wriggled back against him and was gratified when she felt his penis hardening even more.

She raised her bottom and tried to get it inside her, but they were both too slippery and her attempt was unsuccessful. She turned to face him and, in a tangle of soapy limbs, managed to kneel astride him. Making love in a bath which held three people was no easy matter. But by hanging onto his shoulders, Lisa managed to move up and down on his engorged shaft in a way which was mutually pleasurable.

Solange suddenly rose from the water, scented bubbles streaming off her, and stepped out of the bath to give them more room. She perched on a stool with her legs wide apart and began to touch herself as she watched them.

Lisa found she couldn't tear her eyes from where Solange's beautifully manicured hand moved between her own thighs. Her touch was sure and skilful and she achieved a climax while Lisa was still scaling the lower slopes of hers.

But the heat in Lisa's sex continued to grow until it intensified into a bubbling caldron of red-hot desire. She rubbed herself frantically against Alex's rod, desperate for the release which seemed to elude her. Alex fastened his mouth over one of her rose-pink nipples and sucked hard, sending darts of sheer erotic sensation lancing through her body.

'*Aaaaah*!' she cried, as at last her climax overwhelmed her, rolling over her like an avalanche, her internal muscles clutching convulsively at Alex's shaft and making him come too.

They rinsed themselves in clear, cool water and then dried themselves on the hotel's fluffy towels.

Solange had dressed by the time they emerged from the bathroom and she paused just long enough to kiss them both goodnight before leaving.

'I had an interesting experience in Kuala Lumpur,' Alex told Lisa as they lay back against the pillows, their bodies sated and relaxed.

'What was that?' she murmured, toying with his chest hair.

'My agent took me to a brothel.'

'*What*?' demanded Lisa, sitting bolt upright.

He pulled her back down again.

'Don't over-react. I didn't avail myself of any of the many services on offer. Arnold obviously thought the worse of me for it, but I couldn't get excited about the idea of buying sex for money.'

Lisa's curiosity got the better of her.

'What was it like?' she asked.

'I only saw the reception room which had lots of bamboo sofas with pink satin cushions and which were deuced uncomfortable to sit on. All the clients seemed to be expected to buy extortionately priced drinks for the girls whether they intended to go upstairs with them or not.'

'W . . . were the girls pretty?'

'Some of them were absolutely beautiful, some less so. One came and sat on my knee and wriggled around, stroking my neck and hair, whispering in my ear the things she could do for me.'

'Weren't you tempted?' Lisa wanted to know.

'To be honest, yes – or at least I had the usual male

reaction. But all the time I was aware that she'd say the same things to any man in there. It wasn't me she wanted, just my money and I found it off-putting.'

'Did you stay long?'

'Long enough for Arnold to take a gorgeous girl upstairs, but he was only gone for fifteen minutes or so and when he came back he was ready to leave. The floorshow was interesting though.'

Lisa knew she was being prurient, but she couldn't resist asking, 'What was it like?'

'Too depraved for me to describe,' he teased her. Lisa gave the tendril of chest hair she was toying with a sharp yank.

'*Ouch*!' he exclaimed. He grabbed her hand when she did it a second time and held it firmly as he said, 'Two of the girls got onto a small stage at one end of the room. They were both wearing short sarongs and high-heeled western shoes. They began to embrace and then slowly, one girl unwound the sarong from the other to show she was wearing nothing but a scanty pair of camiknickers.

'I have to say that it wasn't as exciting as watching you and Solange together that night. Both of them seemed to be rather going through the motions, but nevertheless it held my attention.

'Then it was the other girl's turn and she too was undressed to show that she was wearing a triangle of scarlet fabric over her sex, held in place by ribbons. They began to dance together, rubbing breasts and grinding their mounds against each other.

'It certainly had the desired effect. When they came to the grand-finale, which consisted of them ripping away each other's last covering against indecency, every man in the place had an erection. As soon as they'd left the stage all the men except me grabbed the nearest girl and headed for the stairs. I was left with the bartender and the Madame, who seemed to assume I must prefer my own sex, or possibly something even more aberrant.'

Alex's tone was so rueful that Lisa burst out laughing. They made love one last time and then fell deeply asleep.

The following morning Phyllis Templeton escorted them to buy some practical clothes for travelling through the jungle. Solange pulled a face as she tried on military-style short-sleeved shirts in fawn and khaki cotton and declared that they didn't suit her. But even she had to admit that her delicate silk and voile dresses wouldn't stand up to much wear and tear.

She compromised by ordering some blouses, skirts and trousers in plain shantung and lovat-green silk which the obliging tailoress promised to have ready for the following day. Neither did Solange care for the stout, flat walking shoes they needed.

'High-heels simply aren't possible on the dirt-tracks,' Phyllis warned her. 'You can wear what you like in the house, but you'll have to have something to change into while you're inspecting the plantation or you'll sink into the mud up to your ankles.'

Solange refused point-blank to wear a solar topi, saying she had several hats and parasols which would be perfectly adequate to guard her from the hot sun.

In the afternoon Alex took them to explore some of the white sand, palm-fringed beaches on the west coast. They drove through sleepy fishing villages, some with lovely old villas overlooking small, half-hidden bays.

They swam in the clear turquoise water and ate freshly caught fish, curried and served with rice, exotically prepared vegetables and cucumber.

Afterwards, while Solange and Phyllis dozed in the shade, Alex and Lisa strolled down the beach and made love in a sandy hollow in a rocky outcrop. Afterwards they dived into the sea to wash the sand, perspiration and mingled juices from their bodies.

Despite the uncertainty of her plans, Lisa felt content and at peace and was determined not to let her misgivings about the future encroach on the present.

The following day they were to travel into the heart of Malaya and as, unlike Solange, she had no fear of physical discomfort, she was hoping to enjoy every moment of their journey.

Chapter Seventeen

Lisa was dazzled by the endlessly unfolding panorama of the Malayan mainland. Tree-covered hills, ridges and peaks undulated into the far distance; at close quarters a deep lush green, but fading to misty purple on the horizon.

They started at dawn when a feathery mist hid the surface of the water as the ferry moved slowly towards the palm-edged mainland.

Solange was not in the best of humours at the early start. She'd wanted to set off at a more civilised time – some time around eleven o'clock. Mark had explained that if they left at first light they should just reach the plantation by nightfall. Her suggestion that they should break the journey met with derision from him.

'That's fine by me – I'm used to camping out overnight in the jungle, but I can't see you enjoying sleeping on the ground with snakes slithering over your sleeping bag. Contrary to your expectations, my dear, there aren't any hotels between here and our destination.'

They'd decided to spend the first night at Mr Varonne's house because as far as they knew, there was a still a full complement of staff in attendance. Mark had sent a message that they were coming so they had every expectation of finding beds prepared and a meal ready. Nevertheless he insisted they take what seemed to Lisa to be an inordinate amount of supplies.

Lisa was excited by the prospect of the trip and unlike Solange, wasn't daunted by any potential discomfort. They spent the morning in the first-class carriage of a train which chugged along belching thick black smoke which settled in their hair and on their faces leaving greasy smuts.

But the seats were comfortable enough for Solange to doze off against Mark's shoulder while Lisa looked out of the window at the spectacular scenery. At first the train passed rice fields and swamps, then as it began to climb higher, tree-strewn hills of a rich, verdant green.

They had a large hamper containing a picnic lunch which the hotel had supplied, but the early start had made them all hungry and by midday nothing remained except a few pieces of fruit.

They left the train in the early afternoon and along with several other passengers transferred to a boat, an ancient ramshackle structure captained by a bearded Australian who took frequent pulls from a brown bottle which contained some lethal local spirit.

As they made their way slowly up the river the trees closed in on them, growing all the way to the water's edge, their roots trailing in the thick, brown water. At times the only sky visible was directly overhead and only where the river was at its widest. Where it narrowed they were travelling under a green canopy, giving their journey an unreal, dream-like quality.

The forest seemed to be full of strange squawks and

screeches, making Solange jump. They saw tiny birds with brightly-coloured feathers swooping over the water and occasionally they spotted monkeys, glimpsed only briefly before they vanished back into the trees.

They passed villages where thatched-roofed houses built on stilts stood at the river's edge. The boat stopped at each village to allow other passengers to get on and off and at every stop they were besieged by beautiful brown-eyed children holding out their hands for coins.

By late afternoon they were the only passengers left and when the tropical downpour began, they sought shelter under an ancient tarpaulin which was slung up at one end of the boat. It dripped water relentlessly onto them through the many weak points in the worn canvas. Solange unfurled her parasol and sat beneath it, but the very air held so much moisture that soon she was as wet as the others.

The noise was deafening as the water thundered down through the criss-crossed branches, hitting the river so hard that the spray alone was enough to drench them.

Lisa was constantly aware of Alex, looking lethally attractive in his khaki shirt and shorts, his tanned well-muscled legs brushing against hers as they huddled under the shelter, setting her on fire despite the all-pervading damp.

Several times Lisa got the distinct impression that Solange was about to embark on a litany of complaints, but that she stopped herself because she was aware what Mark's reaction would be.

The light was fading as the boat dropped them at a rickety wooden jetty at a bend in the river. A red dirt road led into the jungle, but there was no-one waiting to meet them and no sign of any habitation.

They unloaded their bags and then the boat pulled away and continued on its journey up the river.

'Shouldn't someone be here?' asked Solange plaintively as their last link with civilisation vanished into the low-hanging mist. The downpour had ceased, but water still dripped steadily from the trees and the air was thick and steamy with moisture.

'It's more than feasible that my message didn't get here,' said Mark, apparently unperturbed. 'But don't worry, Solange – Alex and I will shoot something so you and Lisa can cook it over an open fire. Have you ever eaten monkey?'

Solange hit him with her parasol and broke into a tirade of abusive French, but stopped suddenly as the unmistakable sound of an engine reverberated through the air.

A minute later a jeep came round the bend and came to a halt beside them. A young man with a thatch of tousled tow-coloured hair leapt out.

'I'm Edward Weston, Mr Varonne's overseer,' he greeted them.

Solange, now all smiles, made the introductions.

'I'm sorry about your guardian's death,' he said awkwardly to Lisa. 'He was very much looking forward to your arrival. I'll stay here to keep things going for just as long as you want.' He turned to Solange. 'I knew your husband, Madame Valois and his death shocked us all, but there's a sound, experienced man running the place. I'll take you over there tomorrow if you wish.'

He began to load their cases into the back of the jeep and then they all climbed in and he drove them along the rutted, red dirt road through the darkness. They passed miles of rubber trees, planted in military rows, briefly illuminated by the jeep's headlights.

They passed the shacks where the plantation workers lived. Work now finished for the day the men sat on the wooden steps of their huts while the women tended to the evening meal, cooking in the open air and making Lisa hungry as she was assailed by the spicy, savoury smells.

At last they came to the palm-flanked plantation house. Lamps were burning on the verandah and Lisa was relieved to see that it was a handsome stone building with a pillared facade. She was glad for Solange's sake that they hadn't ended up in a wooden hut.

A Chinese houseboy with a white jacket hurried out to greet them, bowing as Edward introduced Lisa as the new mistress of the house, which thoroughly flustered her. They stepped onto the wide verandah where comfortable rattan furniture was set in an inviting group, the cushions freshly plumped.

The houseboy, who was called Cheng, led them into the sitting room where Solange gave a small exclamation of pleasure at the sight of the drinks tray.

'Could you make us a shaker of gin martinis?' she asked him.

'But of course, Madame,' he replied, looking offended that she was obviously uncertain whether he would be able to do so.

He busied himself at the tray, measuring out the ingredients very deftly and then placing the five glasses on a small silver tray before pouring the drinks and handing them round.

'At what time would you like dinner served, Madame?' he asked Lisa as he proffered her martini with a flourish.

'I'm not sure,' she replied, taken aback that he should be asking her rather than Solange. 'What do you think?' she appealed to the others.

'As soon as we've had time to bathe and change,' was Alex's opinion.

'Perhaps in about an a hour and a half then,' Lisa suggested tentatively.

'Very well, Madame. What would you like prepared?' Lisa had never been the mistress of a house and certainly hadn't the least idea what might be a possibility in the middle of a Malayan rubber plantation, so she told him to serve whatever he thought best. He reeled off a list of dishes which sounded sufficient to feed an army and she nodded weakly.

'Would you like me to take you around the house now, Madame?'

Lisa would really rather have sat and enjoyed her drink, but Solange had sunk onto the sofa and was drinking her martini as if it were the last she'd ever enjoy on earth and didn't look inclined to come to her aid.

'Yes, if it's no trouble,' she murmured reluctantly.

He showed her the large dining room which had a massive mahogany table and a dozen matching chairs. Five places were set, reminding her that Edward might expect to be invited to dine with them.

There was a study with book-lined walls from which, to judge by the piles of papers and documentation, the estate business had obviously been carried out.

There were also six airy bedrooms, including the one which had been Mr Varonne's, each with a double bed shrouded in mosquito netting. She barely glanced inside the one that had been her guardian's, feeling she was somehow intruding on his privacy, particularly since his personal possessions were still scattered around.

'Five of the rooms are ready for occupation,' Cheng informed her tactfully. 'Which will you require?' She allocated the largest bedroom to Solange and Celeste immediately appeared from behind them and began to unpack Solange's vanity case. Unsure of the form Lisa decided to play safe and allotted them a room each, including one for the maid.

The bath house had a large metal tub with carved feet in the middle of a slatted wooden floor and as there was patently no indoor plumbing, Lisa was apprehensive about Solange's reaction.

'We'll need water heating for baths for all of us,' she said hesitantly, but Cheng seemed to take the request in his stride and nodded.

She returned to the sitting room where Alex had mixed another shaker of martinis and Solange – her good humour restored by finding an oasis of civilisation in the middle of the jungle – was flirting with Edward, while Mark scowled at her from across the room.

'There's only one bathroom I'm afraid,' Lisa told them. 'Solange – would you like first bath?'

'Thank you, *chérie*, I would indeed,' she said rising to her feet. 'I feel as though I have been wearing these clothes for a lifetime.'

It was true that they usually bathed and changed their clothes several times a day, the only way to stay fresh in such a humid climate. Lisa thought her own clothing was so stained and crumpled that it would never launder successfully.

Solange left the room to return five minutes later wearing a clinging garnet-silk robe and with a horrified expression on her face.

'Mark, you must bring your gun and stand guard over me while I bathe,' she told him. 'The floor has gaps in it and anything may wriggle, crawl or slither into the room while I am naked in my bath.' Edward blushed a vivid-crimson and looked at his feet while Alex burst out laughing.

Mark didn't look too displeased by the idea and followed Solange along the corridor to do as she asked.

'Where do you live?' Lisa asked Edward, hoping to relieve his embarrassment by making conversation.

'I have a bungalow about half a mile away. There are six overseers and we have a bungalow each and there's a club house with a billiard table in the same compound.'

'Will . . . will you stay and dine with us? You may not find us the best company, we're all rather tired and certainly Solange, Alex and I have never been in the jungle before and we're finding it rather strange.'

'Particularly Solange,' said Alex dryly.

'Thank you, I will,' said Edward eagerly. Lisa wondered if he grew bored of the same faces night after night and thought that it must be a lonely life so far from civilisation.

There was a lot Lisa wanted to know, but she decided it could wait until the following day. She was relieved when Celeste came to tell her that her bath was ready.

'Shall I come and watch over you?' asked Alex, making Edward blush again.

'No, thank you.' Lisa declined the offer. 'But if you hear me scream, please come running.'

Solange and Mark appeared at dinner with the satisfied air of a couple who had just made love. Lisa wished she'd been able to spend some time alone with Alex, but by the time he'd emerged from his bath, dinner was almost ready.

They dined by candlelight at the huge mahogany table. It seemed incongruous to be in evening dress, using solid silver cutlery and drinking from crystal glasses in the middle of the Malayan jungle. The food was surprisingly good and even Solange didn't complain, although all the dishes were typically Malayan.

Soon after dinner Edward excused himself, saying he had an early start and the other four sat on the verandah for a while enjoying some excellent cognac and listening to the sound of what seemed to be hundreds of different species of insects and wildlife chirruping, squawking and calling to each other.

But they were all tired and soon afterwards Solange and Mark excused themselves.

'I think I'll turn in too,' said Lisa, yawning.

'I'll come to your room in a few minutes,' said Alex, his eyes glittering with erotic promise. 'I'll just have a last cigar.'

But such was Lisa's exhaustion that she fell deeply asleep as soon as she got into bed and wasn't aware of Alex joining her. He looked at her recumbent form with regret, but swathed them both in mosquito netting and then fell asleep beside her.

She awoke as a milky dawn light crept into the room and lay looking around, forgetting where she was for a few moments. It was strange to think this was now her house. It had been a disconcerting experience to have the Chinese houseboy turn to her for instructions and she half-wished they were staying on Solange's plantation, so she could just be a guest.

She slipped out of bed in her eau-de-Nil silk nightgown and padded out onto the verandah on bare feet. She was amazed to discover that the house was surrounded by well-tended emerald-green lawns with beds of bright flowers set at intervals, just like an English country house.

But no English country house – as far as she knew – was flanked by tall palm trees, their fronds a pale-silver in the drifting early morning mist. Just a few hundred yards away on the far side of the lawn lay untamed jungle, also at the moment wreathed in mist.

It was an incredibly beautiful outlook and she leant against the verandah rail taking it in and enjoying the cool air on her bare arms.

A sound behind her made her turn her head, just in time to see Alex stepping out of the bedroom, fastening his dressing gown. He came up behind her and put his hands onto the verandah rail on either side of her, effectively imprisoning her. He pressed himself against her and she felt the hardness of his early morning erection, making her instantly aroused.

He lifted her nightgown at the back and caressed her bare bottom, his hands warm against her cool skin. She sighed with pleasure and leant back against him, enjoying his attentions.

His fingers slipped between her thighs and found the soft, moist tissues of her vulva. She parted her legs for him and he stroked her sex-flesh softly, until it began to unfurl like the petals of a flower.

The situation had a dream-like quality to it, invoked by the absolute stillness of their surroundings. Lisa felt as though they could easily be the only two people for hundreds of miles as he pulled gently at her sex-lips, coaxing them apart.

She realised his intention a moment later as he eased his member into position.

'Alex – not here,' she murmured. 'Any of the staff might come round the corner at any moment.'

'No-one's about yet,' he told her, nuzzling her neck and kissing her ear. She felt herself melting, her female honey trickling out of her, readying her inner chamber by coating it with sticky moisture.

He slipped his hand in front of her and rubbed her mound in a persuasive circular movement over the thin stuff of her nightgown. He probed delicately between her legs and found the rapidly stiffening point of her clitoris. He rubbed it through its silk covering and she found the additional stimulation of the soft silk against the sensitive tissue, made her moan and rub her bottom against his granite-hard shaft.

Too late, she felt his member thrusting firmly inside her, penetrating her to her core and making her gasp. Whenever Alex buried his manhood deep inside her she felt a sense of completeness that was intensely satisfying, but particularly so this morning.

He withdrew slightly and then commenced a determined thrusting that had her holding onto the verandah rail and butting her bottom back against him as he made vigorous love to her.

His fingers stayed on her clitoris and he continued to manipulate it skilfully so that heat flooded her body. She came just before he did and they pressed hard against each other as their bodies were racked with the spasms of release.

He withdrew and they went back into the bedroom to slip into bed and fall immediately asleep in each other's arms.

When Lisa woke up she was alone and a glance at the clock told her it was now mid-morning. She rang her bell, hoping it would be Celeste who answered and not the houseboy. Fortunately her wish was granted.

'Are the others all up?' she asked sleepily.

'Mr Channing and Mr Campion have breakfasted and Madame is still asleep,' Celeste informed her.

'Ask Cheng to have some water heated for my bath, would you, please,' she said, yawning.

'*Oui, Mademoiselle*.'

There was no sign of the men when Lisa went into the dining room, but she was soon joined by Solange. With great efficiency Cheng immediately began to bring in dishes and place them on the sideboard.

'Wh . . . what is this?' asked Lisa weakly, as it became obvious they were curry dishes.

'*Naski lemak*,' he beamed. 'Rice cooked in coconut milk with prawn sambal, cucumber, dried anchovies and roasted peanuts. Mr Varonne's favourite breakfast.'

Solange shuddered. 'Do you have any croissants?' she asked.

'No, Madame. I can bring you bread if you wish, also preserves.'

'Please,' she said faintly. 'That disgusting smell is about to make me throw up,' she complained to Lisa. 'As if it is not bad enough that we must have curry for lunch and dinner, now we are presented with it for breakfast too.'

She poured herself a cup of coffee and watched in horror as Lisa put a little of each dish on her plate.

'You surely can't be intending to *eat* that at this time in the morning,' she exclaimed. 'I am mistaken in you, Lisa – you have no sensitivity after all.'

'I'd much rather have a croissant too,' admitted Lisa. 'Or at least bacon and eggs. But someone's gone to a lot of trouble to make all this. I'll speak to Cheng later and ask him to provide something else for breakfast in future.'

Much as she'd grown to like the spicy dishes of the East, it wasn't what she wanted to eat for her first meal of the day, but she managed to struggle through it.

Mark and Alex appeared as the two women were on their second cup of coffee.

'We've been taking a look round,' Alex told them, 'it's like a steam bath out there already. Are you ready to inspect your properties, ladies? Solange – Edward's waiting to take you over to your plantation whenever you're ready.'

'In about ten minutes,' was Solange's reply. She looked at Mark through her long lashes. 'Will you accompany us or shall I go alone with him?'

'I'm coming with you,' he said determinedly. Lisa suppressed a smile. If Solange were as flirtatious with Edward today as she had been last night, Lisa could envisage fireworks ahead.

'There's another jeep parked at the side of the house,' Edward told Alex. 'Would you like one of the other overseers to take you on a tour?'

'We'll be okay on our own, thanks,' replied Alex.

'Stick to the dirt tracks and you'll come across various of the estate workers and the other overseers. I wouldn't go wandering off on foot if I were you. If you run into trouble and require assistance, fire your pistol into the air once.'

Lisa was delighted to have some time alone with Alex. Shortly after the other three had gone she climbed into the jeep beside him and they set off.

There seemed to be literally miles of rubber trees in orderly rows, all of them with a fork at exactly the same height in their slim, grey-brown trunks. Each tree had the same circle of scarred bark around the trunk above a tin cup held in position by wire. They stopped to inspect the way the milky sap ran down a carefully cut curl of bark into the cup, without a drop being wasted.

The estate workers in their colourful sarongs all smiled at them and the overseer who was in charge of this particular group stepped forward to greet them.

'Miss Cavendish?' Lisa nodded and he went on, 'I'm Hans Van Dorst. Please accept my condolences for your loss.' It was obvious that he was Dutch, although his English was excellent. Lisa thanked him and introduced Alex. They exchanged a few words and then drove on.

They rarely saw the sky. It was usually hidden beyond the canopy of intertwined leaves and branches over forty feet above their heads. The interior of the tropical forest was lit by a dim green light and the estate workers fought a constant battle to keep the area around the trees free from the ever-encroaching foliage which threatened to overgrow it on a daily basis.

SENSUAL STORM

After a couple of hours Alex stopped the jeep on a deserted stretch of road and turned towards her. 'All this barely tamed nature is making me hot for you again,' he told her. 'As if it wasn't already bad enough that the climate seems to render me unable to think about anything else as it is.'

She glanced down and saw that his penis was a prominent ridge under his khaki shorts. She laid her hand on it and it twitched and grew even harder. Careless of the consequences, she unzipped his shorts and drew it out, squeezing and kneading it so that he groaned and leant back against the back of his seat, thighs splayed.

Lisa always enjoyed the feeling of power handling Alex's member gave her. She knew that when she touched it his thoughts were of her and her alone, with no room for anything else.

As she caressed it a surge of primitive lust assailed her, making her determined to have him there and then, even if the dense foliage hid hundreds of pairs of eyes and their coupling was witnessed by every species of wildlife in the vicinity.

She glanced at the forest floor, but decided it was too risky to lie down and possibly be bitten or stung by something. Instead she stood up awkwardly and slipped off her silk camiknickers, then turned and climbed astride Alex, facing him.

With her back braced against the steering wheel she managed to get him inside her and then lost her precarious balance and sat down heavily. His shaft felt huge and hot inside her, filling her up and throbbing in a way which made her tingle internally.

She began to move up and down on him, clutching at his

hardness with her internal muscles. He ripped open her khaki silk shirt and scooped her breasts out of her low-cut camisole, pressing his face between them and then covering each in turn with hot, feverish kisses.

His hands clasped her bottom, helping her ride him, their movements perfectly synchronised. Despite the heat she rode him with increasing ferocity, until rivulets of perspiration were trickling between her breasts.

Alex came in a series of boiling spurts, holding her tightly against him, his lips on her breast. But Lisa hadn't quite made it and reached between her own thighs to stimulate her throbbing bud.

She came at last, crying out and then looking swiftly over her shoulder as an answering cry came from the bonnet of the jeep. A small brown monkey sat there watching with interest, its head on one side, and its expression apparently quizzical.

Lisa couldn't help but burst out laughing which made her expel Alex's member far sooner than she'd intended to.

'Let's get back to the house,' she suggested. 'I'm ready for another bath and then some tiffin. Cheng's going to get tired of heating bath water for us all.'

Chapter Eighteen

Lisa had never quite got used to the fact that dusk fell swiftly in the tropics. The sun was setting as she left her bedroom in the plantation house that evening and by the time she reached the verandah outside the sitting room, pausing only briefly to speak to Cheng, it was already dark.

Fireflies began to flit around in the undergrowth on the far side of the lawn and she leant against the verandah rail to watch them. The lamps were already lit and just inside she could hear Cheng clinking glasses as he prepared a shaker of gin slings.

She breathed in the scented night air and on an impulse walked down the steps onto the grass and began to stroll through the gardens. The night was full of the sound of insects and wildlife and she wondered if she'd ever get used to it. Mark had assured her that very soon she wouldn't even notice the noise, but she wasn't altogether convinced.

It seemed strange to think that only a short while ago her guardian had lived in this house and walked in these gardens. She looked back at the lamp-lit verandah and the solid bulk of the house against the night sky and wondered if he'd enjoyed his solitary life.

He'd obviously read a lot – the study was lined with books and she'd found a trunk full of them under his bed – and he'd had Edward and the other overseers for company in the evenings, if he'd felt like it. The plantation Solange had inherited adjoined this one, so there were also the people who lived and worked there for him to socialise with, although the other plantation house was apparently twenty miles away.

She hadn't seen Solange since her return from her own estate. The Frenchwoman had been taking a nap before dinner and hadn't yet emerged.

Lisa reached the edge of the lawns where they gave way to thick undergrowth and then froze with terror when she heard the sound of some large animal moving through the foliage only a few yards away.

Her heart pounding, she wondered whether it would be better to flee back to the house, or remain immobile. What if it were a tiger or a leopard? She cursed her own foolishness for acting as though she were in a London garden. The creature – whatever it was – loomed up in front of her and she gave a whimper of terror – it must be a bear because it was much taller than she was.

But then her terror turned to relief as she realised it was Mark.

'*Mark*!' she exclaimed, clutching the front of his shirt. 'You frightened me to death – I thought you were a tiger or a leopard!'

'You shouldn't be so far from the house,' he told her. 'Not on your own and after dark.' He put his arms around her and she clung to him, breathing in the comforting aroma of starch from his shirt, together with a whiff of the woody smelling cologne he used.

His arms tightened around her and she was suddenly reminded of their shared carnal interlude when he'd thought she was Solange. It became obvious from the way his manhood hardened rapidly against her hip that something much the same was passing through his mind.

He bent his head and kissed her, sending the blood coursing hotly through her veins and making her knees go weak with lust. His hand found her breasts and fondled them over the soft chiffon of her dress. She felt her nipples harden in eager response and pressed against him, parting her legs as he thrust a muscular thigh between them.

'Lisa!' She heard Alex's voice and turning to look back towards the house saw him silhouetted against the lamps, looking out into the darkness.

She doubted if he could actually see them as they were in the shadows of the trees, but he was obviously anxious about her because he went around the corner where the verandah ran down the side of the house and called in that direction too.

'We'd better go back in,' she said to Mark, but he tightened his hold on her.

'Coming!' Lisa called in the direction of the house. Alex hurried down the verandah steps and walked swiftly towards them, so Mark had no option but to release her.

'You had me worried,' said Alex, as soon as he reached them. He took her hand.

'I thought I'd go for a stroll and then I heard Mark in the bushes and assumed he was a tiger or bear,' explained Lisa. 'I almost dropped dead of fright on the spot.'

'I've told her not to go so far from the house on her own

after dark,' said Mark. 'Has Solange honoured us with her presence yet?'

Something in his tone told Lisa that the two of them were enjoying one of their frequent altercations. This was borne out when they reached the verandah and Solange came out, a vision in silver lamé, a silver circlet around her dark hair. The dress plunged almost to the waist at the front showing an indecorous amount of cleavage.

Instead of looking delighted by the sight, Mark scowled. The reason for his ill humour became apparent when Edward was ushered onto the verandah a few moments later by Cheng.

'Lisa, *chérie*, I have invited Edward to dine with us again,' said Solange airily. 'He was so kind to take me to see my inheritance.'

'I . . . it was no trouble,' stammered Edward, blushing. His eyes lighted on Solange's décolletage for the first time and he blushed again.

'It was most obliging of you,' said Solange taking his arm, leading him to the rattan sofa and pulling him down beside her. 'And some time soon all your other oh-so-handsome colleagues must dine with us too – we will have a party.' She shot a triumphant glance at Mark who glared back.

'Why stop there?' he asked from between clenched teeth. 'Surely you could invite all the overseers from your own plantation too, then you'll have over a dozen men with their tongues hanging out instead of just one.'

Solange tossed her head and ignored him, but Edward looked distinctly uncomfortable.

'It was wise of us to stay here,' Solange told Lisa. 'The plantation house on my estate is much smaller and in a very bad state of repair because no-one has lived in it recently. We are much better here with Cheng looking after us so well.' She accepted a drink from the houseboy, smiling at him.

'I hope you have instructed him to have the cook make us something other than curry,' she continued, as soon as Cheng had gone back into the house.

Lisa had in fact merely assented to Cheng's suggestions for the dinner menu, all of which sounded distinctly Eastern.

'I don't think the cook can make anything else,' she said. 'But why don't you talk to him yourself tomorrow and tell him what you'd like. You're so much better at that sort of thing than I am.'

'Very well,' said Solange graciously. 'I will speak to him in the morning.'

They discussed the current state of the rubber market over their drinks then Cheng came out to announce that dinner was ready. It was as Lisa had suspected, another selection of spicy dishes – all of them excellent – but fortunately Solange was too busy goading Mark by flirting with Edward to complain too much.

Mark was drinking heavily and by the end of the meal was in a dangerous mood. There was a muscle going at the side of his mouth and his hard-boned face had a higher colour than usual.

While they were eating, Lisa could see Edward trying not to look at Solange's creamy breasts, but his eyes kept being drawn back to them. As soon as dinner was over he made his excuses and left, obviously aware the situation was becoming explosive.

There was a gramophone in the sitting room and although

the selection of records left a lot to be desired, Solange insisted she wanted to dance. Alex obligingly wound the gramophone up and she pulled him into her arms and began to undulate against him.

Mark had the air of a man goaded beyond endurance as he watched Solange's shapely rump moving in time to the music.

'Don't just sit there like a stuffed shirt,' called Solange, 'ask Lisa to dance.'

Lisa wondered whether to excuse herself and go to bed. She had an uneasy feeling that the situation would soon be out of control, although Alex appeared to be completely unruffled by it.

To her surprise Mark seemed to get a grip on himself and rose to his feet.

'Shall we?' he asked her. He led her out onto the verandah and held out his arms. Lisa moved into them and began to dance, the skirts of her hyacinth-blue chiffon dress swirling out around her.

She knew that Mark was both angry and aroused – a potentially lethal combination.

Although his knowledge of the country and language had been invaluable to them, Lisa half-wished it had been Roland who'd accompanied them instead. Roland's easy charm and light-hearted approach to life had never antagonised Solange the way that Mark's possessive and confrontational attitude did.

But Mark was a very attractive man and Lisa had thought about the night they'd spent together more than once and always with a quickening in her sex-flesh. She knew he wanted her, she also knew that to a certain extent it was to spite Solange, but she didn't care.

She looked up into his face, saw the desire there and felt her stomach kick with an answering lurch of lust. His hands moved over her body, working the skirts of her dress upwards until he could reach beneath it to caress her stockinged thighs.

They continued to dance and he steered her around the corner where the verandah ran past the bedrooms. Lisa was finding it difficult to breathe, particularly when he slipped his hand between her thighs and rubbed her vulva over the slippery silk of her camiknickers.

She knew that the strip of fabric was damp and knew he realised it too as he inhaled sharply. They swayed against each other as he continued to rub her lewdly, before managing to slip his fingers into her camiknickers and then inside her.

She gasped and pressed herself against him, finding the hard ridge of his manhood and squeezing it feverishly. She became oblivious to the fact that Solange and Alex were still dancing in the sitting room, in fact she became oblivious to everything except her own all-consuming need and the answering one she could sense in Mark.

She ripped open his trousers with trembling fingers, drawing out his hot, throbbing shaft. His hands clasped her bottom and she guided his member up the loose-fitting leg of her camiknickers until she felt it against her sex-flesh.

With one vigorous thrust it was inside her, then he lifted her and she wound her legs around his waist. He supported her with his hands under her bottom and she held onto his shoulders, wriggling so that the full, glorious length of him was deep inside her, filling her up and making her even more desperate for satisfaction.

She began to move on him, raising herself slowly then

grinding against him hard on each downward movement. He grasped her bottom tightly, raising her and jamming her back down on his hugely distended manhood.

The gramophone music filtered out to them, almost drowned by the insect cacophony and occasionally accompanied by the sound of Solange's husky laugh, but neither of them registered anything except their own urgent pleasure.

Their rhythmic movements had become so frenzied that the verandah was shaking beneath them. Mark was just giving half a dozen last desperate thrusts, when over his shoulder Lisa glimpsed Solange, her eyes wide with surprise.

But it was too late to call a halt. As Mark exploded into a volcanic release Lisa ground herself against him, needing just a little more stimulation. She felt her internal muscles contract spasmodically then she too felt the blood thundering in her ears and came, her head falling back on her shoulders and a loud cry issuing from her lips.

Mark staggered the couple of yards to the wall of the house and supported her with her back against it, unable to stop his legs from trembling after such a cataclysmic climax. Lisa slowly unwound her own legs so she could slide to her feet, but continued to cling to Mark's shoulders, afraid she might lose her balance.

The sound of clapping made them both look round; Solange was applauding them, a wanton smile on her face.

'Please continue,' she urged them. 'Come, Mark – I know you can do much better than that once you get into your stride.'

Alex lounged just behind her, his face in shadow, a glass in his hand. As they watched he came up behind the Frenchwoman, slid his hands into the front of her low-cut dress and began fondling her breasts.

Solange arched her back and pressed herself against him, running her hands up and down his thighs. Alex pulled the narrow straps of her dress down her arms, baring her breasts and continued to toy with them. He tugged her brown nipples gently and weighed the ample, creamy orbs in his hands.

His face was no longer in shadow and Lisa could see his long, narrow eyes glittering challengingly as they met first Mark's eyes and then her own.

Lisa took Mark's hand and led him to a rattan lounger. They stretched out on it together then Lisa said, 'We're just taking a breather – it's your turn.' She knew she was taking a calculated risk and that Mark might not be able to endure watching Solange with Alex, but his possessiveness was spoiling their sojourn.

In contrast, Alex who had been so jealous and moody during the early part of the voyage, had become much less so after their group sex-scenes.

She took Mark's quiescent member in her hand and fondled it persuasively, hoping that the implicit promise of more carnal dalliance with her would be enough to stop him erupting into violence.

Alex continued to caress Solange's breasts, then her belly while she writhed against him, still smiling at them provocatively. He picked her up and deposited her on the verandah rail with her back to one of the handsome pillars which were set at intervals around it.

She freed her arms from her shoulder straps so she was naked to the waist and then drew the skirt of her silver lamé dress up her thighs. Her sheer stockings were held up by two black satin garters each of which had a trailing bow of narrow black ribbons. He pushed her knees apart and she hooked the high-heels of her silver kid shoes onto the lower rail and leant back against the pillar.

It was, Lisa was well aware, the sort of scenario her friend revelled in – one lover about to pleasure her while another deeply possessive lover watched.

Solange was wearing a pair of silver-grey camiknickers and Lisa was startled when instead of drawing them down her thighs, Alex hooked his fingers in them and ripped them across the crotch, leaving them dangling in tatters around Solange's mound.

Her sex was now fully on display, a deep glistening crimson. Alex caressed her thighs and then slowly peeled her garter down her shapely legs, so one stocking fell in sluttish wrinkles around her knee.

He took the garter and slowly, with infinite patience, inserted it into Solange's sex with the tip of his forefinger. At last all that remained visible was a bow of frivolous black satin, looking distinctly lewd as it trailed over her vulva.

Mark's shaft which had been hardening slowly as Lisa caressed it, burgeoned into renewed life at the sight.

Alex pulled a rattan stool nearer to Solange and knelt on it. He leant forward and with the tip of his tongue began to trace the slick folds of Solange's sex-lips, delving into the intricate petals and then flicking his tongue wickedly over the swollen crimson point of her clitoris.

Solange, eyes half-closed and lips parted, idly stroked her own breasts while Alex continued with his oral ministrations.

She had the contented air of a sleek cat as she enjoyed all the attention.

Alex took her engorged bud between his lips and began to suck, making her moan softly as her arousal spiralled upwards. She clutched the rail with both hands, as if afraid she might lose her balance and fall, then her head dropped back against the pillar.

Alex began to strum her clit hard with his tongue, moving it faster and faster until Solange let out a louder moan and convulsed into a climax.

Alex took the trailing ribbons of her garter between his teeth and pulled them out of her, letting them fall in a tiny damp heap onto the wooden floor of the verandah. He stood up, bent forward to kiss her and she bit him on the lip hard.

With a muffled curse he scooped her off the rail and strode into the dining room through the open door. Lisa and Mark turned their heads to watch as he laid her on her back on the table, ripped open his trousers and plunged into her.

From where they were it looked almost more like fighting than copulating. Alex held Solange's hands above her head and thrust into her with relentless vigour, while she writhed under him like a maddened cat.

She bucked her hips upwards to meet each virile thrust, panting and moaning beneath him, trying to free her wrists. But Alex had had Solange in this mood before and knew that if he didn't keep her hands imprisoned, she'd lacerate him with her nails or strike him.

Usually making love to her was a voluptuous, infinitely passionate experience, but once in a while her usual serenity was cast aside and she went beyond passion to behave in a way that bordered on violent.

But Alex was more than a match for her and continued to plunge in and out of her until at last, exhausted by her struggles and another explosive climax, she lay passively back and allowed him to subdue her.

At long last Alex was able to let go and enjoy the pleasure of release, pumping his juices into her in a series of staccato jerks, then collapsing on top of her on the mahogany table top.

Mark turned back to Lisa, his eyes glinting with renewed lust. She'd become unbearably excited watching Alex and Solange together, particularly when she recalled some of the times he'd made love to her in the same way.

She rose from the rattan lounger, threw her skirts up over her waist and undid her sodden camiknickers so they fell down around her ankles. She stepped out of them and bent over the end of the lounger, offering him the pert swellings of her shapely *derrière*. His penis towered massively up against his belly as he stood up and moved to stand behind her.

In the balmy evening air, Lisa gave herself up to yet more lewd, carnal pleasure.

Chapter Nineteen

By the time that Solange appeared for breakfast the following day, Lisa, Alex and Mark had already been up for several hours and had been for a walk through the forest. Lisa had been enchanted to spot a miniature mouse-deer as well as several monkeys and – rather less endearing – a huge coiled snake which she'd given a wide berth.

They came back and were enjoying a freshly brewed pot of coffee in the dining room when they heard Solange's high-heeled shoes on the wooden floor as she came down the hallway.

The efficient Cheng had already put out bread and preserves, but nevertheless Solange still pulled a face when she saw the accompanying array of spicy dishes waiting for her.

To Lisa's relief there had been no indication of any awkwardness between Alex and Mark this morning and Solange too appeared to be in a sunny mood and kissed Mark passionately when she came in.

'Today I shall speak to the cook,' she announced. 'Tonight we shall have some civilised food. Perhaps steak in red wine or chicken in a delicate cream sauce with *pommes frites* and whatever fresh vegetables are available. I shall ask him to bake croissants for tomorrow morning too.'

Mark raised one eyebrow but, unusually, forbore to comment.

'What do you want to do today?' he asked her.

'I thought we might enjoy a picnic until the inevitable downpour this afternoon, which is when I shall work my way through the huge pile of papers relating to my rubber plantation which I brought back with me yesterday.'

'Sounds good to me,' commented Alex lazily. 'You'd better speak to Cheng, Lisa, and get him to organise a picnic.'

'I know just the spot,' said Mark. 'One of the overseers mentioned it yesterday; we'll stop off and get directions on our way out.'

Lisa went to find Cheng while Solange strolled to the back of the house in search of the cook. She was rather surprised to find him outside behind the house, chopping ingredients on a massive wooden chopping block.

He was Malayan and ceased chopping to bow courteously as she approached.

'Good morning, do you speak English?' she greeted him. He bowed again and so she launched into her suggestions for future meals while he bowed and smiled politely. Satisfied that her mission had been successful, she thanked him and returned to the others.

They took a jeep and after getting directions from the Dutch overseer bounced along the uneven dirt road. Their destination was about an hour's drive away and was well worth the rather uncomfortable journey.

It was a small freshwater lake fed by a waterfall and surrounded by trees covered in blossoming vine. The surface of the lake was dotted by lotus flowers in pink and white, floating lazily in the late morning heat.

It was possibly the most beautiful scene Lisa had ever laid eyes on. The water was a clear, limpid blue and just beneath the surface hundreds of small brilliantly-coloured fish darted around, swimming in synchronised shoals.

While Alex threw a blanket on the ground for them to sit on, Mark divested himself of his clothes and plunged into the water, sending the fish fleeing in consternation.

Lisa sank gratefully onto the blanket in the shade of a tree and watched his broad shoulders admiringly as he cleaved through the water to the centre of the lake and then floated on his back.

Alex too began to strip off. 'Coming in?' he asked them.

'If you'd told us we were picnicking by a lake, I'd have brought a swimming costume,' said Lisa. She knew she was being unreasonably coy considering how they'd spent yesterday evening, but somehow she couldn't quite bring herself to undress in front of all three of them and step into the water naked.

'Wear your underwear, *chérie* – it will dry in minutes in the sun when you emerge,' suggested Solange.

'Are you coming in?' Lisa asked.

Solange shuddered. 'I prefer not to swim where creatures might bite my toes. There may be water snakes or crabs and I do not care for fish except on my plate. You, I know, have no sensitivity, Lisa, and do not mind such things.'

She stretched out on the blanket and yawned. 'I may take a little nap before lunch.'

Alex dived into the water and swam out towards the centre

while Lisa stripped down to her pearl-coloured camisole and camiknickers and stepped tentatively in. It was colder than she expected, but warm in comparison to the icy waters of the Scottish lochs where she was accustomed to swim.

The lake sloped steeply until the water was waist deep and then shelved more gradually towards the centre. After the sticky journey in the steamy heat of the jungle it felt marvellous to be immersed in cool water and feel it caressing her perspiration-damp skin.

She swam slowly into the deeper water, avoiding the trailing roots of the lotus flowers and then dived under the surface to watch the fish swimming along the bottom.

She struck out for the far side and climbed out by the waterfall, perching on a rock and enjoying the spray falling in a fine rainbow-hued mist over her.

There was a rock ledge which led behind the cascade of water and she decided to explore it. Picking her way with care – it was very slippery – she found herself in a cave hidden from view by the wall of water.

It was noticeably cooler in there and she looked around in the dim light wondering when someone had last entered it. She emerged from behind the waterfall on the other side and found herself among mossy rock pools where a large tree had fallen and was trailing its branches in the water.

She sat astride the tree, her feet dangling in the rock pool and gave herself up to day dreams. It was strange to think that she used to spend a lot of her time sitting in the window high up in the tower of the castle in Scotland, weaving dreams for hours at a time. Now it was becoming an increasingly rare occurrence.

As she allowed her mind to conjure up dark, erotic images she rubbed herself against the tree trunk, using it stimulate her bud. She was almost on the point of climaxing when she heard a sound from somewhere to her rear. Before she had time to jerk her head round she was seized from behind and a hand clapped over her mouth.

She couldn't tell whether it was Alex or Mark, but she remained obediently quiet, every cell in her body tingling with a combination of alarm and anticipation. He took his hand away from her mouth and she felt something soft and dark being tied over her eyes. He grabbed her around the waist and lifted her from the tree, then bent her over it.

She was startled to feel her wrists being tied together and then secured to something. Her legs were pulled apart and then each of her ankles also tied so she was held immobile. It wasn't an altogether comfortable position, but the erotic charge she got from being helplessly tethered while one of the men she was enjoying an ongoing carnal relationship with prepared to do what he wanted with her, made her breathless with lust.

She still wasn't sure whether it was Alex or Mark but thought she'd be able to tell once he touched her. She felt him draw her dripping camiknickers under the overhang of her bottom so her buttocks were exposed and then felt something probing the cleft between them.

She couldn't tell what it was, but she felt herself tensing as it made contact with her sex-flesh. It was smooth and hard with a certain springiness to it, making her think it must be a switch cut from a tree.

He moved it gently along the grooves of her sex-flesh,

teasing and separating the overlapping petals of her labia then circling the entrance to her hidden chamber. She inhaled sharply as she felt it sliding inside her about an inch and then being twitched from side to side.

She felt a certain uneasiness that she was being penetrated by something not flesh and blood and her internal muscles tautened. The switch was withdrawn and then she felt it rubbing against the point of her clitoris with a determined, insidious pressure.

The stimulation was too direct and too hard and she squirmed and tried to move away, but her bonds held her firmly in position and she had no choice but to bear it.

She could feel the perspiration forming between her breasts and the heat rising through her body. The friction against her clitoris was having the intended effect, even if she wasn't actually enjoying it very much.

She moaned and writhed as much as the constraining ties would allow, then worked her internal muscles, hoping to precipitate her orgasm. It broke over her in a wave of drenching heat and thankfully the switch was withdrawn.

A moment later she heard the sound of it swishing through the air and screamed out loud as she anticipated it landing on her bare buttocks with what she could only imagine would be considerable force. But instead it slammed into the tree to one side of her and then she heard it falling into the rock pool with a little splash.

She was reminded of the first time she'd seen Alex as he'd worked a riding crop between Solange's thighs with erotic expertise. Was it him? Was he punishing her for having allowed Mark to have sex with her last night? Or was it Mark, playing some strange game of his own?

She wasn't sure, but part of her wanted him to release her and remove her blindfold so they were on equal terms and part of her wanted the deviant game to continue.

The next thing she felt was her buttocks being pulled apart and then with no warning, whoever it was plunged into her, reaching around her to find her breasts.

It was a rough and careless coupling and if she hadn't been dripping with warm moisture it would probably have been very uncomfortable. He rammed in and out of her so her pubis was worked backwards and forwards over the tree bark, arousing her against her will.

She was so disoriented that she was unable to tell who it was. There was no finesse and no further attempt to give her pleasure, just a coupling so primitive it bordered on the savage.

It was over very quickly and within seconds of obtaining his release he pulled out of her, leaving hot juices trickling down her thighs. The covering over her eyes was snatched away and then he was gone without her having had as much as a glimpse of him.

She blinked a few times, dazzled by the sunshine, and then glanced down and saw that her wrists were secured by a length of trailing creeper. It took her a few minutes to work herself free and then push herself upright before leaning down to release her ankles. She saw the switch floating in the water and picked it up after pulling her camiknickers back up over her hips.

It had been cut from a tree with a knife and the end rubbed smooth with a pebble or something similar. She wondered if he'd actually intended to beat her with it and changed his mind at the last minute, or just wanted to alarm her. Well he'd certainly succeeded in that.

She bent to wash herself in the rock pool then rather stiffly made her way back behind the waterfall and out the other side, thinking she'd soon know which of them it was – he couldn't have had time to swim all the way across the lake.

But she saw immediately that both Mark and Alex were on the opposite bank, Mark lying next to Solange on the blanket and Alex sitting on a rock nearby. Surely whoever it was wouldn't have had time to swim back so quickly?

But if it hadn't been either of them, who had it been? Puzzled, she slipped into the water and made her way slowly towards them.

Something she didn't quite understand prevented her from asking outright. Was it possible that one of the overseers had followed them, hoping for an opportunity to present itself to take advantage of either of the women? She shivered at the thought, even in the warm water.

Perhaps it was best if she didn't know.

After lunch – another selection of highly spiced dishes which Solange ate with a pained expression – she and Mark vanished into the trees leaving Lisa and Alex stretched out on the blanket.

'They'll be ages,' commented Alex. 'Take your underwear off so it will dry properly.' Her camisole and camiknickers were in fact already dry, but now she was alone with Alex, Lisa didn't mind removing them.

She laid them on a rock and then lay down and closed her

eyes, revelling in the steamy warmth and Alex's close proximity.

The heat, the food and drink she'd just consumed and her long swim combined to make her drowsy. Alex picked a brilliantly coloured blossom and began to stroke her breasts with it, then her belly, then her mound.

She became lost in an erotic doze, half aware that Alex was continuing to touch her gently, twirling the blossom by its stem against her thighs and then running it down her leg.

In her semi-somnolent state she enjoyed what felt like hundreds of tiny caresses, like a much loved and constantly petted cat. She felt him toying with her pubic fleece and then her labia, lifting the slick tissues and tugging at them gently.

She was also aware of something else, something she couldn't quite place, as he continued to touch her. He seemed to be sliding something inside her, but whatever it was it had no bulk or substance because when she contracted her internal muscles, there was nothing there.

Then he turned his attention to her clitoris, stroking it softly and tenderly, taking her from a state of being half asleep to one of intense arousal without her ever quite coming fully round.

As her excitement mounted she began to thrash her head from side to side, enjoying wave after wave of mounting heat. She felt as though she'd been poised on the brink of coming for some considerable time, but instead of the urgency she usually experienced, she was content to remain there, revelling in the anticipation.

Her climax was luxuriously languid, leaving her bathed in a voluptuous sense of well-being. She opened her eyes to look at him and then smiled as she saw what he'd done.

Two large white flowers had been laid over her breasts, their overlapping petals and bright ochre centres forming a sweetly-scented bra. Several tiny blue flowers had been woven into her silken fleece, the cool gentian-blue a pretty contrast to her red-gold floss.

But the *pièce de résistance* consisted of several scarlet blossoms apparently growing from her sex, the stems of which he'd secreted among the nestling folds of her vulva and the entrance to her hidden chamber.

'I'd like a painting of you just like that,' Alex told her. 'I'd keep it in my bedroom for my eyes only.'

One by one he plucked the flowers from her vulva then covered her body with his own. He made love to her with languorous skill, moving over her as if they were two parts of the same whole.

When at last it was over and he lay to one side of her, she saw that the blooms on her breasts and in her fleece had been crushed and were little more than fragments of petal and leaf. She felt a fleeting sadness at the sight.

They waded out into the lake to bathe and then returned to the shore to dress. Alex looked at his watch.

'I'd better call the others,' he commented. 'If we don't set off back soon, we're going to be caught in the rain.'

He was right. By the time Solange had dressed and rearranged her hair it was late afternoon and the rain hit them as they drove the last few miles.

Sitting in the back of the jeep with only the blanket to drape over her as the sheets of rain deluged down, Lisa wished there was somewhere they could stop and seek shelter. But she knew there was nowhere between where they were and the house.

The rain thudded down with such force that it was painful. Solange had initially used her parasol to shield herself, but it had been battered into a damp rag within minutes. Now her shrieks and exhortations to drive faster were obviously infuriating Mark.

They began an altercation which made Lisa inwardly groan and it was with a heartfelt sense of relief that she leapt out of the vehicle when it drew up outside the house.

Happily, Solange and Mark seemed to have made it up in the interval before dinner and she appeared gay and smiling in a scarlet gown with a dropped waist and a scalloped hem. It was cut to a deep vee at the back but was decorously high at the front.

Celeste had inserted a scarlet feather into the back of Solange's glossy brown hair which had been piled up rather than left hanging in her usual bob. Her lipstick and nail varnish echoed the colour of her frock and she made an attractive sight as she sashayed onto the verandah with her usual undulating walk.

Alex handed her a champagne cocktail and they enjoyed their drinks to the usual background noise of a million insects.

'Whatever do they do to make such a racket?' Lisa wondered aloud. 'Some of it is a kind of chirruping, but goodness knows what else they do.'

'Do they not rub their legs together, or some such thing?' said Solange brightly. 'Mark – why do they do that?'

'Damned if I know,' he replied. 'Maybe they're trying to start a fire.'

'I'm so hungry,' observed Solange, changing the subject. 'I haven't had a decent meal since we left the *S.S. Orient.*'

'What are we having?' asked Alex. 'Remind me.'

'Either steak or chicken in a wine sauce with *pommes frites* and fresh vegetables,' said Solange happily. 'My mouth is already watering.'

Lisa saw Mark's eyes had a satirical gleam in them and felt a moment's unease. But Solange had a large house in Paris and was used to dealing with staff – surely everything would go smoothly.

The first course was a selection of sliced fresh fruits in a palm-sugar syrup. Solange spooned down the pineapple, starfruit, roseapple and guava with exclamations of delight, pleased not to have been presented with a spicy soup, or battered vegetable fritters.

Cheng removed their plates, then after a pause he carried in a selection of covered dishes. He laid them on the table, bowed and removed the covers, announcing proudly, 'Chicken . . . beef . . . fresh vegetable.'

There was a silence as they all inspected what was patently a chicken curry, a beef curry and dishes of spiced sweet potatoes and yams.

After a prolonged silence Lisa said faintly, 'Thank you, Cheng – everything looks delicious.'

He bowed and left the room. As soon as he was out of earshot Mark burst out laughing and helped himself to a large helping of chicken curry.

'I don't think the cook's grasp of English must have been quite as good as you thought,' he teased Solange. She looked at the dish of curry and then at Mark and for a few seconds

Lisa held her breath, almost certain that Solange was going to pick up the dish and dump its contents on Mark's head.

But then she too burst out laughing and reluctantly helped herself to a spoonful of sweet potatoes.

'We must hurry and conclude our business here,' she said resignedly, 'so we may return to civilisation and proper cuisine. I shall devote myself to business over the next few days and you must do the same, *chérie*.'

Lisa smiled and nodded, but mentally, she had to admit to herself that she was in no hurry to leave this paradise and face the uncertainties of the future.

Chapter Twenty

For the next few days both Solange and Lisa applied themselves to learning as much about their two plantations as they could. Solange soon decided on the approximate price her inheritance should fetch and resolved to put it on the market the day they returned to Penang.

Lisa's situation was more confusing. She knew that the sensible thing would be to sell hers too, but she'd swiftly come to love living in the solid, comfortable house surrounded by so much unsurpassed beauty. She felt that if she parted with the estate she would be completely rootless and more and more she was considering bringing in a manager to run it and keeping it as a base she could return to whenever she felt like it.

Living there all the year round wasn't practical – it was too isolated – but she could imagine spending some of her time there, either with or without guests.

Solange had no such considerations, her plan was simply to get the best price possible and then return to France.

Lisa discussed the situation with Alex who thought that the idea of keeping it was financially sound as it would give her another source of money in addition to her investment income.

When the day came for them to return to Penang, Lisa felt very sad. She'd spent a day going through her guardian's personal possessions and felt that really she knew as little about him as she had before.

She decided that whatever happened she'd return to the plantation before leaving the country. She'd advertise for a manager and then perhaps make the journey with him to get him settled into his new position.

Edward drove them back to the river and they waited for over an hour for the antiquated riverboat to come round the bend and stop to pick them up.

After an uneventful trip down the river they boarded a train where Solange sank into her seat and promptly fell asleep. Lisa stared out of the window watching the glorious panorama, wondering how her friend could sleep when there was so much beauty to observe.

The rhythm of the train transmitted itself through her slender frame and she found she was becoming aroused. It seemed to be making her very sex vibrate with barely suppressed lust and she found herself pressing her thighs together and working her internal muscles. Idly she wondered if it would be possible to bring herself to a climax in this manner.

Her eyes met Alex's and a slow flush spread upwards from her throat as she realised that he sensed her excitement. He leant across and laid his hand on her knee and the heat of his caress made wayward darts of lust shoot up her thigh to make her kernel of pleasure throb demandingly.

He left their compartment and returned a while later, to beckon to her.

'Where are we going?' she asked as he took her hand and led her down the corridor.

'I bribed the attendant to let us have a sleeping compartment for a couple of hours,' he told her. A little squib of carnal anticipation began to fizz high up in her sex at the idea of making love on the train.

The compartment was very small, but it did have a wash basin next to which were two snowy towels and the high, narrow bunk had been let down and made up with clean sheets.

'We won't both fit on that,' said Lisa dubiously.

But Alex was already stripping off his clothes, before hauling himself onto it. It wasn't long enough for him to stretch out and when Lisa climbed up to join him she had to lie on top of him.

She tried to climb astride his lean frame, but the bunk simply wasn't wide enough to accommodate her knees. She got down again to let Alex off and then went back up and crouched on all-fours, thinking that if he crouched behind her, they might just manage to make love. But the position she adopted gave Alex another idea.

'Turn so you're facing the wall,' he directed her. She did so, presenting him with the glorious sight of the pert mounds of her backside.

He eased her thighs apart, opening her up to him completely and then when she felt his warm breath on her private parts, caressing it like an erotic ether, she realised that standing up his face was level with her sex. She felt his lips on her silken posterior and then he kissed and nibbled it, making her wriggle with sheer carnal pleasure.

His tongue began a prolonged exploration of the ridges and valleys of her vulva, flickering in and out of her molten core, bringing her slowly to boiling point.

The train's vibrations continued to add their own salacious edge to the proceedings, so she was soon running with warm moisture which Alex lapped eagerly up as quickly as she could produce it.

The warmth of his mouth was replaced by his forefinger, which he slid slowly inside her, pressing outwards against her velvety tunnel as he swivelled it around. He increased the pressure which made her shiver with longing to be penetrated by something else, something much larger which would fill her completely.

She felt his hands on her waist and he lifted her down from the bunk. With her back to him she held onto it while he grasped her by the hips to steady her.

The lurching of the train made it difficult for him to position his member at the entrance to her hot, slick core, so she reached behind her and guided him to it.

'*Aah*!' she cried as a particularly vigorous movement of the carriage made him plunge into her with a force he hadn't intended. Briefly, she felt she'd been violently skewered on his shaft, before he began to move in and out of her and waves of pleasure replaced the fleeting moment of discomfort.

The rattling of the train added another dimension of sensation as all their movements were intensified. Lisa held onto the bunk for dear life while Alex held onto her. They swayed and buffeted against each other in a gloriously wild coupling until with a gasp and a long moan Lisa came, clenching her buttocks and butting her rump back at him as she was overtaken by a series of convulsions that left her trembling and drenched in perspiration.

But Alex kept going for several more minutes before erupting into her in a scalding rush and holding her tightly against him until they both sank exhausted to the floor.

They took it in turns to wash as best they could in the hand basin. Lisa soaked her small towel and used it to rub over her damp body, then lay on the bunk for a few minutes while Alex performed his own ablutions.

When they returned to the first-class carriage Solange opened her eyes to look at them and smiled knowingly, before dozing off again.

The last leg of the journey by ferry from the mainland to Penang took place in the torrential downpour, but part of the boat was under cover so the discomfort was minimised.

As she walked up the steps of the E & O Solange sighed happily.

'How wonderful it will be to be able to luxuriate in a bath without fearing that some horrible creature will slither up between the slats in the floor and frighten me,' she announced as she waited for her key.

'Does that mean you don't want me to stand guard with my gun?' asked Mark. 'I have to admit that I enjoyed watching you bathe.'

'Then you had better come and guard me again, in case bandits burst in through the door to ravish me and steal my jewels,' suggested Solange sweetly. 'Tonight I shall dine in the hotel and enjoy the finest western food the chef can prepare.'

Almost delirious with delight at the prospect, she took her

key and smiled a cat-like smile of sheer sensual anticipation at Mark.

Once up in her room she ran a deep bath and tossed in a handful of scented essence before discarding her clothes and getting in. Mark leant against the door frame and watched her with his arms folded, his eyes lingering on where the points of her chocolate-coloured nipples just broke the surface.

'Come – wash my back,' she demanded imperiously. He crossed the room and picked up the sponge, rubbing a cake of scented soap against it. Solange leant forward and he moved it in slow circles up and down her slender spine.

'I've got something to tell you,' he said, washing her creamy shoulders.

'What?' she asked, leaning back against the bath as he ran the sponge down her arm and then washed between each finger as if she were a child.

'It's about your husband.'

Solange's eyes flew open and she looked at him warily.

'Tell me what it is,' she said.

'One of your overseers told me that two other owners of rubber plantations in the area were found shot in just the same way in the following months. They caught the chap who did it only a short while ago. It seems he had a chip on his shoulder because his own plantation had failed and he was determined to bump off as many successful planters as he could. I've contacted the District Officer and asked him to let you have full details.'

There was a long silence while Solange digested what he'd told her.

'Murdered,' she murmured at last. 'Poor Maurice – to die like that.'

'I'm sorry for the things I said,' said Mark awkwardly.

'And so you should be,' she flashed at him. 'They were terrible things.'

'I know,' he admitted. 'But I wanted you from the first moment I ever laid eyes on you and it seemed as if you were flitting from affair to affair with just about every man you knew, except me. When I saw you on board the *S.S. Orient* I wanted to make you suffer as much as I'd suffered watching you from afar in Paris.'

Solange's eyes widened at this unexpected confession.

'You must learn not to be so possessive, *chérie*,' she told him.

'I've admitted I was wrong about your husband's death,' he growled. 'But that doesn't mean you're not the most selfish, pleasure-seeking, promiscuous slut I've ever met. But all that's going to change. From now on you're going to be faithful to me if I have to keep you under lock and key.'

Solange sat up so abruptly that a wave of water splashed over the side of the bath and soaked Mark's shirt.

'That will never happen,' she declared flatly. 'I will take to bed whom I please, whenever I please.'

'Then I'll make love to you so often and for so long, you won't have the energy to look around you for other lovers,' he ground out from between clenched teeth. She reached out and patted his cheek patronisingly.

'You must stop getting so angry about things,' she told him. 'Did I make a big scene when I discovered you'd bedded Lisa?' She remembered belatedly that in fact she'd berated him soundly and continued hurriedly, 'If I choose to take every virile man I meet in the street as my lover I shall do so and you will have nothing to say about it if you wish to go on seeing me.'

Goaded beyond endurance he reached into the bath and scooped her out, holding onto her slippery nude body with difficulty as he strode into the bedroom. She squirmed and wriggled in his arms and then hit him on the side of the head crying, 'Let me go or I'll scream my head off and bring everyone in the hotel running!'

'Go ahead!' he snapped, throwing her on the bed and ripping open his trousers. 'If you want an audience for what's about to happen.' He pinned her down and covered her mouth with his, kissing her into silence.

Lisa, in the next room, heard the sound of yet another altercation and smiled, glad that her own relationship with Alex wasn't as stormy. Alex had taken a room at the E & O, having decided that staying with his agent was too restricting to his movements.

They dined in the hotel and Solange gave herself up to an extravagant feast which contained not a single trace of curry, rice or coconut milk.

She finished with *bombe au chocolat* and eventually laid down her spoon with a satisfied smile.

'How thankful I am that this hotel serves other food than the dreadful curry – I can't wait to embark on my return journey to Europe. Mark, how long do you think it will take to sell my plantation?'

'Difficult to say. If you wanted to make a quick sale you

could drop the price. The figure you've decided on is a fair one, but it may still take time to find a buyer. Why not start at that and drop it if there aren't any takers?'

Lisa could see Solange's desire to return home as soon as possible vying with her shrewd business sense.

'And you, *ma petite*, what will you do?' she asked Lisa.

'I'm going to appoint a manager and keep my plantation for a while. I may travel around the East for a few months and maybe even visit Roland. It seems silly to have journeyed all the way out here to go straight back without having seen much.'

Solange's face fell.

'I was hoping you'd travel back on the same ship as me. It was so amusing on the outward journey.'

Mark's expression darkened. 'I can't leave here until at least next year,' he pointed out. 'You seem to have forgotten I've business interests of my own which I've postponed attending to so I could help you with yours. I'm going to have to spend some time in Kuala Lumpur and then Singapore.'

Solange raised her delicate winged eyebrows. 'I'm most grateful to you for coming with us into the jungle which was most primitive and even worse than I expected, but as soon as my estate is sold I shall return to France.'

'I've just told you that I can't travel back until next year,' he growled, his face hardening.

'So I am to delay my trip until you can travel too? Impossible.' Solange gave a haughty toss of her head and then took another sip of brandy. She turned to Lisa. 'Let me urge you not to remain in this uncivilised country, *chérie*. I was hoping you would make your home with me in Paris – at least for a time. We would be so well amused and meet so many charming, delightful men.'

She shot a challenging glance at Mark while Lisa groaned inwardly. Mark pushed back his chair and threw down his napkin, his face like thunder.

'Then it's over between us. You selfish little bitch – have you ever in your life considered anyone other than yourself?'

Solange didn't reply and Mark stormed out of the restaurant, drawing many curious glances from their fellow diners. Solange rearranged her bracelets with an air of studied indifference and then turned back to Lisa.

'Do say you'll come to Paris with me.'

'Solange, I'd love to,' replied Lisa, touched. 'But I really would like to remain here a little longer. Wouldn't you consider staying until the new year?'

Solange shook her head. 'It's the cuisine, *chérie*, I really can't abide it. What about you, Alex? How long do you plan to be out here?'

'A few months at least. First I have to find out where money belonging to my family is disappearing to, then I intend to travel around once that business is resolved.'

Solange made a moue of disappointment. 'Then I will travel alone. If you'll both excuse me, I'm tired and shall return to my room.'

'Another cognac?' Alex asked Lisa as soon as they were alone.

'Please,' said Lisa wondering if this particular row between Solange and Mark would blow over like all the others.

'Let's go for a walk,' Alex suggested when they'd finished their drinks. A warm breeze ruffled their hair and played with the gauzy skirts of Lisa's gown as they walked through the hotel gardens.

'I'm glad you aren't leaving yet,' Alex said as they made their way to the seafront. 'It means we can still spend time together. Why don't you come down to the tin mines with me when I go? It will probably mean roughing it – I don't think there's any accommodation out there as comfortable as your plantation house.'

Lisa's heart leapt at the opportunity to see more of this beautiful country and, even better, in Alex's company.

'When are you going?' she asked.

'Next week probably.'

'I'd love to.'

'I thought we might go down to Singapore after that and visit Roland.'

'It would be good to see him again,' she agreed. In the shadows of a palm tree he drew her into his arms and kissed her, then released her.

'I want to look at you,' he told her. 'Now.'

'Look at me?' she asked, bewildered. 'What do you mean?'

'Show me your sex.'

Lisa glanced around. There were other strolling people in sight, but none of them near.

'Not here,' she protested. 'Someone will see.'

'Here,' he said implacably. 'It will excite me to look at you.' He placed his hand possessively on her mound over her flimsy dress. Lisa glanced anxiously around, but no-one seemed to be taking any notice of them.

There was a frangipani bush growing to one side of the tree and she moved to stand in front of it so she would be hidden from the waist down if anyone walked by.

Slowly, she lifted the skirts of her gown at the front, drawing them up her thighs until he could see the lace-edged silk of her camiknickers. Swiftly, he bent to pull them down her legs to her ankles. She stepped out of them and he buried his face in them for a moment before stuffing them in his pocket.

He gazed at her russet fleece in the shadows then muttered, 'Open your legs.' She did so and he reached out a hand and touched the tip of her clitoris with one finger. It tingled in eager response and he stroked it deftly, making it harden and swell.

She heard a noise behind them and turned her head. Two army officers were walking towards them talking animatedly.

'Someone's coming,' she hissed frantically, trying to move away. He pinched her clitoris between his finger and thumb, holding her immobile. She dropped her skirts, but it was still obvious he was touching her intimately.

He rubbed the trapped bud, making her gasp as her arousal mounted.

'Let go!' she hissed, but his only reply was to grin at her showing his teeth with the unusually long canines in a predatory smile.

To her horror the men obviously knew him and hailed him goodnaturedly. She kept her back to them but half turned her head in acknowledgement of their presence. The frangipani bush hid her from view below the waist, but they only had to step round it to join them for all to be revealed.

A blush of shame at the thought crept up her cheeks, making her glad it was dark, even though the full moon was throwing a silvery light over everything. Alex intensified the movements of his fingers as he exchanged greetings with them.

She willed her body not to respond, but it seemed oblivious to the delicacy of the situation and she felt warm juices trickling out of her and wetting Alex's fingers. Still he kept up the stealthy manipulation of her clit, making her suppress a moan as she felt her knees trembling and hot, tingling pleasure washing over her in waves.

Mentally, she urged the men to continue on their way, but they continued to chat to Alex, who seemed quite happy to prolong the conversation. She gritted her teeth in desperation, trying to hold back her swiftly mounting excitement, well aware what the inevitable outcome of Alex's skilful touch would be.

She bit her lip as she felt the surge of moist heat which usually preceded her climax, swiftly followed by a series of intensely pleasurable spasms which emanated outwards from her female core to every extremity of her body.

She was only half-aware she'd cried out. Just staying upright was hard enough, but as the climax receded leaving her weak and drained, she saw the two officers looking at her expectantly and became aware Alex was saying something. He'd slipped two fingers inside her as soon as her climax broke and was now busy moving them in and out of her in a way which made her want to bear down on them.

'What is it? he asked innocently.

'I . . . I thought I saw a snake,' she mumbled, 'but it was only a shadow.'

The two men moved off, calling 'Goodnight,' as they went. Lisa kicked Alex hard on the shin.

'You bastard,' she said feelingly. 'They must have realised what was going on.'

'What if they did? They'd just be envious that they weren't touching a beautiful woman.'

With a swift movement he fell to his knees and pulled her down beside him onto the grass saying, 'I've got to have you.' He rolled her onto her back, moved on top of her and after ripping open his trousers, thrust inside her.

Her immediate reaction was to struggle, but it only took three thrusts before she was moving with him, mentally cursing him for wanting another public coupling, but unable to resist the sheer carnal pull of her sex which was insisting on satisfaction.

Her best hope was to speed things up as much as she could and hope to bring things to a swift conclusion before anyone else passed by.

She bucked her hips up to meet each thrust, jamming her pelvis hard against him and squeezing his member with her internal muscles.

It was a frantic coupling, and forever afterwards Lisa was unable to smell the sweet waxen scent of frangipani without remembering the occasion.

At last Alex made four last corkscrew thrusts then let out a loud groan as he erupted into her with the force of a dam breaching its banks.

The sound of someone coming their way had Lisa frantically trying to push him off her. To her horror she realised that whoever it was – a woman, because those were definitely high heels she could hear now within only a few yards of them – was getting nearer and nearer.

Alex was like a dead weight slumped on top of her. The woman came right over to them and Lisa was appalled when she left the path and stopped right by them, her heels sinking into the grass.

'Lisa, Alex – I've been looking for you,' said Solange from above them. Alex lifted his dark head to glance up at her.

'Damn it, Solange – you pick your times,' he accused her.

'If you will copulate in a public place you must expect to be interrupted,' she said sternly. 'You are no gentleman, Alex – you should have been underneath. Now Lisa's gown will be covered in grass stains.'

Alex withdrew from Lisa, scrambled to his feet then held out a hand to help her up.

'Just as I thought – her gown is ruined. You must buy her another,' Solange chided him. Alex zipped himself up and then helped Lisa rearrange her clothing.

'I'll buy her a dozen. What's so important that you interrupted us, anyway?'

'I have just been speaking to Roland on the telephone,' said Solange, her eyes sparkling. 'He wishes us to go and visit him.'

'We know that,' Alex pointed out.

'Yes, but what you don't know is that Roland has been lucky enough to hire one of the finest French chefs alive. This master of his art used to be in the employ of the Princesse Valière and people used to kill to obtain an invitation to dine at her house. It seems he came out here with his latest employer – a Duke of my acquaintance – who was inconsiderate enough to die last week. Roland heard of this and managed to secure the chef's services this very day. He knew how interested I would be and telephoned – we must leave tomorrow and make a long stay with him.'

Lisa burst out laughing at the thought that only this could have persuaded Solange to stay in the East for a day longer than it took her to sell her estate and book a passage on the next ship.

'I suppose we could,' she said. 'What do you think, Alex?'

'Why doesn't Solange go on ahead, while we visit my tin mines,' he suggested. 'We can travel to Singapore after that, just as we'd planned.'

Lisa was struck by a sudden thought. 'What on earth will Mark say?' she wanted to know.

'He will be delighted,' said Solange airily. 'Because no-one will be so lacking in diplomacy to tell him the real reason for my prolonged stay. He must come with us too – it will be agreeable for Roland to have an extra guest. Shall we go back to the hotel? This can only be celebrated with champagne.'